Sea of Thieves
HEART OF FIRE

HEART OF FIRE

CHRIS ALLCOCK

TITAN BOOKS

Sea of Thieves: Heart of Fire
Print edition ISBN: 9781803362069
E-book edition ISBN: 9781803362779

Published by Titan Books
A division of Titan Publishing Group Ltd
144 Southwark Street, London SE1 0UP
www.titanbooks.com

First edition: August 2022
10 9 8 7 6 5 4 3 2 1

This is a work of fiction. All of the characters, organisations, and events portrayed in this novel are either products of the author's imagination or are used fictitiously. Any resemblance to actual persons, living or dead (except for satirical purposes), is entirely coincidental.

© 2022 Microsoft Corporation. All Rights Reserved. Microsoft, Sea of Thieves, and the titles of other video games owned by Microsoft are the trademarks of the Microsoft group of companies.

No part of this publication may be reproduced, stored in a retrieval system, or transmitted, in any form or by any means without the prior written permission of the publisher, nor be otherwise circulated in any form of binding or cover other than that in which it is published and without a similar condition being imposed on the subsequent purchaser.

A CIP catalogue record for this title is available from the British Library.

Printed and bound by CPI Group (UK) Ltd,
Croydon CR0 4YY.

*Dedicated to my Grandad, Reg,
who had a smile as wide as the horizon
and a heart as boundless as the sea.*

Historian's Note

This story takes place roughly eight years before the events of *The Seabound Soul*, the fateful day that saw Sir Arthur Pendragon and a pirate crew inadvertently revive the notorious Skeleton Lord, Flameheart. The prologue takes place roughly two decades prior to the rest of the adventure.

PROLOGUE

THE MAGPIE'S WING

Whenever Ramsey closed his eyes, he began to drown. It had been like this every night since the battle, and the nightmares showed no signs of granting him respite any time soon. Sometimes they would lie in wait for hours to ambush Ramsey during a peaceful sleep, washing away pleasant memories and casting him down into the inky void of the ocean. On other nights, it took mere moments of slumber before his treacherous imagination plunged Ramsey back beneath the waves.

With a grunt of annoyance, Ramsey forced himself upright and clambered out of his bed, which seemed destined to spend another night unoccupied. He lit no lamp, for his cabin was bathed in moonlight. Truth be told, he knew it well enough by now that he could have moved to sit behind his desk, as he did now, even while blindfolded.

This was his ship, his *Magpie's Wing*, and she was as familiar to him as his own bearded face in the mirror.

Having almost lost her in the fateful encounter that continued to plague him in his dreams, Ramsey spared no expense when it came to refitting and restoring the little galleon down to the last detail, and the gold he'd surrendered set several lucky shipwrights up for the rest of their lives. Not that money was hard for Ramsey to come by; he was a pirate, and a hugely successful one at that. He had captained the *Magpie's Wing* during the perilous voyage that led them to an untouched paradise, now referred to as the Sea of Thieves, and her crew had availed themselves of all the plunder they could carry home from those lawless, untamed lands.

Things, Ramsey mused as he settled into his chair, were very different now. Others had followed in his footsteps and, while the Sea of Thieves remained as mysterious and unpredictable as the day he had arrived, there were now plenty of people in the region who also had their eyes on treasures that had once been his for the taking. Not just shipwrights, but merchants, tavern-keepers, weaponsmiths and any number of competing crews out on the waves. Whether they were seeking adventure, looking to seize some forgotten fortune or simply hoping to live out their lives free from rules and responsibility, the Sea of Thieves called to pirates far and wide.

At first, Ramsey had resented the intrusion of other pirates into 'his' waters, though time and experience had softened his anger. Nowadays, he found himself enjoying first encounters with fresh-faced men and women who already knew him by his fearsome reputation. Many of the younger crews he encountered spoke of him only as the Pirate Lord, founding father of the Sea of Thieves, and the sight of his sails on the horizon was normally enough to stop any would-be rivals dead in the water.

The problem with having a reputation, of course, was that one needed to maintain it. The days when Ramsey could walk into a grog-house and enjoy a quiet drink were long behind him. Now he would be besieged by pirates seeking a story, a job or a fight – sometimes all at once – the minute his wooden leg clattered over the threshold. Ramsey's natural ambition, coupled with a significant sense of pride, compelled him to sail out day after day to prove, as much to himself as to others, that 'Pirate Lord' was a title he still deserved.

It was that ambition, the urge to pursue the impossible, which was responsible for the totem that rested on his desk, shining softly in the light of the moon. The totem that would, Ramsey hoped, ultimately lead him to the… blast, what the devil had he called it?

Ramsey reached out, fumbling with the lantern overhead until its warm glow overtook the steely moonlight and fully revealed the notes he'd scrawled down in his journal. 'Shroudbreaker', that was it – the name he'd chosen for the object of his quest. Yes, with a little luck and a fair wind, that strange name would be the talk of every tavern for years to come.

A decade ago, there had been no journey deemed more dangerous to a sailor's life and limb than a trip into the Devil's Shroud – the dense, deadly miasma that concealed the Sea of Thieves. Its boundaries ebbed and flowed, sometimes swallowing up entire islands for years at a time and rendering them entirely uninhabitable, as the fog choked living things, rusted iron and rotted away wood as if the ravages of time itself were crashing down upon them.

Ramsey and his crew had braved the Devil's Shroud and lived to tell the tale, eventually leading others to follow in their wake, but its true nature remained a mystery, as did the nature of any islands that might currently lie within its borders. Pirates, who revelled in gossip and could spin the most mundane journey into an enthralling yarn, soon began to spread rumours of vast treasure hoards and forbidden temples languishing just out of reach, and one such tall tale quickly grew in popularity. There was an island somewhere within the Shroud, so the story went, so overburdened with gems and precious metals that the very shores themselves were formed from gold.

The prospect was almost too ludicrous to imagine, but then, hadn't the Sea of Thieves itself been dismissed as nothing more than a fairy-tale by the sailors back home? Ramsey had consorted with merfolk, battled with an enraged kraken and single-handedly forged cursed chests whose properties could only be considered magical by all sane thinkers. Still, upon first hearing about these supposed Shores of Gold, Ramsey did not pay the tale too much heed, even if he did not discount it entirely. An island lost within the Devil's Shroud was, after all, lost. Until now…

Ramsey toyed with his quill, pondering how many of these thoughts were worth committing to the journal in front of him. He avoided reading when possible and wrote only when absolutely necessary, but the clues that had set the *Magpie's*

Wing on its current course were subtle and strange. Trapping them on paper was the only way Ramsey could trust them to make sense. As he reached for his inkwell, however, a familiar knock at the cabin's door made him pause. "Come in, Mercia," he called, his voice roughened by fatigue.

The door swung open at once and Mercia backed inside, balancing a bowl of steaming broth and a flagon of the hot, bitter tea she had taken to brewing at nights. "Your light was on," she said by way of a greeting. "We missed you at dinner," she added pointedly, turning to set the meal down on Ramsey's desk in a manner that suggested continued fasting was not an option.

Ramsey merely grunted, but picked up the bowl in both hands and supped from it gracelessly. Mercia pivoted the half-completed pages towards her and pulled a face as she deciphered Ramsey's scrawl. "I thought you said you were keeping a journal," she remarked. "This looks more like a jigsaw puzzle. I can't imagine anyone else making head or tail of it."

"Good," Ramsey replied gruffly. "I don't want anyone to know what we're doing until we've done it. Words can betray you."

"If it wasn't for words, we never would have learned about the Pathfinder—"

"Shroudbreaker."

"Really? I liked Pathfinder. Anyway, this is the big adventure you were yearning for, isn't it? A chance to get back out at sea, where we belong."

Mercia span the journal back around and leaned forward, eyes bright as she locked gazes with her captain. Side by side the two of them made an odd pairing: Ramsey was a great, roaring bear of a man who wore his heart on his sleeve, while Mercia was deliberate and meticulous in everything she said and did. History, however, had proven that they could be a formidable team when they worked alongside one another. Together they had constructed the *Magpie's Wing*, breached the Devil's Shroud, and been the first pirates in Ramsey's lifetime to converse with the strange, glittering race known as merfolk.

Having spent years studying the mysteries of the Sea of Thieves, it had been Mercia who uncovered legends of an artefact capable of dispelling the Devil's Shroud, at least for a short time. A ship that held such a relic could, in theory, sail directly into the fog and emerge again unscathed, allowing its crew to escape pursuers or visit unexplored islands with ease. Whether the Shores of Gold existed or not, any pirate who could wield the Shroudbreaker would be the first to know for sure.

Suddenly feeling in much need of some fresh air, Ramsey set down his empty bowl and stood, moving swiftly around Mercia and throwing open the door of his cabin as if to greet the moonlight. At once, he was immersed in the brassy, boisterous chatter of the remainder of his crew, the two men keeping themselves awake and amused with a steady stream of conversation as they worked the sails to catch every gust of wind.

The patient, lyrical voice drifting down from the upper deck was unmistakably Shan, oldest and most unflappable member of Ramsey's crew. Shan was a tinkerer, and many of his quirky inventions had become ubiquitous across the

Sea of Thieves in recent years, a fact that pleased the bald little pirate more than he would ever have admitted.

Shan was engaged in a lively, mostly shouted conversation with George, the *Magpie's Wing*'s newest and youngest shipmate, who was stationed at the front of the galleon's three sails. Ramsey hadn't quite made up his mind about George yet, though he could see that the lad's inquisitive nature might well give Mercia a run for her money. When George wasn't singing or making up rhyming couplets about their adventures – a habit Ramsey was working hard to disabuse him of – he spent his time aboard soaking up information like a sponge.

"What I don't understand," George continued, voice raised over the sound of spray, "is why everybody calls them Ancients!"

"What's that?" Shan squinted a professional eye at his own sail then tweaked the angle to be just-so. "They lived here in ancient times, didn't they? All across the Sea of Thieves, I mean. That makes them the Ancients."

"Right, but when they *were* here, it wasn't ancient times," George persisted, wiping one meaty arm across his face to mop away the sweat of a hard night's work. "It was now. So what were they called?"

Shan appeared to consider this very deeply. "No, I think you're wrong, see," he said at last. "It was definitely ancient times, because they wrote everything down as pictures and built big temples for everything. That's why the key on the captain's table looks like a carved animal. They did a lot of that sort of thing in ancient times, carving animals. Not to mention, if it was now, we'd be talking to them, wouldn't we?

We could just ask them about their Shroudbreaker instead of all of this sailing about."

George, who was still too green to realise that Shan was teasing him, opened his mouth in what would surely be yet another doomed attempt to make his point. Ramsey decided to put the boy out his misery and coughed loudly. "What's important is not what the Ancients called themselves," he declared, striding out onto the deck. "It's that they were cunning, and liked to set traps.

"If Mercia says the totem's a key to some treasure vault or other, then that's the case. *I* say that once we're inside it, if we should tread on the wrong tile or pick up the wrong gewgaw, it'll be the last mistake of our lives. Focus on where we are here and now, and save your flights of fancy until we're back in the tavern." Eager to please his captain, George lowered the brim of his hat and set his jaw in concentration, his banter with Shan quite forgotten.

Looking to set an example, Ramsey began to climb the ladder that led to the crow's nest, intending to scan the horizon for other ships whose presence might introduce an unacceptable element of chance to his plan. He had barely laid his gloved hands upon the wooden rungs, however, before his keen eyes spotted the merest flicker. Something was imperceptibly wrong with the skyline. Nothing so threatening as another set of sails, at least not yet, but… something.

Ramsey redoubled his efforts and all but flew up to the top of the mast, pulling out an ornate spyglass and meticulously examining the choppy sea around them. A storm they had passed an hour before still brooded on the horizon, but beyond the large island they were about to sail past, the way ahead seemed clear.

If there was nothing untoward on the waves, then that only left...

"Drop anchor!" Ramsey bellowed, so harshly that George actually jumped. "I have business on that island!" It was Shan who moved to the capstan and sent the ship's anchor crashing into the waves, bringing the ship to a halt with a protesting screech as the wind strained in her sails. Having sailed together for so many years, he had learned to obey Ramsey's orders, however confounding they might be, without question.

Despite his bulk, Ramsey could move with a turn of speed that had caught more than a few foes off guard over the years. By the time the *Magpie's Wing* had been set back in motion, now easing her way as close to the shoreline as Shan could manage, Ramsey was already clinging to the ship's ladder, readying himself to drop into the shallows. He waded to shore without another word, striding swiftly across the curving shoreline, cutlass in his hand, until at last he found what had caught his attention.

A little way up from the beach lay the smouldering remnants of a cooking fire, nestled in a shallow gully hidden from the view of passing ships. Quite by chance, Ramsey had spotted the last wisps of smoke as the fire had been hastily extinguished. Someone had been resting here – several someones, judging by the flurry of footprints around the campsite. Either they were nearby and concealed, which was bad, or they were currently boarding a ship of their own, which was worse.

Ramsey plunged back into the foam, leaping for the ship's ladder and hauling himself aboard, his face set in grim determination. He wrenched at the ship's wheel the moment it was within his reach, sending the prow of the *Magpie's Wing* veering directly away from the island and out towards the open sea at a sharp deviation from their original course. That was why the first volley of cannonballs, shots that came thundering over the island in a deadly parabola, struck the rear hull of the ship instead of toppling its sails.

Ramsey cursed loudly, but had no need to bark orders – Shan and George had begun to weigh anchor as soon as they'd spotted their captain's flight along the sand. Mercia was ducking below deck to repair the damage, a supply of stout wooden planks balanced on one shoulder and a look of grim determination on her face. She knew as well as Ramsey that the barrage had been aimed with expert accuracy, and only the ship's sudden, unexpected motion had prevented the *Magpie's Wing* from being crippled by the surprise attack.

A second round of cannonballs followed, striking the waves where the *Magpie's Wing* should have been, fizzing and smoking in the water as if filled with some malevolent power beyond mere metal. Ramsey continued to twist the ship this way and that, looking to confound their enemy until they were out of range, while Mercia emptied out buckets full of the seawater that had flooded in down below. Shan and George returned to their posts at the sails; there was no banter to be heard now – only two pairs of eyes fixed on the horizon to catch a glimpse of their unseen foe.

She sailed out from behind the island at last; a galleon with rich crimson sails and a hull the colour of old charcoal, her distinguishing features now clearly visible as the ship's lanterns flared into life ready for the hunt. Her defiant figurehead was a roaring dragon, but it was the crest on her billowing flag that made Ramsey certain of what he was seeing. This was the *Burning Blade*, and her short time upon the Sea of Thieves was shrouded in mystery, for no shipwright would admit to constructing her and nobody could remember her arrival.

Her current commander, too, was an enigma. Known as Captain Flameheart by those out in the wider world, he had made his mark as a bold and merciless pirate who gave no quarter to any who crossed his path. As far as Ramsey knew, Flameheart had made no attempt to plunder treasures to increase his own fortune, nor did he visit drinking dens to mingle with fellow pirates. He simply sailed from place to place, often lying in wait for victims, and frequently engaging in ferocious ship-to-ship combat seemingly for the fun of it.

Mercia returned to Ramsey's side, her boots squelching with seawater. "We're patched," she informed the others, then turned to glare at the vessel that had blindsided them. "This makes my teeth itch, Ramsey. Tonight, of all nights, is when Flameheart decides to pick a fight with the Pirate Lord?"

He knows, Ramsey realised, brow furrowed as he stared at the galleon that had begun to match their course. *He's come for the key.* His gut churned at the thought of Flameheart taking the totem for himself, and using it to snare the Shroudbreaker from its resting place. By abusing its power, the *Burning Blade* would be free to flit in and out of the Shroud at will, attacking and doubtless destroying new arrivals to these waters before they had chance to get their bearings. Before long, without a steady influx of fresh blood, the Sea of Thieves itself would surely wither and die.

No, Ramsey decided with a sudden swell of fury that emerged as an audible growl. *He never gets the Shroudbreaker. Not ever.* Though it humiliated Ramsey deeply, for the sake of their quest – and perhaps even to protect the Sea of Thieves – this was one battle the Pirate Lord would try to flee.

Much to Ramsey's consternation, the flight of the *Magpie's Wing* did nothing to deter Flameheart's pursuit, and though they extinguished every lantern, the *Burning Blade* showed no sign of losing her quarry in the darkness. Staring moodily at the waves as he considered their next move, Ramsey felt George's presence beside him at the helm. "I've angled the sails as best I can," he said, "but they still seem to be gaining. How can that be, though? We have the same wind they do, and we're both galleons."

"There's more to a vessel than her crew and how many sails she has, lad," Shan replied. "If you don't mean to take in cargo, you can shape a hull that cuts more neatly through the water. Scrap your stove if you want to shed some weight and don't mind a crew that's fed on ship's biscuit. Besides, the *Wing* is an old ship, patched and re-patched a hundred times. That slows her down. Not much, but enough."

"We'll have to fight after all, then? And risk losing the totem?" Mercia sounded decidedly unimpressed by this suggestion.

"Aye, though it wouldn't be my first choice," Shan replied. "I can't quite put my finger on it, but there's something odd about that ship's cannons. The way they catch the moonlight…"

Ramsey harrumphed, but knew the truth when he heard it. "To arms, then," he commanded. "If we're going to fight, let's try to land a few good blows." Trusting the others to work the cannons with their usual skill, he span the ship's wheel sharply so that the starboard side of the *Magpie's Wing* faced directly towards the *Burning Blade*'s prow.

As he had hoped, this burst of aggression seemed to take Flameheart by surprise. The *Burning Blade* began to turn, but not before three good shots had made their marks upon her hull. Ramsey could spy at least one breach below the roaring dragon figurehead, and nodded in grim satisfaction. If they could deliver a few more volleys like that, it might make Flameheart think twice before locking horns with the Pirate Lord.

The *Burning Blade* was quick to return fire, and a single shot rang out from its port cannons. But this was no ordinary lump of pig-iron. It glowed from within like an enormous firefly as it sailed towards them, striking the *Magpie's Wing* and shattering as if the whole thing were made of glass.

Shan and George turned their heads away in alarm, expecting to be showered by a thousand tiny shards of white-hot pain. To their surprise, though, nothing remained of the mysterious projectile save for a few ethereal strands of light that quickly began to fade away.

"They're toying with us," Ramsey roared, and tugged at the wheel with all his might. "Hit them again, and not with any silly baubles!" To his crew's obvious alarm, however, their own cannons seemed to have seized up completely. No amount of exertion could force them into position, and the fuses stayed stubbornly unlit.

Mercia's eyes widened in sudden realisation. "It's the—"

Her thought hung in the air uncompleted as another glowing cannonball, this one sickly green in hue, struck the centre of the deck, sending a billowing wave of green smoke washing across the crew in a matter of seconds. Ramsey was a hard man to surprise, but even he could not hide an audible gasp as Shan, Mercia and George suddenly crumpled before his eyes, clutching at their legs with expressions of agony on their faces. A moment later, Ramsey felt a spear of pain lancing up his own good leg, stumbled, and almost toppled to the deck along with his crew.

The cannonballs, Ramsey thought, realising what Mercia had been trying to tell him. *They're cursed. One seized up our cannons, another our bones.* He glanced down grimly at his lion's claw with unaccustomed gratitude. A wooden stump, at least, could feel no pain.

The *Magpie's Wing* rocked again and this time Ramsey heard the splintering of wood. Having incapacitated his enemies with curses, it seemed as though Flameheart now aimed to sink their ship via more traditional methods. Hardly honourable for someone who claimed to love the thrill of a good battle, but Ramsey had no time to dwell on that now. He alone could still move, and that meant he alone would have to take responsibility for what happened next.

Relying solely on his wooden claw, Ramsey crashed into his cabin with all the grace of a wounded animal, snarling and muttering to himself as he reached for the crudely carved stone container from which he'd first retrieved the key. It was heavy enough to sink swiftly, at least. With a twinge of remorse, Ramsey plucked the ancient totem from its spot on his desk and flung it angrily into the chest, his heart lurching in time with his ship as more cannon fire tore great rends in her hull.

Throwing open the door to the balcony that adjoined his cabin so that the ship's bulk hid his actions from the *Burning Blade*, Ramsey raised the chest above his head, waited for another explosion to rock the *Magpie's Wing*, and hurled the chest into the sea with all of his might. *Gone*, he thought sombrely, *but not lost. Mercia has been keeping logs. One day…*

Pushing that line of thought to one side, he retreated through his cabin – where Flameheart's latest broadside had created an unwanted extra porthole – and back to the main deck, noting with relief that his crew appeared to be recovering from their supernatural affliction. The ship itself was still lurching, however, and sat noticeably lower in the water than she should.

George moved past him, looking sick to his stomach. "I'll get ammunition…" he began, in a low, rasping voice, but Ramsey laid a hand on his shoulder. "Belay that, lad," he said softly, though his voice seemed to echo in a sudden silence. Mercia's eyes narrowed, but she said nothing. "Now pay heed. The key is sunk, but I'll be damned before Flameheart learns that. Now, our task must be to draw him as far away from this place as we can, before we're scuttled for good. Lead him towards the Wilds, perhaps, and find a place to make our stand."

He looked to each of them, then, old friends and fresh young face alike. His heavy heart lifted a little at the sight of their expressions: not hopeless, not doubtful, but determined and proud. Ignoring the bombardments as best they could, the crew set about keeping the *Magpie's Wing* alive long enough to reach her final destination.

Furniture was hurled overboard to lighten the load or torn apart to make repairs. George and Mercia patched and bailed relentlessly, wading around in the rising water and stumbling as the ship swayed from side to side. At the helm, Ramsey drew on his lifetime of experience to keep their foe at bay, tacking towards familiar ocean currents that would help speed them along. The *Burning Blade* continued to pursue, taking pot-shots now and then in the way a cat bats at a wounded mouse in search of more amusement.

Only when the *Magpie's Wing* began to slow, its lower deck now completely submerged despite the crew's struggles, did the executioner's blade descend. One final volley of cannon fire struck the ship's central mast, toppling it with an almighty crash and a tangle of rigging and cloth that came within inches of pinning Shan helplessly against the deck. Ramsey used the last of their inertia and steered the ship into the shallows near a tiny island, so insignificant it lacked so much as a name, and told his crew to carry whatever valuables they could to the shore.

Side by side with swords drawn, they watched helplessly as the *Magpie's Wing*, the first little galleon to sail upon the Sea of Thieves, surrendered to those same waters. A pile of trinkets – Ramsey's journal, Shan's latest music box and a few strange-smelling bottles Mercia used in her research – were all they had left to guard, but guard them they did. They stood defiantly as the *Burning Blade* drew closer, expecting a thunderous hailstorm of buckshot or bullet to strike them down at any moment.

"They're certainly taking their time," Shan grumbled at last. "If I'm going to die here, I'd at least like it not to be of boredom."

"They seem to be turning..." Mercia, who had lowered her blade to peer through a spyglass of her own, announced. "There's – I don't believe it. There's another galleon coming around Crook's Hollow, and the *Blade* is changing course to pursue her!"

"What?!" Ramsey roared. "Are we no longer sport enough without a ship? They can damn well get back here and fight me after costing me the *Wing*!" He pulled his great tricorn hat from atop his head and waved it furiously like a flag of war, as if it might somehow goad Flameheart into re-joining their battle.

Mercia laid a placating hand on the heavy leather of Ramsey's coat. "I've lost quite enough for one day, thank you," she soothed. "I don't need to lose you too. Any of you," she added, flushing slightly.

"Good, because you're stuck with us." George was scanning the horizon, a look of abject glumness settling on his face for the long haul. "If that ship doesn't come back to rescue us, we'll be marooned here."

Mercia shared a glance with Ramsey. "Do you really think so?" she asked with a tinge of amusement in her voice. She strode over to the young pirate and span him around so he could look to the west, where several foaming trails were slicing through the water towards them. One vanished beneath the surface only to arc out of the ocean in a graceful backflip, and George caught the briefest glimpse of silvered scales glinting in the first rays of dawn.

"Merfolk," Mercia said when it became obvious George had momentarily lost the power of speech. "We have an… arrangement, you might say. They'll get us back to an outpost right enough, though you might want to keep your eyes closed during the journey. Saltwater stings." She gave George a push, and he waded slowly into the water as if hypnotised.

"We'll need to buy a new ship," Shan said as he helped Ramsey gather up their belongings, bundling them neatly into an oilskin pouch. "That is, if you mean to retrace our steps and find that key of yours. The Shroudbreaker's still out there, somewhere."

To Shan's surprise, Ramsey shook his head slowly. "Let the totem sleep for now," he said, hoarsely. "At least until the seas are a calmer place to explore." He strode into the sea, reaching for the outstretched hand of a patient mer, and Shan caught his last words before the Pirate Lord was borne across the waves.

"Sooner or later, someone's going to have to put a stop to Captain Flameheart…"

1

The Morningstar

Things were going to be different this time, Jill told herself firmly. Her plan was absolutely, *definitely* going to work. The trouble was, she knew herself to be a very bad liar.

When Jill dared to raise her head and peek over the edge of the building upon which she was currently splayed, she had an excellent view of the path that snaked its way through shops and stalls towards the shoreline. It was almost dark, which was also part of her plan, but from here she could still make out the distinctive canopy of the shipwright's storefront, which served as her landmark. She knew it very well indeed, for the business was her livelihood, the closest thing she had to a home, and – unless she did something about it, and soon – the stall in which she'd be stuck working for the rest of her life.

Jill was an apprentice shipwright, and that meant her place was down at the outpost docks where she could serve her customers. Out here on the Sea of Thieves, that usually meant talking with passing pirates looking to spruce up their sails or celebrate their fortune with a gilded figurehead. The shop gave Jill an unparalleled view of the horizon as she worked, and afforded her the opportunity to watch, dreamily, as nimble sloops and stately galleons sailed back and forth. Only out there, on the wild waters, did the ships Jill helped to shape become real.

Suki, who owned the business, took a very different view of… well, the view. Every capstan carved and every sail sewn by Suki were nothing short of exquisite. Gems would be set against deep mahogany, nestled snugly in an intricate web of golden brocade that Jill supposed must be as fine as the lace on a petticoat – not that she'd ever seen one. Striking splashes of paint brought attention to the way a handle tapered, or drew the eye away from minor blemishes and imperfections in the grain of the wood. Nothing on the Sea of Thieves was truly new, but Suki could take any ship part, even one that had mouldered on the ocean floor for years, and bring it to the lustre of a freshly painted masterpiece.

This was a skill, Suki had been clear, that Jill would only learn with her gaze fixed firmly on the workbench and not on the waves. "I have raised three daughters," she would say sternly. "I did not waste my days worrying that they might face adversity, for it was certain that they would. I spent my time making certain that they would endure it. So it must be with our ships. If you do not distract yourself with thoughts of grand adventure, you will not make mistakes. A fine ship built with no mistakes will, of course, endure adversity of its own. How could it not be so?"

Had Suki learned of Jill's intentions, she would almost certainly have dismissed her at once. A shipwright taking an apprentice at all was an unusual occurrence, least of all one as talented as Suki. That was part of why Jill was currently hiding on the roof of a tall, stilted building underneath which the Order of Souls had stationed their representative – one of the highest spots on the outpost, and somewhere she was unlikely to be spotted. It also gave her an excellent view of incoming ships, though there was only one she cared to spy this night, and it had sailed into port at dusk.

The *Morningstar*. Few pirates, particularly new arrivals, knew her proud history upon the Sea of Thieves, but Jill had spent many sunny days at her post, hammering and sawing gently enough that she could overhear the old salts talking. The *Morningstar* had sailed in an alliance with the Pirate Lord, stood firm against the Twisted Knife at the Siege of Crescent Isle, and had once been split clean apart by a kraken – only to be salvaged by merfolk and restored through the hard work of the grateful traders she'd protected. The gleaming stars upon her burgundy sails that gave the ship her name, along with the wooden bear carving affixed to her bow, showed how much pride her crew took in their ship's pristine appearance.

Despite her best efforts, this was the third time Jill had attempted to speak with the *Morningstar*'s captain, and that was the other reason she had hauled herself up onto a windswept rooftop for the evening – it was uncomfortable and certainly precarious, but she was running out of ideas. When she'd first tried to make contact in the tavern, a runaway grog barrel slipped from Tracy the tavern-keeper's grip and careened over Jill's foot, leaving her able to do little more than gasp breathlessly while her swollen toes were held in a bucket of icy water by an apologetic barmaid. By the time Jill had recovered enough to stand once more, the *Morningstar* and her crew were gone.

A week later, the same ship had appeared unexpectedly during a bright afternoon, and Jill had risked Suki's wrath by slipping away to pursue the crew as they ambled along the docks. Through sheer bad luck, an argument between two pirates haggling with the Merchant Alliance had erupted into a full-scale brawl, and a wayward elbow had knocked Jill off balance and sent her tumbling off the dock. She'd been more embarrassed than hurt, but the commotion drew Suki's attention and Jill was unable to sneak away for the rest of the day.

"I'm never one to gossip," Tracy had said cheerfully to Jill as she drowned her sorrows afterwards, "but ol' Eli comes in here every month, regular as you like, and never leaves without paying his bill. He'll stop by again, I'm as sure of it as I'm sure Madame Olive's sweet on young Tyler down at the weapon shop, not that you heard that from me." This, at least, seemed like information Jill could use to finally meet the man face to face.

Jill had waited impatiently for what seemed like an eternity, but on the day of the *Morningstar*'s expected arrival, the fates once again conspired against her. An unexpectedly cheerful Suki had informed Jill that they'd be shutting up shop earlier than usual, because she was meeting her friend Sharon for a drink that night. As there was only one tavern on the small outpost, Jill would certainly be spotted by her mentor if she stepped inside and began conversing with pirates. That was why she'd come up with her new, admittedly rather desperate, plan.

There was a spot at the back of the tavern colloquially known as Tanner's Alley, a name that Jill hadn't immediately understood the full implication of. It was, Tracy had explained, a haven for pirates in search of some privacy and a chance to deal with the consequences of a night spent drinking. Jill's vantage point offered an excellent view, though it made not getting spotted all the more essential. She doubted pirates would take kindly to being caught with their breeches down, as it were. No, best to stay quiet as a mouse until nature took its course and the *Morningstar*'s captain stepped outside for a moment's relief…

She was so caught up in her own musings, Jill nearly missed her moment entirely. Her quarry had appeared and, having gone about his business, was now making his way back around to the entrance of the tavern. Stifling a curse, Jill shuffled gracelessly to the edge of the roof and swung her legs over, scrabbling down onto a balcony that ringed the building and tottering down the steep wooden stairs at speed. She nearly collided with Madame Olive when she stuck her head outside to see what the commotion was, and mumbled a hasty apology before making a beeline for the tavern's steps, rounding the corner to find—

Nobody. The walkway was deserted. Dumbfounded, Jill stared at the spot where the man should have been, confident that he'd been out of her sight for a couple of seconds at most. Pirates could be fast, but not *that* fast. Had he somehow slipped back into the tavern via a side entrance and denied Jill her opportunity to speak with him?

Something – a sixth sense, perhaps, or the slightest crack of a snapping twig – made her turn back towards the pathway down to the docks. There was Jill's target, having suddenly changed course to veer away from the bright lights and bawdy shanties of the tavern. She hadn't the slightest idea how he'd slipped past her so easily, but that didn't matter now. If she didn't act quickly, she'd miss her chance.

A life spent clambering over and around half-constructed galleons meant that Jill was a lot nimbler than most people assumed from looking at her, but she wasn't used to sprinting. She sprinted now, though, thundering across the distance to the docks as quickly as she could. The pirate was climbing the gangplank of the *Morningstar* now, apparently eager to get underway. "Hoy!" Jill called, cursing the breathlessness in her voice. "Captain! I want to talk to you, please!"

All at once, he stood before her: Eli Slate, Commander of the *Morningstar*. Though his build was slim and his hair and beard were white with age, there was something about his demeanour and impeccable appearance that made him seem somehow larger than life. His face was impassive and his gaze hard as Jill skidded to a halt in front of him. "I am well aware of that, young lady," he said offhandedly as Jill reached the jetty. "Have you considered that I may have little interest in talking to you, however?"

He's been avoiding me, Jill realised, and felt her stomach drop clean out of the world at the revelation. *We've only just met and he doesn't like me.* "I..." she began, feeling the beginnings of a blush spreading, and hoping furiously Slate would think she was simply flushed from sprinting. *Well, at least now I can't say anything to make things worse.*

"Ach, don't let the cat catch your tongue, lassie." This unexpected interruption came from another, younger pirate as he slung himself over the railings of the *Morningstar*, his bulky frame causing the jetty to creak as he landed. One good-natured eye, framed by the bushiest beard Jill had ever seen, sparkled as he looked her up and down; the other eye covered by a large patch. "We don't bite. Speak what's on your mind, that's what I always say!"

Jill stared at the man for a moment. *This must be Dinger*, she thought, *the one even Tracy thinks is a chatterbox.* She'd tried to find out as much about the *Morningstar*'s other crewmembers as possible, and it turned out that every tavern-keeper across the Sea of Thieves recognised Dinger – or at least, the sound of Dinger's voice as he approached and started the tankards rattling. If the rumours were true, he'd been banned from singing indoors after one too many shattered bottles.

"I want to join your crew!" It took Jill a moment to realise that the words were hers; that she'd blurted them out instinctively. The sentence seemed to hang in the air, twisting slowly under Slate's scrutiny. "As a pirate," she added, suddenly feeling utterly foolish. "Not as..."

"A shipwright?" Slate's visage was stern, but his voice sounded amused. "I should think not, Jill." He caught sight of her startled expression, and added, "Now, there's no need to look quite so surprised. Tracy means well, but she was hardly likely to resist the temptation to tell me all about you and the questions you'd been asking. This in turn leads me to question – why? What makes a shipwright down tools and aspire to the pirate's life?"

Here goes nothing, Jill thought. *I hope I can explain this better to Slate than I can to myself.* "It's… about the future," she said, slowly, feeling the words out as she went. "The shipwrights here, they've been making sloops and galleons the same way pretty much forever. Yes, they'll carve a new figurehead or add some jewels to raise the prices but that's not the same as making things better. For that, you'd have to spend time with a living ship. Working aboard her out there, in the real world, learning all about her quirks and her shortcomings. Sensing her soul."

Slate observed Jill for a long while before speaking. "I knew a chap once, used to be a bit of a tinkerer," he remarked, "and I have to say that he would have agreed with you. It's one thing to handle a ship in the calm waters at port and quite another when she's straining against a storm, riddled with holes, with her wheel spinning fast enough to wrench your arms off. It's correct to say that no-one knows a ship better than her crew. But why come to me?"

"Because it's the *Morningstar*, sir," Jill replied, promptly. "She's a fine vessel. Well, more than fine – she's got the Merikov capstan design, with the double-linked chain they used to forge out at Tortuga. That's not the strongest, but the load gets offset by an interleaved bracing mechanism most shipwrights wouldn't even attempt on a galleon… Oh, and there's the classics in there too, because you've got the Epping oak masts and what I think is an original Chapman rudder, but I'd have to get under the bilge to see if I could find his initials..." She trailed off, aware that the two men were staring at her with blank expressions, and felt another blush stirring.

"Well," said Dinger after a moment's stunned silence. "I may not have understood anything you said afterwards, but you're right about her being a fine vessel! Isn't she, skipper?"

"You have an appointment to keep, Mister Dinger," Slate said evenly. "You know how the Senior Traders dislike it when we tarry." Dinger looked like he was about to protest, but instead shuffled mutely past Slate and ambled away up the dock towards the small, hut-like building that served as this outpost's office for the Merchant Alliance. Jill thought he might have given her a cheerful wink as he passed by, though it was hard to say for sure in the gloom.

"I should say that you must be an excellent shipwright," Slate said. "That much is obvious just from speaking to you. Perhaps one day you will even be a capable pirate. The situation aboard the *Morningstar*, however, is somewhat unique. I run her much as I would a vessel in the merchant navy. There is a chain of command I expect to be obeyed and each member of the crew has a defined role I expect them to excel at."

Slate's voice softened very slightly as he continued. "It hardly seems fair of me to demand that you make best use of your skills as a pirate when you do not yet know what they are. No, I think it would be best for you to find a more... informal... set of shipmates, shall we say. A post aboard a sloop or a brigantine, perhaps, where the rules are more relaxed and you can find your sea legs."

Jill stared. She'd expected laughter, or dismissal, or even anger at brazenly approaching a crew of seasoned pirates and asking to be counted among their number. She hadn't expected *kindness*. But this was still a refusal, no matter how neatly gift-wrapped, and the worst part was that Slate's argument was entirely reasonable. Even so, Jill's brain was spinning as she tried to think of something, anything, she could say to prevent the majestic piece of engineering that was the *Morningstar* from sailing out of her life forever.

Something large and leathery brushed against the back of her neck, and Jill let out an involuntary yelp, spinning around to see what had touched her and nearly getting a mouthful of salad as a result. Someone had placed an enormous green plant down next to her while she'd been lost in thought, and its thick, moist leaves swayed around as the wind picked up. As she watched, Dinger staggered down the causeway carrying more of the oversized greenery, clearly struggling to see where he was going through the mass of foliage.

Slate looked distinctly unamused, snatching at the order slip pinned to the crate of plants. His brow furrowed as he read through the manifest, Jill seemingly forgotten for the moment. "Rare silks… spiced tea… a snake…" he muttered, before his voice pitched up to a roar. "MISTER Dinger! This isn't a cargo run you've organised, it's slave labour. We'll be here all night!"

"Chief Trader Mollie drives a hard bargain, sir!" Dinger said cheerfully, his voice muffled by leaves. "Wouldn't give us the animal cages without us taking the cargo too. Fontaine, get your backside down here and give us a hand before you take root like these plants, eh?" A pale, hitherto unseen pirate aboard the *Morningstar* made an audible sound of disgust before appearing at the railing, then began to clamber down the ship's ladder with all the speed and enthusiasm of continental drift.

"And you forgot to tell her we were short-handed, I suppose," Slate grumbled. "We'll be lucky to get all this stowed aboard by suppertime, let alone get underway."

"Well..." Dinger began, pausing and looking meaningfully between Slate and Jill, then back to Slate once more. "Permission to make a suggestion, Captain?" he added, slyly.

"Permission denied," Slate said. "And don't think these old eyes are so blind they can't see when you're trying to play me for a fool. However, we have agreed to the work, and as such..." He turned to Jill, and spoke curtly. "A shipwright needs strong arms as well as a strong heart. I'm not saying that one trip will make you a pirate, but if you really want a taste of life at sea, I cannot deny that we could use an extra pair of hands tonight."

"Yes!" Jill cried. "Uh, I mean, aye! Aye, Captain! Sir." Eager to show willing, she turned and hefted the nearest plant with such enthusiasm she nearly uprooted it from its pot.

Slate's moustache twitched in what might just have been the beginnings of a smile. "First things first, crewman," he said mildly. "Everyone who serves aboard the *Morningstar* wears the same uniform, however brief their journey. Go with Fontaine and he'll find something in your size."

"First I am a pack mule, now I am a tailor..." the pale pirate moaned. "Perhaps you had better follow me before I am also tasked with repainting the hull, or counting all the grains of sand on the beach, eh?" Even so, he beckoned Jill up the gangplank and led her below decks.

Fontaine, Jill soon discovered, was at his happiest when he was complaining. While not as relentlessly talkative as Dinger, he nonetheless had an opinion about anything and everything – the state of the outpost, the moral quandaries of trying to build a legitimate business empire based on immoral foundations, the transience of wealth – and how he, as a self-styled student of philosophy, was best placed to advise those around him on such matters, if only they would have the wisdom to listen.

One matter on which Fontaine would not be drawn, however, was the whereabouts of the *Morningstar*'s fourth crewmember, sombrely informing Jill that while there were no foolish questions, there were certainly foolish times to ask them. Having procured her an ill-fitting and rather musty uniform from the depths of an old chest on the mid-deck, he headed back up the creaky wooden stairs to offer Jill some privacy and help get the voyage underway. Before long, she heard them weigh anchor, and felt a slight lurch as the ship began to move.

Jill dressed quickly, then briefly investigated the rest of the wares they'd agreed to transport before hastily retreating, not least because the sizeable cargo included a large and very aggravated snake, which now sat coiled up in a cage in the hold and spat at anyone who dared to approach it. Dinger had named the creature 'Chomps', a moniker Jill considered entirely too friendly for such an ill-tempered serpent.

Once she'd tucked and tightened the uniform as best she could without a mirror, Jill took a moment to drink in her surroundings, feeling the gentle rocking of the ship as its prow cleaved a path across the sea. Her practised eye took in the gleam of a fresh nail in the steps weathered by years of heavy boots tramping up and down. In her old life, she'd have been tempted to grab some sandpaper and even them off, but she was a pirate now, if only for tonight.

Jill had been shocked the first time she'd seen a grubby crew of pirates swagger past her stall, belching and cursing, only to halt in their tracks and make polite conversation with a prim, slender woman stood nearby. The Merchant Alliance, she came to learn, had long ago discovered that upon the lawless Sea of Thieves, the best way to keep your valuable goods safe from a crew of cunning buccaneers was to make those same buccaneers responsible for their safety, paying them handsomely for doing so. The pirates got gold either way, and their personal sense of pride was – mostly – enough to see them defending the cargo, even with their lives if necessary.

Giving Chomps a wide berth, Jill grabbed an old bucket and filled it with water, making sure to tend to each of the thirsty plants before ascending to the main deck. She stood for a moment, savouring the creaking of timber as the *Morningstar* soared across the sea. A flock of gulls wheeled lazily in the night sky, attracted by some bobbing flotsam, and the spray in the air tasted of salt. In this moment, it felt like anything and everything was possible.

Everyone else was at their posts, casting watchful gazes

at the horizon, and Jill – who lacked a spot of her own – couldn't help but feel slightly awkward just standing there. She was about to duck back down below decks when she spotted a dark shadow detach itself from the silhouette of a nearby island. "That's a sloop," she muttered to herself before raising her voice. "Captain Slate, there's—"

Whether Slate's keen ears had overheard Jill or if some other detail had alerted him to the little ship's presence, Jill couldn't tell, but he was already striding to the rear railing of the galleon with his own spyglass in hand. "I see her," he said. "Looks like a lone pirate, unless they've a friend hiding below deck."

"They won't attack us, will they?" Jill asked, cautiously. She'd hoped to get some time alone to practise with a cannon before needing to try one out in a fight to the death.

"They'd be mad to try." Dinger declared, "We outnumber and outgun them. But then, there's plenty of madness to go around out here."

Slate seemed to concur. "Why don't you head on up to the crow's nest and keep an eye on them?" he suggested. "Just in case."

Grateful for the opportunity to be useful, Jill ascended the central mast with a shipwright's familiar ease, turning to track the mysterious sloop. It was closer now, sailing in the wake of the *Morningstar* and slowly gaining ground. Not a single lantern aboard her was lit, but the figure at the helm was still dimly visible by the light of the stars. Was their intention to stalk them all the way to their destination, Jill wondered, and then strike while the *Morningstar* was docked? Or perhaps attempt to sneak away with some cargo while it was being unloaded? She realised she had absolutely no idea what was going to happen next and shivered with excitement.

She had her answer soon enough. The sloop continued to edge forward until its prow was practically brushing against the *Morningstar*'s stern, at which point the lone occupant began to act strangely, abandoning the helm entirely. Jill rang the ship's bell three times to alert the crew before dropping back down the ladder in case she could help, following Fontaine into the Captain's Cabin so she could get a better look at what was happening.

Slate's quarters were as well appointed as the man himself, with little sign of clutter and the bare minimum of personal effects. Were it not for a few tattered books and a few small curios on the captain's table, Jill might just as well have been standing in the unclaimed cabin of a ship without an owner. The rear wall was dominated by a large window through which the encroaching sloop was clearly visible – as was Fontaine, who had darted through a small side door to reach a narrow balcony, his pale hands grasping the railing tightly.

As she moved to stand with her shipmate, a blur of motion caught Jill's eye. Having surrendered the wheel, the sloop's pilot was now racing down the length of the ship with considerable speed. Their footsteps rang out as they hurtled up the prow and made a great leap, launching themselves towards the *Morningstar*. Now it was the stranger's turn to grasp the railing, and Fontaine stepped back, startled, as the unfamiliar pirate hauled herself upwards. Behind her, the unattended sloop veered off course as the wind and waves took their toll.

Jill hesitated, uncertain whether she should be helping the strange woman clamber aboard or searching for a weapon instead. The stranger didn't seem to need any assistance, however, and a moment later her scrawny frame was hunched over, balanced on the railing like an acrobat as she stared wildly around. Jill thought she might possibly have been beautiful once, but now her eyes were unnaturally sunken, strands of hair sticking limply to her gaunt face. *A sickness*, Jill wondered, *or something worse?*

"I caught you!" cried the woman triumphantly in a haughty, sing-song voice. "Chased you down, took you by surprise, boarded – all fair and square!" She began to laugh, a harsh and rasping sound. "So now you'll hand over all you own to Captain Rooke, that's the rules, or I'll take my little knife and—"

Fontaine reached out with an open palm, and shoved Rooke into the sea.

There was a furious screech as the haggard pirate dropped out of sight, followed by a splash a second later. Jill peered over the balcony and squinted into the choppy water behind the *Morningstar*, but there was no sign of the unfortunate Captain Rooke, only a distant crunch as her errant sloop ran aground on some rocks.

Jill glared at Fontaine. "Was that really necessary? We don't even know who she is."

The pirate gave a lazy shrug and moved back through the captain's cabin. "A cursed pirate is always dangerous, as much to themselves as others. She was too wild, and too thin. But then you live on the land, I think? Perhaps you do not see the signs as I do."

"Signs?" Jill frowned as she followed Fontaine back to the main deck. Slate, as unflappable as ever, was now back at the helm as if nothing unusual had taken place, and rogue pirates tried to board them on a daily basis. "What are you talking about, exactly?"

Fontaine gave a long sigh and waved thin fingers vaguely in the direction of the outpost. "Oh, life. Death. What falls between them. Let us make a bargain, Jill. When we arrive, you will carry the heavy boxes, and I will attempt to explain…"

2

THE *PRIDEFUL DAWN*

There had been three fistfights in the Captain's Head tavern so far tonight, and Tina was worried. If things didn't get livelier soon she'd have to start throwing punches around herself, for she was in favour of a good bar brawl so long as it resulted in spilled grog. Spilled grog needed to be replaced by fresh tankards and, as owner and proprietor, she had a business to maintain.

She brightened up a little when she spotted Harry Harkly walking through the door, making a beeline to his usual table with a particularly irritable expression on his face. Harkly was one of her regulars, and Tina knew him to be loud, opinionated and generally angry at the world, especially when he was drunk – a combination of qualities that meant his starting an argument with someone was practically inevitable.

Harkly tended to win his arguments decisively, for he was a large, thickly built young man with a shock of fiery red hair and a permanent scowl on his freckled face that tended to dissuade most people from standing up to him. Those that did usually found themselves in the grip of two large, scarred hands itching to thump, shove or – in extreme cases – throttle.

To Tina's surprise, Harkly had company this evening. He was being followed closely by a tall pirate dressed in an assortment of ragged brown leathers, her dark eyes glittering in the firelight as her gaze swept suspiciously around the room. Harkly's temperament made it hard for him to stick with any one crew for long and most of his days were spent on a sloop by himself, but if Tina was any judge, his latest companion would be more than a match if the two should come to blows.

Rather than approach Tina, Harkly and his new accomplice began poring over a sea chart as soon as they were seated. They were so engrossed, it was almost an hour before Harkly reached out for a drink he hadn't yet ordered, by which time the tavern had filled up considerably. He hauled himself to his feet and pushed his way through the crowd to the bar. "Two grogs," he demanded gruffly. "To start with." He leaned on the bar moodily, towering over a little Gold Hoarder named Hugh who was slumped morosely on a stool next to him, waiting as Tina hurried to fill two tankards with some of her special stock.

The presence of a Gold Hoarder at her bar was something of a rare occurrence. Members of the infamous Trading Company were, as their name implied, traditionally tight-fisted to the point of being miserly. Most Gold Hoarders considered money spent on drink money wasted, especially when rain filled up a water barrel for free. Something had driven the hunched-over figure into the tavern tonight, however, and he'd surrendered three shiny coins for drinks so far. Noticing that one of Hugh's fingers was partially golden, a common hazard of handling so much cursed treasure, Tina had carefully donned gloves before accepting the money.

"Sling another my way an' all, gal," the Gold Hoarder moaned as Tina deposited Harkly's drinks on the bar. "I need it after the day I've had. Six crews sent out with me best treasure maps, and not one of 'em made it back with the loot! I'm startin' to think it's a mug's game to rely on pirates," he added, mournfully, which Tina privately considered a foolish thing to say, particularly given the company Hugh was keeping. While Gold Hoarders amassed a sizeable fortune from opening treasure chests that nobody else could, it was the pirate crews they hired who unearthed them to begin with.

There was a loud thunk as Harkly set his tankard down with rather more force than was necessary. "Maybe *real* pirates have too much self-respect to do the dirty work of a grubbing little bean-counter like yourself, eh?" he growled. "Perhaps we'd all be a lot better off if you sail out yourself and give the sharks something to chew on!" Several pirates in the outpost shifted uncomfortably at this remark, for they had turned a tidy profit from their own visits to the little green tents where Gold Hoarders traditionally did their business.

"Leave him alone, Harkly," called another pirate whose name Tina struggled to remember. "And you keep your trap shut, Hugh, you don't know nothing about what it's like out there right now. More skellies than ever, new forts being built every day. Not to mention..." The pirate trailed off, as if suddenly aware that everyone was listening to him in relative silence. "Well, it's hard times for everyone."

"Yeah," spat another pirate from across the room, startling a sleeping macaw from its resting place on her shoulder. "And we all know whose fault it is. I barely made it here with my head still on my shoulders thanks to... him."

"Listen to yourselves!" Harkly had turned and was addressing the room, pounding his fist into his hand in irritation as he spoke. "You're supposed to be pirates, but you can't even bring yourselves to speak a name? I say that if you are all so terrified of Captain Flameheart, he deserves to sink your ships and take your treasure!"

"Some names are best left unspoken, lad." The voice was soft, and melodious, but it cleaved neatly through the rising tide of grumbles and muttered objections that Harkly's outburst had caused. Cartwright, an elderly pirate with an obsidian hook where his left hand used to be, had recently retired to the outpost and was now one of Tina's most loyal customers. Despite his advanced years, he remained a commanding presence and often held a large crowd enthralled with his fireside stories. "I stood eye-to-skull with Captain Flameheart in my final days on the seas," he continued, "and I tell you that he is no longer merely a pirate, nor is there now much about him that can be called human."

"Really?" Harkly deadpanned. "Then tell us. What is Captain Flameheart now?"

His companion folded her arms and smirked, clearly enjoying the theatre.

"War," Cartwright declared, sombrely. "Aggression. Hatred. He has become all of these things personified, a Skeleton Lord filled with an unquenchable fury that burns brightest in his chest when he plunges into battle. Mark my words – nothing good can come to this Sea of Thieves while Captain Flameheart sails our waters."

In response, Harkly tilted his head back and drained his tankard, wiping his mouth with his sleeve and unleashing a satisfied belch. "Finished? Then I'll tell you what I think," he declared. "I think people are far too comfortable with the way things are. Running errands for shopkeepers, then creeping back home to spend the coin before somebody steals it from you. You're all terrified of Captain Flameheart because he still remembers what it means to really be a pirate – to show no mercy, take what you want because you can, and rain hell upon anyone who gets in your way!"

As Harkly spoke, Tina saw his associate nodding in approval, but was equally aware that other pirates were starting to stir angrily in their seats. It hadn't come about in the way she'd imagined, but it looked like the bar brawl she'd been hoping for had finally arrived.

"In fact," Harkly continued, "if it takes a Skeleton Lord to help a few of you remember the kind of lives we're meant to be living, ones where miserable little worms like *him*" – he jerked his thumb at the Gold Hoarder, who looked like he'd appreciate the ground swallowing him up right now – "get strung up and left to rot when they try and order us about, then I say: *good for Flameheart!*"

"And I say you need a fat lip!" The pirate with the macaw launched herself across the room, scattering drinks and feathers as she struck Harkly in the side of the head. Her blow took him by surprise and he staggered against the bar, sending a pint of cold grog straight into the lap of the Gold Hoarder, who yelped and tumbled backwards from his stool.

That turned out to be a mistake, as Hugh landed squarely on top of a young pirate who'd spent the entire evening asleep by the fire with his colourful bandana pulled down over his eyes, snoring loudly, oblivious to the fight brewing around him. The startled pirate reacted furiously as he jerked awake, pushing the luckless Hugh away with a hard shove that sent him down onto the flagstones.

"Stinking Trading Companies!" the pirate snarled, springing to his feet and glaring down at the fallen Gold Hoarder. "First you try to swindle us out of treasure, and now we can't even relax in a tavern without you making our lives worse!" His hand went to his sword, but it was his turn to hit the floor as another pirate kicked his legs out from under him. "Stay out of this, stranger!" he hissed.

The interloper, a bearded old goat of a man known as Lampwick Larry, stared down at him contemptuously. "We don't brawl with the Company types!" he spat. "You trying to get our entire outpost blacklisted, you filthy little deck-wipe?" That seemed like quite a plausible outcome, for the terrified Gold Hoarder was scuttling for the door on his hands and knees, but he had already been forgotten.

The bandana-wearing pirate launched himself at Larry instead, embroiling them both in a tussle that nearly sent them both rolling into the fire.

Larry's leg splayed out as he fought, his foot hooking around the leg of a stool and yanking it out from underneath another pirate who had been deeply engaged in a game of Chō-Han and was pointedly ignoring the growing tumult because she was currently winning. As her seat went out from under her she screamed and toppled backwards, landing roughly on top of Lampwick Larry, who assumed that he was being ganged up on and lashed out viciously with his other leg, sending yet more grog everywhere as it struck the table.

Tina pressed herself into the darkest corner behind the bar, a shaky feeling spreading out from her stomach as she realised that this wasn't like the normal kind of bar fights that helped her turn a profit. Something in the air had turned sour, and more and more pirates were starting to fumble for swords and, in a few cases, pistols. One got as far as readying his flintlock and aiming it at Harkly, who was busy repeatedly thudding another pirate's head against a wooden beam, before Harkly's companion picked up a large bench and, without much effort, hurled it across the room with a blow that laid out the would-be assassin for the night.

Lampwick Larry was back on his feet and grabbed the bandana-wearing pirate by his collar, shoving him roughly back towards the bar to stand alongside Harkly and his shipmate. "Traitors, the lot of you!" he declared, to a loud chorus of agreement. "You'd sell your own mothers to earn a place on a stinking skelly ship with the likes of Flameheart! Well, we don't want your kind here! And that goes for you, too, missy!" He aimed another kick at the pirate who'd landed on him, and she shot him a murderous look before backing out of his reach to stand alongside Harkly and the others.

Fairly or not, Tina realised, lines had been drawn, and this was no longer just a brawl. The tavern was now united, having turned its pent-up rage against Harkly and the three who they believed, rightly or wrongly, supported him. Accusations of treachery and cowardice rang out from the crowd as peanuts were hurled from the rear of the room, and a throng of enraged pirates were already edging closer. In a matter of moments, a blade would flash in the lamplight, and either Harkly or one of his comrades would be the first to die tonight.

CLANG!

CLANGCLANGCLANGCLANG!!

Every pirate in the place froze solid as Tina rang the tavern's bell for all it was worth, causing a deafening cacophony until she had everyone's attention. "Out," she said tonelessly, jerking a rum-stained thumb at Harkly and his accidental allies. "Get out and don't come back. You're… barred, or whatever. Just don't be here."

A dark shadow of fury passed momentarily across Harkly's face at this decree, but he turned to his companion. "Let's find somewhere else to drink," he said, icily. "It *stinks* in here." She – along with the other two pirates, who were still both disoriented by the brawl and very keen to escape the angry crowd around them – nodded, and as a group they moved swiftly to the door of the tavern and out of sight.

Tina sighed, dropping her bell back onto the bar with one final clang that served to diffuse a lot of tension. "All right, everyone," she called. "A free pint for anyone who sets their chair or table straight, and wipes the blood away while they're about it."

That did the trick, and pirates were soon at work helping put the tavern back to rights as normal conversation resumed. Only Lampwick Larry and a few of his friends refused to help, slipping out into the darkness on a mission of their own. Tina sighed, watching as her profit for the evening evaporated one complimentary grog at a time, but at least her pub was still in one piece. *Be careful what you wish for*, she thought grimly. *Out here, wishes come true.*

Skip-skip-skip-*plunk*!

Cursing and muttering under his breath, Harkly stooped and picked up another stone, tossing it from one hand to another as he brooded. He and the others had retired to the western part of the island chain that made up Golden Sands Outpost and now sat far away from the shining lights of any buildings, lurking in the shadow of an unoccupied galleon so that they could lick their wounds and talk freely.

"It's always the same," the bandana-wearing pirate said morosely, once the others had explained the night's events. "People don't like to hear the truth. My old man, he came out here when everything was his for the taking. He plundered lost gold from temples or pried it from the cold dead hands of anyone who picked a fight with him. It would have made him sick to see how soft people are nowadays, with all their Gold Hoarder money."

"True enough," Harkly grunted. "What's your name, friend?"

"Can't remember," said the youth, and shrugged. "Everyone calls me Scraps, on account of I can make a meal out of pretty much anything. That's good enough for me." He tugged at the knot of the bandana, revealing a mane of long black hair, and blew his nose on it noisily before shoving it into his boot for safekeeping.

"Harkly," said Harkly. "And that's Karin. We have a mutual destination in mind." Karin gave the slightest tilt of her head in acknowledgement and then went back to whittling away with her knife at a chunk of driftwood, much of which had already been reduced to a pile of sawdust at her feet.

They stared expectantly at the fourth pirate, who had yet to say anything – although now that Harkly came to think of it, he wasn't entirely sure she *was* a pirate. Her clothes were as opulent as anything he'd seen since coming to the Sea of Thieves, her fair hair was clean and fell in gentle tresses across her shoulders as she stared, apparently mesmerised, at the motions of Karin's knife. Only a magnificent scoped rifle strapped to her back, the kind known informally as an Eye of Reach, suggested that she might be anything other than a lady of high society who'd somehow wandered into the wrong tavern.

Suddenly realising that she had a part to play in the conversation, the woman blinked once or twice. "Oh, I'm Jewels," she said meekly. "Well, Juliet really, but Jewels is fine." She let out a little sigh. "Figures I'd get chucked out of the game when I was actually winning for once."

"Well, who needs that filthy old hut and its overpriced drinks to have a good time?" Scraps asked, trying to force a cheerful note into his voice. "I've got a grog barrel aboard my sloop, some dried plentifin left over... I could cook us up a meal and we could say what we damn well think without people getting in our faces about it."

"The little red sloop anchored alongside ours?" Karin scoffed. "Good luck getting there." She passed Scraps her spyglass and through it, much to his dismay, he could make out several patrolling figures marching up and down the docks. It seemed as though Lampwick Larry and a number of other pirates had yet more to say on the subject of Flameheart and those who might sway to his cause, and were waiting for Harkly and his associates to return to their vessels.

"I count at least nine of them," Karin said grimly. "It won't be long before they realise that's more than enough to watch our ships. Then the others will start searching for us. Where are you moored, Jewels?"

"Oh, this is the ship I came in on," Jewels said, jerking a thumb at the galleon whose silhouette was currently giving them respite. "All of her other crew are back in the pub. I doubt they'll let me back on board now, though," she added sourly. "Just take my gold and sail away, I shouldn't wonder."

"You know…" Scraps was staring thoughtfully up at the galleon's hull. "Just because we can't reach our sloops doesn't mean we don't have a ship at our disposal. There's four of us now…"

Harkly stared at Scraps for a moment, then slapped him roughly on the shoulder, "That's thinking like a pirate!" he roared, loud enough that the others cast worried glances across the island, fearful that their hiding place might just have been exposed by the sudden noise. Unwilling to stay and find out, they followed Harkly as he leapt from the jetty and caught the ship's ladder with both hands, ascending it to stand aboard the deck of the unfamiliar ship. "The *Prideful Dawn*," he remarked, examining the nameplate outside the Captain's Cabin. "She'll do."

There was no discussion of who should take command; Harkly was already making for the helm, barking orders as he went. "Keep those lanterns sheathed, Karin. Scraps, Jewels, get on the capstan. Once we lower the sails we'll be easy enough to spot, but the wind's on our side and the outpost's between us and their ships."

Unwilling to risk any argument that might scupper their escape plan, Jewels and Scraps shared a brief glance and then moved to raise the anchor as instructed. To begin with, Karin lowered the galleon's central sail the tiniest fraction, enabling Harkly to swing the ship in a tight circle so that it was facing away from the outpost. Only when he bellowed "NOW!" did she allow the great folds of canvas to tumble downwards and billow in the rising wind.

The *Prideful Dawn* burst onto the open sea with a start, and Harkly was pleased to see that although her crew had barely done more than exchange names, they were already working together well, listening for his instructions and dividing up the work between them. Karin made her way up to the crow's nest and a moment later, a plain black flag was fluttering atop the mast for the world to see. It sent a clear message: *leave us alone*.

Harkly waited until the outpost was little more than a dot on the horizon, and the view clear of pursuing ships, before ordering that the *Prideful Dawn* be slowed to a more manageable speed. "All right, you three," he said as Jewels, Karin and Scraps gathered around the helm. "We're all from different lives. I'm sure we all have places we want to be, but only one ship. So what's it to be? Do we go our separate ways, or do we claim this galleon as ours for good and make a go of it as a crew?"

"I don't have anywhere else to be, actually," Jewels said quietly, staring intently at the floor. She was toying with an ornate bracelet on her wrist, twiddling absent-mindedly with its intertwined chains.

"Yeah, and I'm sick of working with crews who want to spend their days sucking up to the merchants and the Gold Hoarders to make their coin," Scraps grumbled. "If you and Karin are trying to live like proper pirates, then wherever you're heading, count me in."

Harkly stood in silence for a moment, lips moving silently as though he was struggling with a particularly difficult puzzle. Finally, he straightened. "I've decided to trust you," he declared. "That means telling you where Karin and I are heading, and believing that you'll not choose to jump ship. If you try, you'll end this night in the brig. Clear?"

He waited for Scraps and Jewels to nod, mutely, before continuing. "There are others who feel like us, that the Sea of Thieves has been overrun by shopkeepers and gutless wretches who don't have the strength to fight for their own freedom. It's plain to see who's got the best chance of taking back everything we've lost. Karin and I are on our way to join with Captain Flameheart."

3

The *Morningstar*

The morning sun beat down. Fontaine talked. Jill sweated.

Even shopkeepers and shipwrights, protected as they were by circumstance, had heard tell of the many skeletons roaming the Sea of Thieves. If you made an outpost your home for long enough, sooner or later you'd bump into some pirates bruised and limping from an unexpected encounter with a pack of walking, snarling corpses with a grudge against the living, but this was only the beginning of the mystery.

Where did the skeletons come from? What did they want? Those were questions that even a self-proclaimed philosopher like Fontaine lacked any real answers for, he explained from his perch atop a barrel. True to his word, he was leaving much of the heavy lifting to Jill, and she strained under the weight of a cargo crate as he spoke.

"It is supposed that they must once have been pirates, or something similar, for they are often to be found wielding swords or lying in wait near treasure," he informed her. "Once they are given a sound thrashing, they return to the soil from which they sprang. This is the way most will meet a skeleton, but it is not the only way. Twice in my life, I have encountered unfortunate pirates who had been transformed, at least in part, into bones without ever having shuffled off this mortal coil. It seems that certain objects can curse a flesh-and-blood pirate in this way, if they should be handled without due care."

"And that's what you think is happening to Rooke?" Jill looked mortified. "She's going to turn into a skeleton, just because she touched the wrong thing or stood in the wrong place one day?"

Fontaine gave another of the shrugs he so often used to punctuate his sentences. "Perhaps a skeleton, perhaps some other fate awaits her. Perhaps she will go mad first, which would be a kindness, I think. Ah, but here we have the last of our cargo, and I see Dinger is negotiating our payment." He stooped, picking up a small box of tea, pointedly leaving the larger, heavier crate of cloth for Jill.

Jill considered giving Fontaine a withering glare as he departed, but knew fully well her patience was being tested as part of her initiation, if that wasn't too strong a word. Together they tottered down the stout wooden beam that served as a temporary gangplank, and deposited the last of the provisions at the feet of a prim-looking woman who tutted loudly and made a great show of striking out one figure before replacing it with another. "That had better be the last of it," she said icily, "I don't appreciate having to correct my arithmetic."

"Oh, yeah, that's the lot," Dinger – who was sat cross-legged on the merchant's table – assured her. "Delivered promptly and with a smile, which is no extra charge, although we do hope you'll consider us in future for all your transportation needs."

"For now," the merchant sniffed, "I would like you to transport yourself off of my paperwork and out of my sight so that I can get on scheduling my other deliveries. And!" – she wagged a finger as Dinger opened his mouth once again – "Your money, before you remind me, is here. Already accounted for." She deposited a large brown bag of gold into Dinger's outstretched hands, and winced as he hopped to his feet with a careless motion that toppled a stack of neatly arranged parchments.

"I really wish you wouldn't irritate the merchants like that," Fontaine complained as they ambled back towards the *Morningstar*. "One day you're really going to upset them and they'll refuse to do business with us."

"Your trouble, my friend, is that you think everyone takes life as seriously as you do," Dinger countered. "And that I'm incapable of delivering the best insincere apologies the world has ever seen, should the need arise. Besides, I think she likes me."

"You're hopeless."

"No, I'm hope*ful*. Just in general. A bit of optimism never hurt anybody. Isn't that right, Jill?"

Jill said nothing. Truth be told, she was feeling a lot less than optimistic, for she'd realised that their voyage was over.

Her one shot at being a pirate, maybe, and what had she really accomplished? Carried some boxes around? There had been no chance to prove herself reliable in a crisis, no opportunity to rally alongside the crew, and certainly no opening to impress them with her pirate potential. It seemed that the same thought had crossed Dinger's mind, as he pressed the matter no further and they walked back to the ship in silence.

Slate was in his cabin when they returned, meticulously filling out the ship's log, capturing the details of their journey in lines of flowing ink. He looked up, unsmiling, as Jill stepped inside. "Well now," he said briskly, replacing his quill and folding both hands onto the captain's table as he stared up at her. "Ours was not a particularly eventful journey, but perhaps that was for the best. Did you enjoy yourself?"

"No, sir," Jill replied at once. "The boxes were heavy and the plants were a pain in the ar— a pain, and I didn't much like hearing that we might all wind up like that Captain Rooke one day if we're not careful. Even so… It was hard work and a lot of lessons, but I think I needed to learn them."

"A good answer," Slate replied. "But be that as it may, I think—"

What happened next took place with such speed, Jill later struggled to remember the order in which events unfolded. The air in the cabin shifted ever so slightly, as if a sudden breeze had slipped through a crack in the window and stirred things just enough to make the lamplight flicker. And then…

Jill screamed. She hated herself for doing so, it hardly seemed a thing pirates would do, but sheer surprise got the best of her. A man now leaned against the side door of Slate's quarters, looking as relaxed as if the cabin was his own. Jill was absolutely sure he hadn't been there a second ago, and equally certain that he hadn't entered the room by normal means. Judging by the way Slate's pistol was now aimed at the stranger's heart, he was definitely an uninvited guest.

The intruder wasn't particularly imposing, though he was dressed ostentatiously in a broad-brimmed hat, his black leather jacket offset by a striking purple sash. His right leg was missing, and silver chains wrapped around the pegleg that now replaced it. Far more disquieting than that, though, were his eyes, for they shone as brightly as the lamp on Slate's desk.

Despite his otherworldly looks and sudden arrival, though, the man didn't *feel* threatening, not in the way Rooke had done. Slate appeared to think so too, for he lowered his pistol almost as soon as he'd raised it – or was that a look of recognition on his face? Jill couldn't be sure.

"If you're going to board a ship and enter a man's cabin without permission," Slate growled, "the least you could do is knock. Or are good manners something you left behind in that hideout of yours?"

"I apologise," the stranger replied unabashedly. "I had it pressed upon me, in no uncertain terms, that the message I carry is urgent and to be delivered as swiftly as possible. The Pirate Lord wishes to speak with you immediately – you and your crew," he added, with a slight bow towards Jill.

"Does he indeed?" Slate harrumphed. "Arrogance begets arrogance. And what, might I inquire, is the proposed topic of discussion?"

The stranger leaned forward, a mirthless grin on his blank-eyed face. "Oh… Mostly, it's about the end of the world."

The inside of the tavern smelled of sweat and last night's beer, and was mostly empty of customers save for a couple of snoring pirates slumped in front of the smouldering hearth. Even the tavern-keeper was occupied, up to her elbows in soap suds and humming tunelessly as tankard after tankard was dunked in kettle-warmed water, swilled around and then dumped on the side to drain dry. She paid them no attention whatsoever as the mysterious stranger led the way to the only part of the rickety building that was free of furniture. It was as if he were invisible and so, being in his company, were they.

Jill was privately amazed that she was here at all. She'd expected that Slate would inform the stranger of the truth and that he'd been about to dismiss her from his ship, but he'd spared her that humiliation. And so here she was, forming a mute crocodile along with the crew of the *Morningstar* as they traipsed past cluttered tables and old grog barrels.

The lumbering figure came to an abrupt halt, then he opened his mouth and whistled a shanty that Jill had never heard before. As they watched, there came a low grinding sound and the flagstones of the floor rearranged themselves as if they were living things scuttling for the shadows, sliding neatly into cracks and crevices. Beneath them lay a rough-hewn staircase that seemed to have been carved into the rockface itself. Jill was on her hands and knees at once, eager to catch a glimpse of whatever mechanism had kept the passageway so elegantly hidden, but could spot no sign of any devices and was soon forced to scramble to her feet and race down the steps after the others so as not to fall behind.

Stumbling through a twisting corridor of natural rock as quickly as she dared, Jill was encouraged to find that the passageway had been shored up with handrails and decking here and there, along with oil lamps and strings of hanging lights to guide her way. These led her at last to an immense cavern, far and away the largest she'd ever ventured inside, and to a long walkway flanked by streaming waterfalls, the natural echo amplifying their sound to a deafening roar.

At the heart of this great cave rested a huge galleon; one that had been cleaved open along its side, exposing its decks to the salty air and allowing the sounds of merriment to spill forth from within. Jill found the sight both astounding and upsetting, for no shipwright would ever make her seaworthy again. Slate's crew were standing a little way ahead, taking in the incredible view, and Jill hurried to re-join them.

"Oh crikey…" Dinger breathed as she approached, staring around them all with a big, daft grin splitting his face. "This is the place, isn't it! The Tavern of Legends, I mean. Where the Pirate Lord drinks."

"This place is a tavern?" Jill squinted through the spray, trying to get a better look inside the ship. "Hidden beneath another tavern. That seems a little unnecessary…"

"I believe the term they prefer is 'exclusive'," Fontaine said, trying to look unimpressed and only partly succeeding. "Only pirates who have earned a reputation as truly fearsome adventurers among the Companies are welcome here, to drink and trade inside what was once the ship of the greatest pirate to ever sail the Sea of Thieves. I presume our guide awaits within."

Slate took the lead as they entered the galleon, stepping briskly across the threshold. Inside, voices were raised in chatter and song as grog flowed freely, and several pirates were gathered around a troupe of musicians as they broke into the chorus of an unfamiliar shanty. It took Jill a moment to realise what was wrong, at which point she grabbed Fontaine's sleeve and tugged on it urgently. "The musicians!" she hissed. "They're *see-through*!"

Her whispered exclamation earned a wry chuckle – not from Fontaine, who looked just as disquieted by the ethereal band, but from the mysterious stranger, who was leaning against the bar in anticipation of their arrival. "Not scared of ghosts, I hope," he said with amusement as he ushered the group through the merry throng and into a side-room. "You'll see far more disquieting things before the day is out, be certain of that."

The chamber in which they had arrived might once have been used as a place of rest and relaxation, but now it buzzed with purpose. Pirates moved this way and that, adding pins to sea charts spread out across tables and lighting lanterns so that they could better pore over old scraps of parchment. "Reminds me of a battlefield," Slate murmured, and Jill suppressed an involuntary shiver at this unwelcome comparison.

The far end of the room was occupied by a captain's table of the kind found aboard any galleon, and its seat was filled by a stout, bearded phantom whose outline wavered unsteadily as he carried on a low conversation with a woman dressed much like their guide. *Definitely the Pirate Lord*, Jill decided. She had heard the stories, of course – it would have been impossible to spend more than a few weeks on the Sea of Thieves without learning of the legendary explorer who'd first discovered the place – but they hadn't prepared her for the effortless way the spectral figure commanded the room. This tavern was his, and he wore it like a king wore a crown.

As the Pirate Lord glanced in their direction, their guide bowed ever-so-slightly before settling back into a corner until he was needed. The Pirate Lord placed one ghostly hand upon the cane at his side and got to his feet, giving Jill her first glimpse of his carved, wooden leg. "Welcome, my friends," he said, heartily. "Or if we have not met before, then I should like to consider you as such. This is a time when we can all use a little kinship, I suspect."

"And are friends permitted a seat?" Slate asked mildly. No sooner had he spoken than an incorporeal tavern-keeper bustled in, evidently able to rearrange the furniture despite her insubstantial nature, and found stools for each of the *Morningstar*'s crew. Once they were seated, the Pirate Lord returned to his own chair, leaning forward over his desk.

"Allow me to share in your candour, Captain," he began. "The legendary pirates you see around you in this tavern know more than most about the state of the seas, and what we see troubles us greatly. More than the greed of the Gold Hoarders, more than the cowardice of those who prey on pirates weaker than they." A stout finger jabbed at the map in front of him. "Here, here… Here too. New emplacements, constructed by skeletal hands. Great keeps and fortresses springing up under our very noses, built by cursed pirates unwaveringly loyal to their master."

"You mean Flameheart, right?" Dinger sat forward in his seat, looking more attentive than Jill had ever seen him. "That bony old braggart sank my mate's galleon three weeks ago while they were having a knees-up on the beach. He's quite potty."

"I thought so too, at first," the Pirate Lord replied. "Flameheart has always been a vicious and violent foe, keen to prove his strength against anyone he considers a worthy opponent. He can be cruel, but he has always been most concerned with proving his superiority in battle – yet in recent months, his aggression has given way to wanton destruction. Ships without crews, scuttled for no reason. Merchant cargo destroyed while valuable treasures lie unheeded. At first I assumed that his skeletal curse was eating away at his mind, causing him to lash out like a wild dog. However, patterns have begun to emerge. Flameheart no longer fights for fun. I am convinced that he and his followers are arming for war."

Jill frowned. "War against whom?"

"Us," said the Pirate Lord soberly, glancing in her direction. "The living, the dead, anyone who will not bow to his might and swear to serve him. I have no doubt that he intends to one day breach the Devil's Shroud and assail the wider world, possibly even seek conflict with the Grand Maritime Union, but not before all those who oppose him on the Sea of Thieves have seen their ships torn to matchwood."

"If you want peace, you must prepare for war," Fontaine muttered. "Is that why we are here? Is this our call to arms?"

To Fontaine's surprise and obvious irritation, the Pirate Lord laughed at this. "Hardly, my young friend. We have much to do before seeking open conflict – and that is partly why I have asked for your company tonight. You see, the world believes that the Pirate Lord has retired. I have done my best to maintain that misconception, and yet my envoy was recently handed a letter, intended for me. Inside it were promises of information vital to defeating Flameheart once and for all. It's a message I hope you will respond to on my behalf."

"Sounds like an obvious trap to me," Slate declared. "I'm not surprised that you haven't sent these Pirate Legends of yours to investigate. What baffles me is why you expect that my crew and I might choose to stick our heads in a noose on your behalf."

"Frankly, even if it is a trap, I'm not sure it's one we can afford to ignore," The Pirate Lord said, looking extremely grave. "Even an ambush might offer us the chance to capture someone with solid ties to Flameheart, or who at least knows where we might find him. My Pirate Legends, however, are currently occupied, struggling to stop his ships from reaching positions where they would be able to cut off supply lines or even blockade an outpost entirely. We know each other of old, Eli. I would not summon you here to take part in a lost cause – at least, not yet."

Slate was silent for a moment, and then got to his feet, turning to address the *Morningstar*'s crew. "Fontaine, I hear there are supplies for sale down here that I'm sure we could make use of," he commanded. "Dinger, use that silver tongue of yours to ensure we get a good price. Jill, I suggest you take advantage of this invitation and look around the place while you can."

Slate waited, still as a statue, until his crew had spread themselves around the tavern and out of earshot. Only then did he place both hands upon the Pirate Lord's desk and demand, "All right, Ramsey, what the hell is really going on? Why us?"

The Pirate Lord sighed. "The letter made it very clear that any ship I sent must not be detected on her journey," he explained, "and although my Pirate Legends can inspire fear in those who sail the Sea of Thieves, they also attract attention. Likewise, my envoy is rather too conspicuous for his own good. He prefers to stick to the shadows nowadays. Put simply, Eli, I need the help of a crew that's…"

"…Neutral," Slate finished, resignedly. "Unaligned with the Pirate Lord, and therefore unlikely to be followed. I'm still not sure this anonymous tip-off is worth the risk to my ship, or my crew."

The Pirate Lord leaned forward, dropping his booming voice to a murmur. "The truth of the matter? We're not merely preparing to fight this war. We are preparing to lose it." He noted Slate's look of dismay, and added, "Oh, we'll make a fight of it, of course, but there isn't a galleon on these waters that can stand up to the *Burning Blade*. I've learned that the hard way. I laud your desire to keep your crew safe, Eli, but I'm afraid that if we do not act, everyone, even the *Morningstar*, will face Flameheart sooner or later."

Slate did not look happy, but he pressed his point no further, changing the subject instead. "There is another matter... If we're to undertake this expedition of yours and meet with whoever sent that letter, I could do with an experienced fourth aboard. Young Jill is very determined, but she's hardly what you'd call a qualified pirate."

The mischievous twinkle was back in the Pirate Lord's eyes as he leaned back in his chair, sliding a sheaf of papers across the desk to Slate. "Curses, betrayals, krakens... I hardly think you or I could have been considered 'qualified' to handle those back in the day, but we still muddled through well enough. Besides, if I'm not mistaken, that's one of your uniforms she's wearing. Experienced or not, that means that she's part of the *Morningstar* crew, or I don't know Eli Slate."

To that, Slate had no response.

They returned to the *Morningstar* laden with supplies, for Dinger had spotted many rare and exotic items for sale in the Pirate Lord's den and had completely emptied his gold pouch by the time Slate ordered them back to the ship. No further mention was made of Jill's presence; rather, she was both surprised and delighted to be issued with a spyglass and several other tools as she was told to take her station in the crow's nest.

Fontaine was far less pleased upon discovering that Chomps was still aboard the ship. Dinger had covered the snake's cage with a heavy tarpaulin to avoid any venomous outbursts, and thus the creature had been completely overlooked when the rest of the cargo was handed in. Jill wondered why the merchant hadn't mentioned the missing animal, but suspected she'd been rather keen to get Dinger back on the waves and well away from her stall as swiftly as possible.

Once all their new belongings were safely stowed away, Slate led them all down to the mid-deck of the *Morningstar* and over to the large map table, neatly marking a nondescript island in the western region known as the Shores of Plenty. "We'll be picking up some business from the Gold Hoarders here before we depart," he said in a low, clipped voice. "That way, if we should be followed, we'll look like any other crew looking to earn coin. Once the sun sets, we'll double back to the spot I've marked and meet with our mysterious informant."

After a brief discussion it was decided that Jill should be the one to collect their voyage, as her lack of reputation with the Gold Hoarders would mean they offered her a cheaper treasure map. As Fontaine pointed out, there was little purpose wasting gold on an assignment they had no intention of completing. She found the Hoarder's tent easily enough, and tried not to look offended when the hunched, muttering figure inside thrust a battered old scroll at her without even bothering to charge for it. "You're doing me a favour by taking it away," he chortled.

Even though she knew it was little more than a prop for Slate's piece of theatre, Jill unrolled the map carefully as she wound her way along the dock. There was a drawing of some atoll or other, detailed enough that she imagined a ship's map would help her work out which one, and an inviting red X in the lower corner. *This is my first pirate treasure map*, she thought proudly. *Even if Slate puts me off the ship after all this, I'm going to find that island and finish my voyage.*

Knowing that they had time to kill before sunset made for a relaxed journey, and it wasn't long before Slate suggested Jill take a turn at each of the ship's stations. As a shipwright, she was more than familiar with the basics, but it was one thing to spin the ship's wheel in the still waters of a harbour and quite another to hold the ship's course out on the choppy, open sea.

When night fell, Slate ordered their lanterns extinguished, and they sailed silently to the island he'd marked on the map while keeping a watchful eye on the horizon. Once, Jill thought she spotted the silhouette of a galleon parked among the mists, but it turned out to be an oddly shaped watchtower whose builder had long since abandoned her to the elements.

"Perhaps I should keep lookout?" Fontaine asked as they made to lower the anchor. "If there's some sort of ambush set for the Pirate Lord, they may come for the ship while we roam the island."

Slate shook his head. "If this is a trap, I want my crew watching one another's backs, not scattered about where we can be taken hostage or picked off one by one."

Jill looked warily at the heavy pistol Dinger pressed into her hands and wished she'd had chance to try some target practice, since Slate had forbidden her to fire any weapon while aboard the *Morningstar* and risk drawing more attention than necessary. She placed it gingerly in its holster and took a deep breath before leaping over the side of the ship and into the sea, kicking out with her legs until she broke the surface and paddling to shore. Jill liked swimming, but not when she was weighed down by what felt like a small armoury at her waist.

Though Slate had not shared the contents of the letter bequeathed to him by the Pirate Lord, the others supposed it must have contained precise directions, for he set off along the shoreline until they reached a narrow stream, trickling out of a long, thin tunnel that appeared to bisect the island. They moved inside cautiously, and only then did Slate permit a single lantern to be unhooded. The light was sorely needed, for the path Slate picked next was both gloomy and confined – little more than a crevice in the wall, and so well disguised that Jill doubted she'd have spotted it even in daylight.

"Nice place for a hideout," Dinger breathed, and Jill had to agree with that assessment. Whoever had taken up residence on this distant island had clearly had the same thought, for around the next corner they realised that there was a crude wooden door erected to block the passageway. The soft glow of firelight spilled out from underneath.

Drawing his sword, Slate knocked smartly upon the ageing wood with a strange, staccato rhythm that had been specified in the letter, stepping back cautiously once he had done so. There were light footsteps, the sounds of heavy bolts being drawn back, and the door swung open.

"Oh, you're here at last!" the skeleton declared. "I must say, your timing couldn't be better. Is anybody else partial to a spot of late-night tea?"

4

THE *PRIDEFUL DAWN*

Tom Toggs would be the first to admit that he wasn't much of a pirate. He'd spent most of his life ferrying cargo from one place to another, at least until his old legs started to ache one morning and he'd started thinking of somewhere pleasant to retire. What Tom was at heart was a gambler, and a poor one at that, so he'd decided that the Sea of Thieves was the perfect place to live out the last of his days – it was warm, sunny, and mercifully free of people who were good at remembering numbers or, more importantly, knew his name.

He'd used the last of his betting money to buy himself a little sloop and make his way through the Devil's Shroud, and now spent his days avoiding the taverns and any islands where skeletons were known to roam. It was a simple life, but bountiful enough, with rock pools for fresh water and plenty of wild fruit to fill his belly – not to mention the chance to catch a fine, fat fish for your breakfast, which is what Tom was doing now.

Lying on the canopy of his sloop with some wiggling leeches at his side, Tom squinted down into the water, watching intently as the first oblivious splashtail darted closer and closer to his line – only for the morning sun to disappear, casting Tom and his potential meal into darkness. His sloop had been swallowed up by the shadow of a galleon which had crept up to him while he'd been fixated on his food. Its crew were all smiles, waving cheerfully down from the railings.

Somehow, this didn't make Tom feel the slightest bit safer, particularly when the first of the crew leapt from the galleon's deck and landed by the wheel of Tom's sloop, making no effort to introduce herself. She was tall, over a head taller than Toggs himself, and looked like she'd been carved out of granite as she stood on guard, wordless and motionless.

"Ahoy down there!" The voice was loud and boisterous, washing over Tom from on high. It came from another huge pirate, this one with a shock of red hair and eyes that glittered dangerously despite the friendly tone of his voice. "We're so pleased to spy you out here!" He spoke so warmly and with such familiarity he and Tom might have been the oldest friends, but Tom was sure he'd have remembered spending time in the company of this fiery giant.

"I've no plunder," Tom said swiftly, "and no means to find any, neither. I'm in these waters to fish for my supper, that's all."

The red-haired pirate beamed widely, as if this was the best news he'd heard all day. "A fisherman, eh? Excellent! I like to try my luck myself, but I don't have much patience with the small fry. What do I call you?"

Tom wasn't entirely sure if he was being befriended or insulted, only that the unwavering smirk on the face of the woman behind him was making him nervous. "Name's Tom," he grunted. "And if you're here to fish, there's a lagoon on that island over yonder that's fit to burst with pondies." *And is very far away from me*, he added silently.

"That's *so* good to know, Tom! I'm Harry, by the way, you've already met Karin, and here we have Scraps. He's already made us a fine feast this morning." Something seemed to occur to Harkly at this point. "Scraps, now that we're all friends, why don't you take some of our provisions aboard? We wouldn't want Tom missing his breakfast now, would we?"

Tom opened his mouth to protest, but now another of the galleon's pirates was aboard his ship, swaggering down the stairs below deck like he was part of the crew. Tom could hear the frying pan start to sizzle, and had to admit that whatever the stranger had started cooking really did smell wonderful. "Very kind of you," he said, grudgingly, as Scraps reappeared to stand at Karin's side. "But I'll wager you're seeking something in return."

"You're not wrong there, Tom," Harkly said, still grinning. "Have you ever forgotten a special day? Someone's birthday, maybe, and then had to rush around hunting for a gift? That's the sort of day I'm having, because we're on our way to meet a very discerning group of people."

Tom frowned, for he could see where this was going. "I've told thee I've no treasure." He jerked a thumb at Scraps. "Your man here's seen my hold for himself."

"Oh, I'm sure you're a man of your word, Tom," Harkly said, "but the fact remains that you do have something aboard that caught my eye – that remarkable flag you're flying. It's such a striking design, it almost took my breath away."

Tom glanced up suspiciously at the flag atop his mast; an unassuming old thing that had come with the ship when he'd bought it. Sunlight had faded the pattern and it was a bit frayed at the edges, but he was willing to play along if it meant getting this madman away from his sloop. "Well..." he said slowly. "Since you've offered me a meal, I suppose I'd be willing to part with it. I'll just climb up and—" He stepped forward, but Karin's arm was suddenly in his path. Colliding with it was like bumping into a yardarm.

"Come on now, Tom," Harkly said, his expression now akin to that of an advancing shark. "Friends, remember? I'm not going to make you climb all the way up that ladder at your age, not when there's an easier way..." He sauntered over to one of the cannons that lined the deck of the *Prideful Dawn*, taking a moment to buff out a mark with his sleeve before swinging the weapon skywards and taking aim at the mast of Tom's sloop.

Realisation dawning, Tom darted forward as if he could somehow ward off the attack, but Karin snagged him by the scruff of the neck and lifted him bodily off the deck. Tom Toggs was left to dangle, twisting and swearing as Harkly tweaked the cannon's pitch just-so... and fired.

There was a horrible cracking sound. Dark fracture lines

flooded down the length of the wood, and then the whole thing – sail, ladder, crow's nest and the wretched flag atop it all – crashed sideways into the water. A moment later, there was another, smaller splash as Scraps leapt into the sea and hacked at the ropes with his sword, freeing Tom's flag from the jumble of rigging and dragging the soggy fabric triumphantly aboard the *Prideful Dawn*.

"That wasn't so hard, eh?" Harkly asked conversationally as Karin dropped Tom carelessly onto the sloop's deck like a sack of potatoes. "I'd offer you passage, but something tells me you wouldn't care for our destination. Still, I'm sure someone will pass by before long. Think of all the time you'll have for fishing."

Harkly turned away, and that was when Tom Toggs made the biggest mistake of his life.

"You call yourself a pirate?!" Tom spat. "You're nothing b-b-but a swaggering thug!"

Harkly froze for a moment, and when he turned around slowly, the shark-like smile had been replaced by a look of pure antipathy. "Why yes, *fisherman*, in fact I do. A cruel, vicious, bloodthirsty pirate. The kind of pirate who might take an old fool like yourself prisoner for getting in his way. The kind of pirate who is going to teach you a lesson in respect, *Tom*."

Karin grunted. "Want me to bring him aboard?"

"Certainly not," Harkly replied, gruffly. "I'm sure Tom has a brig aboard his own ship. Get him acquainted with it, and we'll be on our way."

Karin nodded, hauling the terrified pirate to his feet and frogmarching him below the deck of the sloop. A moment later, there was a loud reverberating clang as a metal door slammed shut.

Jewels, who had been standing well back with her Eye of Reach at the ready, hurried to help Karin clamber back aboard the *Prideful Dawn*, then turned to Harkly with a look of discomfort upon her face. "We're not just going to leave him locked up with food on the stove, are we? It'll burn his sloop to cinders!"

Harkly was already heading back to the wheel and didn't break his stride. "I'm sure the Ferryman won't care if the fisherman arrives smelling a little singed. He'll be back in the world of the living sooner or later, and next time he'll know to mind his manners when he deals with pirates."

Jewels looked uneasy. "And what if he tells people what we did?"

"Good." Harkly turned away from her, indicating that the conversation was over. "Ours is a ship that deserves a reputation. Get that flag dried and folded, Scraps. We're finished here." With the prize stored safely in the Captain's Cabin, the *Prideful Dawn* set sail once more, sails billowing in the wind – a wind that carried the acrid scent of smouldering wood.

As they sailed into the gloomy, unforgiving region that had come to be known as the Wilds, Jewels found herself fumbling with the coarse ropes of the rear sails and dwelling on what they'd done. What Harkly had said was true, of course – the luckless souls who met their demise upon the

Sea of Thieves would find themselves aboard an ethereal vessel known as the Ferry of the Damned, whose sole pilot seemed eternally condemned to rescue wayward souls from oblivion and return them to the living world – so long as they treated him respectfully.

Rumours persisted, however, that the Ferryman could be stern and temperamental, and that a return trip aboard his vessel was by no means a certainty – particularly if a pirate was judged to be particularly dangerous or disreputable. A man who failed to hold his tongue like Tom Toggs had might easily say the wrong thing and find himself lingering aboard the Ferry for years – perhaps much longer.

And what about pirates who side with a Skeleton Lord…?

Deciding that she didn't like where that train of thought was taking her, Jewels shook herself out of her reverie. Far better, she knew, to learn more about her shipmates and what their destination might be. Karin was closest, so she whistled to get her attention, then asked, "Have you and Harkly known each other long?"

Karin considered this. "Not long. A few weeks, maybe a month. You could say that some mutual enemies introduced us. They didn't last long pinned between both of our vessels, and it was a useful alliance, so we decided to join forces."

"To try and find Flameheart?" Jewels pressed. "How'd you even do that? I mean, I thought his lot were all skeletons…"

"Most of them are," Karin affirmed, giving the sail one last tug and then striding over to lean against the railing at Jewels's side. "But don't let the lies you hear at outposts sway you. There are plenty of pirates who are just like you and me, ready to sail in Flameheart's name." She made a grand, sweeping gesture across the deck of the ship. "Kindness can't raise your sails, and a good story won't patch the holes in your hull. What really matters out here, the only thing a pirate needs, is strength. A strong arm, a tight fist and the courage to use them. You got any brothers or sisters?"

The question felt oddly intimate coming from someone like Karin, and it caught Jewels by surprise. Blinking once or twice, she replied, "A sister, yeah. Back home somewhere, I should think, being all respectable and sticking her pinky out for afternoon tea while everyone else does the hard work." She made a face. "Why?"

Karin paused before replying, as if making conversation was an unfamiliar art. "I had a brother. There wasn't always a lot of food on our table, so he and I made a game out of it. We found one of those boxes they bury people in back home, you know the ones. We'd take it in turns to get inside and the other one would keep it closed just as hard as they could. If you managed to force your way out, you got to be the one who ate that day." She smiled, as if recalling a fond childhood memory.

Jewels looked aghast. "That's dreadful!"

"That's life," Karin retorted. "Mind you, we both got in trouble when Dad found out."

"I'll say! He must have been livid."

"Furious. He made us lug the thing back to the graveyard *and* put all the bones back inside."

Jewels started to laugh, but choked it down because Karin's expression was unreadable. Instead, she asked, "And that's why you want to fight alongside Flameheart? Because you admire his strength?"

"*Respect* his strength." This time, Karin's response was immediate. "So what if he robs or wrecks ships that can't stand up to him? They made their choice to be out here, didn't they? Pirates in these waters have had it easy for too long. It's time someone shook things up."

"Fair enough," Jewels said diplomatically. "Still, though, it can't have been easy to find him. I heard his crew have fortified a bunch of islands but no-one knows where Flameheart's hideout is, or even if he has one."

"Honestly? We got lucky," Karin admitted, lowering her voice so there was no chance of Harkly overhearing. "We stumbled upon one of his ships, in a bad way after it had bumped into a kraken. Most skellies can't string two words together but we managed to coax a heading out of their captain. All it took was the right kind of persuasion."

Intrigued, Jewels opened her mouth to ask how you went about threatening a skeleton, but a change in the wind and a bellowed order from Harkly saw Karin step smartly back to her station at the sails, bringing their conversation to an end.

The fog rolled in soon after, and the last stretch of the *Prideful Dawn*'s journey into the Wilds was still and silent, save for the occasional curt command to trim a sail or check for pursuing ships using the mist to their advantage. They needn't have been concerned, however, for the gloomy waters they were sailing were clear of other vessels – and this was to be expected for, as Scraps pointed out, their current course was taking them towards the edge of the map.

Harkly left the helm only once through the long journey, clambering up to the crow's nest to fly an ominous-looking flag which Karin called a Reaper's Mark – a symbol that, she had been told, would inform Flameheart's allies of their approach and might just prevent the *Dawn* from being blown out of the water.

They gradually became aware of a large, low shape that separated itself from the misty horizon. Despite its size, it was absent from their ship's map, nor could any of them recall hearing of anything quite like it. Harkly did not protest when Karin suggested raising all but one sail and approaching cautiously, as there was an uncommon amount of flotsam and jetsam in the water. The closer they crept to whatever was looming ahead, the more battered sections of hull, tangled lengths of rigging and other debris they had to navigate, rising and falling on murky ocean waves.

The fog eased away and they could finally make out their destination, though none of them could quite believe what they were seeing: the *Prideful Dawn* was sailing through a vast shipwreck graveyard. Prows jutted from the water at odd angles, making an already treacherous seascape even harder to navigate and slowing their progress to a crawl.

As they got closer, bridges and gangplanks more frequently connected the old wrecks into a single, maze-like mass. Many of the ships they passed now had been shored up with fresh cannons and flags daubed with strange, scratch-like markings.

Flameheart's secret bastion; dozens of ships seized after his many battles, salvaged and strung together to create an immense pirate hideout from scratch. The more victories Flameheart achieved, the more ships were added to the great construct and the better fortified he and his followers became. There were no visible signs of life, but their battle-honed senses left the pirates in no doubt that they were being watched.

At last, the *Prideful Dawn* sailed through an enormous gateway, large enough to admit the galleon with ease – and that was when a crude wooden approximation of a portcullis dropped into the water with a great crashing sound, sealing their ship within the belly of Flameheart's stronghold and forcing them to drop anchor at once. Distant chittering sounds echoed around them, as though unseen creatures were laughing at the capture of their latest prey.

Once the ship had come to rest, there was a loud *thonk* as a makeshift gangplank, little more than a crossbeam encrusted with barnacles, was poked against her hull. There were still no visible signs of life, only more growling and chattering from dark corners, but the instruction was clear. Karin seized the flag that they had taken from Tom Toggs and held it tightly as, one-by-one, they stepped onto the slippery wood and moved cautiously forward.

Only when all four had reached a walkway that seemed to lead into the heart of the labyrinth did one of the hideout's occupants appear. A skeleton peeled itself away from the shadows and moved to confront them, though she was like no skeleton they had seen before. Unlike the rank-and-file undead that roamed in the wild, she was well dressed in a heavy greatcoat with a pair of tough boots. By far the most remarkable part of her attire was an ornate hat fused together with long bones, the broken ends of which glowed so fiercely, Jewels thought the accessory might well have come fresh from a bizarre blacksmith's forge.

"Your ship flies the Reaper's Mark, and your course tells me that this is no chance encounter," she said as they approached. Her voice was raspy as the desert wind, and sounded amused and intrigued at their presence. "I am Captain Adara. Tell me, outsiders, what it is that you are holding."

"Tribute," Harkly declared, urging Karin forward to place the folded flag at the skeleton's booted feet. "Taken from the ship of one who was not worthy of sailing the Sea of Thieves, as an offering to Captain Flameheart, in the hope he might consider our request."

Adara tilted her head down towards the flag at her feet, as if considering something nasty she had come close to treading in, then fixed her eyeless sockets on Harkly. "A request? State it."

"We wish to join with Captain Flameheart," Harkly informed her. "To fight to reclaim the seas from those who have lost their way, or want to transform the pirate life into just another form of servitude."

"And to kick the Companies out of here once and for all!" Scraps blurted. Harkly glanced across at him, but said nothing, for Adara seemed to be considering their words.

"You will surrender your weapons and follow me to a holding cell," she said at last. "You are not the first crew to have approached us in so brazen a manner, but that does not mean we can trust you. Is that understood?"

"You can't just—" Karin began hotly, stepping forward with her fists clenched, but Jewels put a hand on her arm. "There are five more skellies up in them towers with cannons aimed at us," she hissed.

If Adara seemed perturbed by the pirates' obvious anger,

she didn't show it. "Certainly we 'can just'," she croaked. "You will be confined while your fate is considered, and if your request is denied, then you will be taken prisoner permanently. Warden Chi has space for you in her dungeons, I am sure, and we cannot allow outsiders to tell others of this place. Either you shall join us at our king's decree, or you shall remain clapped in irons for the rest of your lives."

INTERLUDE

Amidst the fire and fury of war, a boy was born.
When he was old enough to walk, he would pick up sticks and use them to strike the other boys in his village. When he was old enough to talk, he would threaten to hit them again, but harder, if they cried. He was a bully, though he did not know that there was any other way to be and he soon had lots of friends because being this boy's friend was far, far easier than the alternative.

The day that the boy became a man was also the day he learned that there were other, bigger bullies in the world. Two stout fellows from the Grand Maritime Union came to his home and informed the boy that his father – a man the boy had never met – had been accused of piracy. The boy's home was to be searched, he was told, and anything of value retrieved and repatriated as payment for the father's misdeeds. He was forbidden from serving his country in its conflict, for no army could trust the son of a filthy, rotten pirate.

That day, one stout fellow from the Grand Maritime Union walked away with a bloody lip and a handkerchief clutched desperately to his streaming nose. The other had to crawl.

The boy who was now a man thought about all that he had learned and decided that a pirate must be a pretty fine sort of a person, as if such things mattered. The next day he took a few of his belongings and made his way down to the docks, where he watched the sailors at work until the stars came out and they went off to the tavern to sing seafarers' songs, which the man considered a strange and wasteful use of time.

The next day, the man went to watch the sailors again. He watched them on the third day, too. On the fourth day, when he had seen all that he needed to see, he walked up the gangplank of a ship, put its captain to the sword, threw the first mate into the harbour and informed the rest of the crew that they would be setting sail immediately.

He took the nickname Captain Flameheart in his stride, for his men used to whisper that you could practically see the fury burning in his chest whenever the sails of the Grand Maritime Union appeared on the horizon. He pursued their ships relentlessly, and became a force so feared that not even mercenaries would accept the bounties placed upon him by frustrated traders.

And then, one day, Captain Flameheart disappeared.

As always, there were plenty of rumours. Some said that a cabal of soldiers had teamed up and taken Flameheart down while they still had ships left to do so. Others said that he'd been eaten by a whale. One or two of the more outlandish stories even suggested that, bored with hunting the same terrified merchants, he'd set a course for strange and distant waters known as the Sea of Thieves, without so much as looking back. That story was true, of course, although few knew it.

Having left behind a vast estate built from his ill-gotten gains, Flameheart found fresh purpose in his surroundings. He soon discovered that his fellow pirates made far better sport than greedy merchants in their ermine cloaks or stuffy, unimaginative soldiers who followed orders blindly and who killed only because they were told to, not because it was fun. If a ship flew the Jolly Roger, he accepted its challenge with glee, slaughtering the crew and then leaping aboard their battered, flooding vessels to claim a memento of their battle.

That was how he stumbled upon the new-born.

The baby had been tucked away in a woven basket, gurgling contentedly at nothing in particular. Whether Flameheart felt guilt, remorse, or simply saw a chance for his lineage to continue, not even his closest crewmates could say for sure. They knew only that Flameheart returned to his ship and retired to his cabin with the boy tucked under one arm, but not before ordering his first mate to set the fastest possible course out of the Sea of Thieves.

The child was returned to Flameheart's estate, and many on the Sea of Thieves hoped that taking on a new mantle, that of a parent, might bring an end to his dark legend. This was not to be. Although Flameheart made sure the boy was well educated and never wanted for anything, having filled his son's head with tales from the Sea of Thieves, he slipped away and returned once again to a life on the waves.

This brief diversion had seen Flameheart's influence wane, and so – in need of troops and transportation – he set his sights upon a legendary vessel which had gained a fearsome reputation on distant waters – a ship now known as the *Burning Blade*. He took his place as part of her crew, biding his time until the day he overthrew the ship's captain and claimed the ship as his own. Already planning a triumphant return to the Sea of Thieves, Flameheart and his new crew plundered the hold, drinking a mocking toast to their former "Cap'n" from a set of chalices they discovered locked in an obsidian casket.

Flameheart's visits home became increasingly infrequent. Though he and his crew did not yet know it, their misdeeds had done much to change them. The changes occurred so gradually they were easy to ignore, and none among them took the time to ponder that they seemed hardly to use any rations when they sailed, or marvel that nowadays, you really could see the burning fire in their captain's chest…

By the time the crew of the *Burning Blade* accepted their fate as skeletons – pirates for all eternity – Flameheart had long since lost any desire to return home and see his son one last time. His attacks became even more ferocious and indiscriminate. Anyone was fair quarry, even if they were sick or slumbering or surrendering, and none were to be spared the sword. The *Burning Blade* became a ship of reavers, feared and hated by all – except for the undead, more of whom appeared to pledge their loyalty to Flameheart with every passing day. Captain Flameheart, Skeleton Lord, had been born in the fires of war – a war of his own creation.

5

The Morningstar

"What I really want to know," Dinger whispered in a voice only Jill could hear, "is how he's able to drink the tea."

After shaking off the shock of being greeted by an articulate, affable skeleton at the doorway to a secret lair at the heart of a distant island, Slate had cautiously allowed his crew inside, though he hadn't yet sheathed his sword. The interior of the hideaway looked like nothing so much as a library, with books and journals stacked here, there and everywhere.

The skeleton had introduced himself as Edmond as he pottered about among the piles of parchment, lighting lamps and filling a kettle with water from a large jug before hooking it over a small campfire. "'Fraid there aren't enough chairs for you all," he apologised. "That's the thing about a life in exile. Very few guests."

"I can imagine," Slate said dryly. "Exiled by whom, may I ask?"

"Oh, by Flameheart himself," Edmond replied, as breezily as if Slate had been inquiring about the weather. "I was part of his crew once, you know. I'd even go so far as to say I was one of his most trusted shipmates. Ever since I was old enough to totter about I had an adventurous streak in me, so it was only a matter of time before the sea called my name. Born to be a pirate, I suppose. I had a few scrapes and came to find myself aboard the *Burning Blade* around the time she reached the Sea of Thieves."

"Whereupon you and your captain started waging war on the rest of us," Fontaine interjected, leaning against the cave wall and puffing on a long, thin pipe. "You speak of Flameheart as though he is some free spirit, a rogue to be admired."

Edmond appeared to take the rebuke in his stride. "Flameheart is not the man he once was, there can be no denying that. You must realise that back then I thought nothing of the future. I sought excitement, the thrills of adventure and the illusion of independence. I say illusion, for Flameheart had us all entranced by his vision of eternal freedom. Even when curses robbed us of our flesh, we swore to honour our oath and follow him to the ends of the earth."

"And yet here you are," Slate pointed out. "I always like to take a man – or what's left of him – at his word, Mister Edmond, but your story hardly lends credence to the idea that you would betray your former captain."

"Flameheart betrayed us first, long ago," Edmond said levelly. "Not consciously, perhaps, but through his deeds and the corruption of our pirate code. Picking on the weak and defenceless is no sport. Razing an outpost to the ground and leaving the gold to bubble and melt…" He sighed. "Loyal as I had been, I could see where that would lead us. One person's freedom cannot come at the cost of another's."

"Hear, hear," said Dinger, breaking the sombre mood. "So, you stood up to old Burning-Bonce and he chucked you off his ship, eh? Why didn't he just finish what the curse had started and kill you?"

Slate looked as though he was about to admonish Dinger for his bluntness, but Edmond waved a skeletal hand in placation. "I have spent many hours wondering that. I can only think he wishes me to witness his total conquest, so that I can see how wrong I was to oppose him."

"That, or this whole story's nothing but a pack of lies," Dinger persisted. "What's your goal in all of this? Atonement? Revenge?"

Edmond waved this away too, somewhat impatiently. "You don't understand the threat that Flameheart represents. He won't stop. He can never have his fill of battles and bloodshed, not anymore. He'll turn the Sea of Thieves into nothing but a charred wasteland and wait for people to return from the Ferry of the Damned just so he can kill them all over again. That's not piracy, it's insanity."

"I agree with your assessment, but I trust you can understand our scepticism," Slate countered. "You claim that Flameheart has left you alone all this time, but that seems unlikely if you really do have knowledge that could lead to his defeat. His Achilles' heel uncovered precisely when we need it most. It all seems incredibly convenient."

"Hardly," Edmond replied, irritably tapping the papers

on his desk. "I don't need to sleep. I rarely need to eat. I have spent every hour of my isolation searching for a way to defeat or contain Flameheart once and for all, and only recently succeeded. Once I was finally confident enough in my findings to act upon them, however, I realised that I had no way to do so." He sighed. "I have no ship, you see, it was destroyed some time ago, and the merfolk will not offer aid to a skeleton like myself. I have been marooned here with the books I was able to save, scavenging from any cargo that washes ashore."

"You did send a letter, though?" Jill asked, curiously. "How did you manage that?"

"I resorted to messages in bottles," said Edmond promptly, "luring pirates to this island with washed-up promises of gold until I finally tempted a ship that flew the flag of the Pirate Lord. Sneaking my message aboard her was tricky, but one advantage of my… condition… is the ability to last underwater. In my letter, I requested assistance from any and all crews that Ramsey could rely on, knowing that we would be facing fierce opposition. And now here's the *Morningstar* – not exactly the fleet of warships I expected. So where does this leave us?"

"At risk of our tea going cold." Slate drained his cup and placed it carefully on the small fraction of Edmond's desk that wasn't covered by books. "Trust must be earned, as always, so perhaps you had better tell us this plan to defeat Flameheart. To the best of my knowledge, there isn't a single sailor on the seas with the means to overpower him."

"Perhaps not in this day and age," Edmond said, steepling his bony fingers. "So now, let us talk about the Ancients…"

Jill's head was reeling as she staggered out of the cave, the stack of books in her arms tucked neatly under her chin to steady the pile. Getting a history lesson from a walking, talking skeleton certainly hadn't been something she'd predicted would happen when climbing out of bed that morning. *Yesterday morning*, she reminded herself. *You haven't slept in over a day. No wonder you're woozy.*

From what she'd been able to absorb through her cloud of fatigue, Jill learned that 'Ancients' was a name given colloquially to a mysterious and possibly magical civilisation that once made its home in the Sea of Thieves. They shared some traits in common with pirates, particularly a love of treasure and a kinship with the merfolk. They also had a great understanding of the region's natural power, using it to craft curses and make medicines far beyond the reach of current knowledge.

Some of this understanding was fashioned to make great weapons, and it was one such creation that Edmond believed would end Flameheart's tyranny and bring peace – or at least, a more traditional level of chaos – back to the Sea of Thieves.

Things had gotten rather tense when Edmond admitted that he knew very little about the form this weapon would take, nor its precise location. He was confident that his work pointed to a particular mural deep in the Ancient Isles, and that answers would be found there – once he had led the *Morningstar*'s crew to its location.

This did not sit well with Slate. "I agreed to hear what you had to say," he declared. "At no point did I swear the *Morningstar* into service as a passenger vessel, least of all for someone of your... past allegiances, shall we say. No, you can tell *us* the location of this mural and get back to your research. Who knows, there may be more than one way to skin a Skeleton Lord and you just haven't found it yet."

Edmond had proved to be just as stubborn as Slate, insisting that he act as a guide in person. "The *Morningstar* represents my only way off this island," he had reasoned. "If you leave me behind, I have no guarantee you or anyone else will ever return. Trust works both ways, Captain." Not only had this argument secured Edmond passage aboard the ship, but also the lion's share of his belongings, including plenty of trinkets and treasures. Skeleton or no, it seemed that Edmond had retained a pirate's predilection for hoarding valuables.

Jill clambered into an old rowboat they'd procured to speed things up, as Edmond had demanded that everything be kept safe and dry on its short journey to the ship, and glanced curiously at a large, crimson box on Dinger's lap. "What's that? More books?"

Dinger shrugged. "Not a clue, but it looks important and has weird symbols carved into it, so I wasn't about to leave it behind and get shouted at." He took the oars in both hands and began to ferry them towards the nearby *Morningstar*. "I bet this isn't what you were expecting from your first day as a pirate, eh?"

"Maybe not," Jill said, "but at least I'm learning. I've got an idea for a faster way to load cargo onto galleons. Maybe we could try using…" She trailed off as a large yawn interrupted her train of thought.

Dinger looked sympathetic. "Tell you what, I'll take care of all this business. You find a spot below decks and get forty winks while you have the chance."

"I'm not that—" Jill began, only for a second yawn to escape. "Yes, all right, fine," she amended, a little sulkily, and hauled herself onto the ship's ladder once it was in arm's reach. "But you're to wake me if anything happens!" she added.

"We're on a secret mission to save the Sea of Thieves from a genocidal Skeleton Lord," Dinger called up cheerfully. "What could happen?"

It was Fontaine, waiting at the stern of the ship, who answered. "Krakens, marauders, sudden storms, an unexpected collision with gunpowder…" A recent refit of the *Morningstar* had introduced a mechanism for docking rowboats and Fontaine used it now, bringing Dinger up to eye level. "Or were you speaking hypothetically?"

"Why, do I look frozen stiff to you?" Dinger clambered over the railings and retrieved the mysterious box he'd been safeguarding. "I think this is the last of the skelly's stuff. Where is our underfed passenger, anyway?"

"Down in the hold among his belongings, on Slate's orders," Fontaine replied. "Even if we can trust this Edmond, which is by no means certain, the captain feels that having a skeleton seen aboard might erode our reputation if we are spotted. We might even be taken to be traitors, or allies of Flameheart."

"Fair enough," Dinger agreed. "Makes you think though,

doesn't it? We've smacked our share of skellies over the years. I wonder if any of them ever took to having tea parties when we weren't around. P'raps not all of them want to fight us over treasure? We could all just get along."

Fontaine snorted. "Do you think so? There is a word, my thick-skulled friend, used to describe any pirate, living or dead, who wishes to abstain from violence. It begins with the letter P."

"Peculiar? Principled? Pacifist?"

"Poor," Fontaine informed him, scooping up the remaining books. "Now hush. It is time, *dieu merci*, to go."

So, you have made your opening gambit... Do you remember our games?

Edmond, sat snugly within the overstuffed hold of the *Morningstar*, jerked upright, dislodging a stack of journals as he did so. Had he still been a being of flesh and blood, he would have dismissed the mocking voice that had startled him as nothing more than the start of a dream, that moment where you balance on the knife-edge between the waking world and slumber. As he had so recently reminded Captain Slate, however, skeletons did not need to sleep.

The voice had been Flameheart's, Edmond was sure of that; the rasping, panther-like growl of a man stripped of all mercy. A memory, then? His subconscious trying to connect the dots by dredging up some long-forgotten moment of the past? Or was he finally, after so many years alone, going mad on the very night his work was to be completed?

Edmond greatly feared the latter possibility, though he knew it was perhaps inevitable. Since the fateful day they had unwittingly placed a skeletal curse upon themselves, the crew of the *Burning Blade* had fought a losing battle with their own sanity. Edmond had often wondered if the inability to sleep – to linger in dreams while the mind sorted out the day's events in peace – had something to do with it. Perhaps the curse was of deliberate design, and madness a part of the intended suffering.

It didn't really matter to Edmond – his descent into obsession and darkness was inevitable, he was sure. What mattered was stopping his former master and commander while he still had some sense in his head, ensuring that the Sea of Thieves remained a place for pirates to be wild, lawless and above all free. Freedom, *true* freedom, had to include the potential for peace.

The next move is mine…

Edmond was on his feet in an instant, glancing wildly around the maze of his belongings. His sudden movement was enough to startle Jill, who *had* been sleeping – an exhausted, dreamless sleep atop a stack of old sacks. She bolted upright and looked around, bleary and uncertain. Then recollection washed over her and she clambered to her feet, looking curiously at the wary, skeletal figure. "Something wrong?" she asked, guardedly.

"I'm just hearing things," Edmond replied, which wasn't exactly a lie. "I've been on my own for so long, the sound of a ship and her crew going about their business can startle me, it seems." Jill decided to help and scooped up his research from the floor, stacking the pages atop the glyph-covered box, the lid of which had been knocked slightly ajar during its transit.

Edmond sighed. "I suppose I'll never feel completely at ease around pirates, nor they with me."

Jill could sympathise. "It's not much fun being the outsider." Now it was Edmond's turn to look curious, and she realised that with her *Morningstar* uniform on she must have seemed indistinguishable from Slate and the others. "Don't let the clothes fool you, I'm not a pirate. Not yet, anyway," she added stubbornly. "But this is my first time out at sea since I arrived." Jill thought back to the cramped hold in which she and two other hopefuls had been crammed for the journey through the Devil's Shroud, having used most of her life savings to reach the Sea of Thieves.

"Ah," Edmond nodded. "I must say, I'm always surprised how many merchants, shopkeepers and so on have tried to make a home for themselves out here. It seems a pretty hard existence if you're used to a life on land."

"Freedom isn't something invented by pirates, you know," Jill replied, clambering to her feet. "Back home, I could never have been a shipwright. Out here, I can be anything. At least, I can unless monsters like Flameheart are allowed to run free. No offence," she added swiftly. "It's who he is, not what he is, that makes him a monster."

"It would be nice to think that others would agree with you," replied Edmond, "but I suspect that my options are few and far between. Even if Flameheart is defeated, those of us who remain cursed will always be outcasts. And targets, too. I shall have to go back into hiding, assuming Slate will permit it."

"I'll make sure he does," Jill reassured him. Suddenly realising that she had no idea how long she'd been asleep, she eased her way past the mounds of cargo and made her way above deck, hoping that her absence hadn't caused too much of a burden. The cool blue light of an approaching dawn suggested she'd been napping for some time, and she'd never be taken as part of any crew if she didn't pull her weight.

"Is our guest behaving himself?" Slate asked, by way of acknowledgement, when Jill emerged, taking in a deep breath of fresh air free from musty papers and dusty sheets. "If so, you can take up your position in the crow's nest and scout the horizon for ships. We should be able to see our destination soon enough."

Jill was grateful to have been granted a station of her own and quickly did as Slate had ordered, scrambling up the wooden rungs of the central mast and into the crow's nest. It was a cramped space buffeted by warm ocean winds, and Jill's eyes watered slightly as she pulled the spyglass from her belt to begin a slow, methodical examination of the waves.

She could just about make out Fontaine and Dinger's conversation over the sighs of the wind. They were bickering, which seemed to be how they passed the time while sailing, and Jill considered that Slate must be far more patient than he appeared. A less tolerant captain might have put the pair off the ship rather than suffer through their endless arguments. Currently, the two seemed to be squabbling over – Jill strained to hear – their visit to the Pirate Lord's Tavern of Legends.

Dinger was on the offensive. "All I'm saying, mate, is that you call yourself a pompadour—"

"You may call me that," Fontaine interrupted, sounding weary, "for your wits are dull enough that they would bounce off butter, but others would correctly use the term *philosopher*."

"Maybe, but I say that no self-respecting philatelist would have passed up that opportunity like you did!"

Fontaine looked as though he was debating whether to indulge Dinger, or to take the easy way out and jump overboard. "To what opportunity are you referring, my cranially curious colleague?"

Dinger gave an exasperated snort. "The ghosts, of course! Actual phantoms, pirates who have shuffled off this mortal coil, and you didn't want to ask them about it? To find out what really happens when you die, and how they were able to come back?"

"The life of a philosopher is to muse upon the ineffable, not dwell upon that which can be explained," Fontaine stated. "Besides, since you are so infamously amiable with strangers, why did you not broach the subject yourself?"

Dinger shivered. "No thanks. What if I didn't like the answer?"

"I think," Slate cut in, "that discussions of the next life are best discontinued so that we can properly focus on this one. I for one spy land ahead. Dinger, go and fetch Mister Edmond, ready to direct us towards this mural of his. The shorter the time we spend on shore away from the *Morningstar*, the better. Is our coast clear, Jill?"

"I can't see anything that looks like a ship," Jill confirmed.

"Of course, if someone came here in a rowboat they'd have been able to disguise it easily enough." She gave the island – a large, rocky peak noted on the map as being named Devil's Ridge – another careful inspection as Slate, guided by Edmond's instructions, cut a gentle, curving path into the shallows and brought the ship to a halt on the island's southern shores.

"There are no more landmarks between us and the Shroud," Fontaine mused. "At least we're less likely to be spotted by inquisitive passers-by."

"An advantage we'll squander if we're incautious," Slate pointed out. He insisted that the sails were furled and the anchor lowered as quietly as possible, so that the *Morningstar* was properly at rest before they made it ashore. A damp mist rose from the ground as they waded onto land, and the morning was silent save for drips of condensation, for not even the birds were awake yet. Jill was acutely aware of her own heartbeat as they tiptoed through the jungle, and was grateful when Slate eventually permitted them to light a single lantern to dispel the early-morning fog.

Edmond led the way with a compass clutched tightly in his bony grip, muttering to himself and stopping frequently to assess his surroundings. His slow, studious path eventually guided the *Morningstar*'s crew to the base of a high cliff almost completely choked in thick vegetation, though the lamplight revealed a few scrapes of faded paint, still just about visible behind the ivy and creepers.

With no more efficient tools to do the job, the pirates pulled out their swords and spent an exhausting hour hacking away at the greenery, felling shrub after shrub until the Ancient scripture could at last be viewed in its entirety. Much of the mural was made up of angular, scratch-like glyphs, though a daubed image of a shining warrior standing tall among many fallen foes was also visible along with several smaller depictions that meant nothing to Jill. Edmond knelt before it, apparently entranced, scribbling into yet another journal. Slate, meanwhile, stepped away on some private mission of his own. Jill and the others formed a loose, watchful circle around the mural, keeping an eye out for any threat – animal or otherwise.

At last, Edmond got to his feet with a slight clattering noise. "I was correct!" he exclaimed. "The images here depict a great weapon, a powerful creation of the Ancients that was hidden away for use in times of great calamity."

Dinger perked up. "Oh, aye? I'd say a great fiery maniac waging war on the Sea of Thieves qualifies. Are we talking a magic sword or what? Never mind, let's dig it up and find out!"

Dinger's hand was halfway to his shovel before Edmond laid a hand on his wrist, causing the pirate to jerk back in revulsion at the touch of bone. Edmond didn't appear to notice. "The weapon, whatever it may be, won't be here. If my time on the seas taught me anything, it's that the Ancients liked to store their most powerful artefacts in treasure vaults, which were normally protected in one way or another."

"Protected?" Fontaine looked grim. "You mean booby-traps, that sort of thing?"

"Almost certainly," Edmond agreed, "but if I'm understanding all this correctly, the first line of defence is that the weapon is locked away, and three keys are required to reach it. Unfortunately, the locations of those keys appear to have been written in some kind of code. These glyphs here, here and here, you see? I have copied them down, but we'll need help to decipher what they mean."

Fontaine looked annoyed. "You mean to say, now that we have found this mural of yours, you tell us that you cannot understand it?"

Edmond had no expression to read, but he certainly sounded put out by this accusation. "I was born to be a sailor, not a scholar! Given my limited resources, I think I did quite well. Unfortunately, as to the glyphs themselves, I can only think of one or two people who might be able to understand them."

"Translated or not, if you've copied down everything the mural has to say, it sounds like we're finished here." Slate had returned, and in his hands he held a large, red gunpowder barrel acquired from a cache somewhere on the island. "Aside from one last precautionary measure." He placed the keg at the base of the mural, solemnly.

"We're going to blow it up?" Dinger scratched his beard thoughtfully. "The whole mural?"

"To prevent Flameheart from learning what we have learned and possibly more besides, correct," Slate affirmed. "I trust that your note-taking has been properly diligent, Mister Edmond. You will not get a second chance at a transcription."

They retreated well along the beach before Slate unloaded a shot into the barrel from his flintlock pistol. Even so, Jill could feel the heat of the explosion, and winced as the cacophony made her ears ring. When the dust settled, there was nothing left of the mural – only fallen rock and scree that tumbled loose from the cliffs overhead. Whether the writing of the Ancients had been meant as a warning or an invitation, its message was now lost forever – save for one journal in Edmond's clutches.

Once Slate was satisfied that all was well, and after a brief consultation with Edmond, he bade the crew make sail for a nearby outpost. Jill took her place in the crow's nest once again, watchfully scanning the way ahead. Which was a shame, for if she had thought to glance behind at the retreating landmass of Devil's Ridge, she might well have caught the glint of a distant spyglass. From atop the rocky peak that gave the island its name, someone watched the *Morningstar* depart.

6

THE *PRIDEFUL DAWN*

Scraps had decided that it was time to panic.

"We're dead. We're dead and we just don't know it yet. We've smeared ourselves with honey and walked into the lion's den!" he said while pacing rapidly up and down the length of the small prison cell in which he, Karin and Jewels had been confined, shaking each of the metal bars in turn for what felt like the hundredth time in case any had magically worked themselves loose.

"Lions don't eat honey," Jewels pointed out, twirling her bracelet. "And would you just relax? They'll be along to let us out soon enough."

"And if you still want to have all of your teeth when they do," Karin growled across at Scraps, "you can sit the hell down and stop whining."

Scraps gawped at her. "How can you be so calm?! You

heard what Adara said – if they decide we don't get to join them they're going to lock us up for the rest of our lives. I don't know about you but I'm not exactly feeling like one of the family right now!"

"Well, Harry's not here," Jewels said. "That's got to be a good sign, right? They must be grilling him as to who we are and where we came from, and that'll prove we're telling the truth. Right?" She looked back and forth from Karin to Scraps, who snorted. At Adara's insistence, only the captain of the *Prideful Dawn* was permitted an audience with Flameheart, and Harkly had acted without a moment's hesitation. He had left in the company of Adara and three other skeletons several hours ago, and the pirates had been completely alone since then.

"All I know is, they can *try* and lock me up forever," Karin said darkly, "but sooner or later, one of the skellies is going to let their guard down, and I'm going to be ready. And if I can't escape, I'll find some way to send myself for a ride on the Ferry. Anything beats being locked up like this. We just—"

Scraps held up a warning hand, then brought a finger to his lips. Fleshless feet were clattering on the rocky passageway outside of their cell, getting louder with each passing second. The three pirates tensed, ready to hurl themselves into the corridor if an opportunity presented itself – even if it meant facing a skeleton's blade.

As it turned out, they needn't have worried. Here was Harkly, standing alongside Captain Adara, grinning like the cat that got the cream and flourishing a set of keys in his left hand. He fumbled with them slightly as he worked the lock, and the others couldn't help but notice that his right arm was covered in a swathe of heavy bandages. He didn't seem the worse for wear, however, and gave a hearty laugh as the prison's door swung open. "Why so glum? Our new lives begin today, as part of the most fearsome fleet on the seas!"

"Your captain has done much to affirm your loyalty," Adara rasped, not seeming the least bit apologetic about their prolonged incarceration. "Moreover, a most unusual situation has arisen. Captain Harkly will explain that to you once you have returned to your vessel."

"We're leaving already?" Jewels sounded surprised. "I thought we'd rest for a while, stock up on some supplies for the ship…"

"All taken care of," Harkly assured her. "Our new friends have seen to that. Now get moving. We've got new orders, straight from Captain Flameheart himself…"

Barely had the crew returned to the *Prideful Dawn*, which had indeed been repaired and refitted in their absence, before Harkly summoned them to the Captain's Cabin. They found him behind the desk with his feet up on the table, swigging from a bottle and looking for all the world as if he owned the place – which, they supposed, he now did.

As promised, there were plenty of fresh supplies, including a large box on the bed that didn't look like any treasure chest they'd ever seen, but Harkly paid no heed to their curious stares. "This is a great day," he thundered. "We're finally where we belong, and we've got a crew of cowards to put to the sword."

"Oh yeah?" Scraps began to root through a weapon chest that had been wedged in the corner of the room, eager to replace the rather rusty blade at his hip with a more formidable example. "Anyone we might know?"

"We'll find out when we catch up to them," Harkly said loftily. "A gang of desperate fools, nosing around Devil's Ridge looking for some treasure that they hope will give them a fighting chance against us. We're to follow their trail, learn if what they're searching for really exists, and see to it that their little scheme is brought to an end! Maybe we'll make an example of them," he added, with a mirthless grin. "Show pirates what it means to defy the will of Captain Flameheart!"

"We're a long way from the Ancient Isles," Jewels said. "How does Flameheart know all of this? And what—"

"And what happened to your hand?" Karin's blunt interruption earned her a brief scowl from Jewels, which she ignored.

"I took an oath of loyalty, for all of us," Harkly said enigmatically, and then his expression grew stern. "I didn't question Flameheart's power, nor his methods. Neither should you. What matters now is finding that rogue ship as quickly as possible, so we can prove ourselves once and for all! Think of this as a test of our abilities."

Karin nodded. "It's about time, and the wind's on our side. I'll get us underway."

"And I'll prepare some provisions," Scraps added,

following Karin out of the room. "Never fight on an empty stomach, not when your food barrels are full to bursting."

Jewels stepped aside to let them pass, but lingered in the cabin with Harkly, looking troubled. "Um…" she began. "I wondered if you had any jobs for me. Scraps is making dinner, and Karin's setting sail…"

Harkly guffawed. "Do as you like!" he replied, magnanimously. "Arm the cannons, fuel the lamps. Swab the deck if it makes you happy. When I have orders for you, you'll know about them."

Jewels flushed a bit. "If it's all the same to you, I'd rather not take the cannons if we're going to be fighting. Nothing important."

Harkly was taking another drink, but his heavy brows furrowed as he paused mid-swig, and he placed the bottle deliberately back on the captain's table. "Poor pirates don't last long out here, so I know you must be skilled at fighting," he said slowly. "What aren't you telling me?"

Jewels swallowed, wondering why her tongue suddenly seemed to have swollen to the size of a powderkeg in her mouth. "I'm having a run of bad luck," she said in a small voice. "At first it was just little things. My cutlass would get stuck in something right when we were caught in a fight. If I signed onto a ship, its grog would go sour the first night. I used to think I was imagining it, but accidents just kept happening."

Harkly looked decidedly unimpressed. "If things don't go our way in a fight, well then, we fight all the harder. You should never rely on luck, but you can count on a sharp blade and the strength of your own two hands. Sooner or later we're going to be getting into a battle with experienced pirates. I want to know you'll be there with us, weapon ready, not worrying you're going to shoot yourself in the foot." He grinned. "If the worst happens, I'll buy you a pegleg."

Jewels smiled weakly and backed out of the cabin, allowing her expression to falter only once she was safely out of Harkly's sight. Other pirates never believed in her constant misfortune, no matter how many treasures slipped from her hands during a storm. Nor did they notice that she could barely take the helm for an hour without the ship encountering a kraken's inky clutches. The Trading Companies, on the other hand, *did* notice – noticed their missing treasure and broken promises. None of them would employ Jewels anymore, not after fate had rolled the dice against her so many times.

Karin had taken the wheel by the time Jewels left Harkly's new quarters, carefully threading the *Prideful Dawn* back through the shipwrecks on the border of Flameheart's great bastion, a look of furious concentration on her face. Rather than disturb her, Jewels opted to wander below the deck, where she found Scraps pouring a good quantity of wine into a pan. "This is the proper stuff," he said cheerfully as she descended the steps and took a seat at the ship's map table. "Not like that filth the Merchants palm off to the tavern-keepers around here."

"Why d'you hate the Companies so much, anyway?" Jewels asked, as she took in the welcome scent of their imminent meal. None of Adara's lackeys had offered them so much as a gulp of water while they'd been locked up.

Scraps gave her an unfriendly glance. "You're saying you don't?"

Jewels shrugged. "It's them that don't like me, t'be honest. I'm more of the shoot-things type of pirate, so Merchants don't have too much use for me." *Especially now that they've blacklisted me*, she thought.

"You ever been to the Americas?" Scraps asked. Jewels shook her head, and he continued. "I was born there. I don't remember much, but I remember my dad's little store at the portside. Sometimes, when the weather was fine, he'd take me along and I'd sit on the counter, watching the ships coming and going. He'd sell the sailors lantern oil, tar, fresh powder, parchment, whatever they needed, and often he'd just take some fresh fruits or fish they'd caught on their travels." He sighed. "Those were the nights we ate well."

Jewels could sense "And then…" lurking just out of sight, and sure enough Scraps's dreamy expression clouded over once more. "And then, one day, a man came to our store. My father sent me to the back room, but I could hear them arguing, not that I understood it." Scraps paused to stir the pot before continuing. "My mother tried to explain. The Grand Maritime Union wanted to build their own store in place of our own, she said. My father was very firm, and said no. They offered him money, but still he said no. It was about the community, he explained, the give and the take that made everyone better-off." Scraps sighed. "He was an honest man, and he paid for it."

"What happened?" Jewels leaned in closer.

"They bought out the pier. Increased the rent on my father's spot so that he couldn't afford to keep the store in business. He swallowed his pride, took his hat in his hands, and went to the Union. To apologise. To sell them the store like they had proposed. They said no."

"That's awful! What did your dad do?"

Scraps was at the stove again, grinding herbs between his fingertips. "He brought me here. Said if there was no room in the world for honest men, we'd have to learn about the alternative. It was rough going at first, but like I told you, he thrived out here. He was lucky – he died without ever seeing the flag of the Merchant Alliance on his seas. He died free."

Jewels realised she was nodding sympathetically. "What about your mum?"

There was a pause. "Not everyone makes it through the Shroud." Scraps turned back to her, his dark eyes shining. "No-one's ever asked me that before."

Jewels shrugged as casually as she could manage. "It's a small ship," she said, a little hoarsely. "Not much room for secrets."

"Yeah, about that…" Scraps stepped away from the stove and took a seat opposite Jewels. "What did they do to Harkly, exactly? What was that oath he mentioned?"

Jewels scowled. "Dunno. Rather him than me. He wants to be captain, he can do the weird ritual stuff and call me when it's time to shoot something."

"Sounds like that something's going to be other pirates," Scraps said, grimly. "But if whatever they're hunting for can really beat Flameheart, what would it do to us?"

"Maybe they won't even see us coming." Karin lumbered down the stairs and gave Scraps's bubbling stew an appraising stare. "Smells okay," she said grudgingly. "Anyway, we're not skeletons yet. They have no reason to think another crew of pirates would turn on them, not if we play nicely. We might even get them to trust us. And then…"

Scraps began to ladle a thick broth into unadorned tin bowls he'd found at the bottom of a storage crate, making sure to include a fourth for Harkly, who hadn't been out of his cabin since they returned. Karin did not join them at the table, but turned on her heel with a portion in each hand, leaving her unspoken threat hanging in the air.

The two seated pirates ate wordlessly for a few moments, and then Scraps suddenly began to choke so ferociously that Jewels had to vault over the table and thump him on the back. "You okay?" she asked, concern etched on her brow.

"Yet!" Scraps gasped. "What did she mean by *yet*?!"

Jewels set her bowl down and rose to her feet. "Let's get back up top," she muttered. "I think I just lost my appetite."

Only when the *Prideful Dawn* had moored itself at Devil's Ridge did Harkly emerge from the Captain's Cabin, now wearing a pair of thick gloves and a heavy greatcoat that struggled to contain his bulky physique. Dark rings under his eyes hinted at fatigue, but he leapt onto the prow of the ship and struck a bold pose, sword raised with aggressive fervour. "Time to go hunting," he declared. "Let's not waste time." The others nodded, taking hold of the ship's ladder one at a time and making their way ashore.

"It would have to be Devil's Ridge," Scraps sighed, staring up at the craggy outcrop that cast the ship into shadow. "This place is huge, not to mention riddled with caves! You know the one about needles and haystacks?"

"Hunt with your head, not with your heels," Karin retorted. "Look for signs that pirates have been here. Footsteps in the sand, trampled vegetation, a snake slain by a blade… They must have been in a hurry. Swiftness is the enemy of stealth."

"We'll split up to search," Harkly informed them. "Scraps, you're with me. When one of us finds something, light that old campfire on the beach there as a signal, and we'll meet back here."

"Wait!" Harkly and the others turned curiously in Jewels's direction. She was crouching ever-so-slightly, peering through a gap between two trees. "Someone's in the bushes. We're being watched, and they're coming closer."

Harkly glanced at Karin, which was all the instruction she needed to melt away into the shadows. For his part, Harkly pulled a compass from his belt and made a great show of holding it before him as he took paces from tree to tree, counting aloud. Bemused, Scraps and Jewels raised their lanterns to illuminate his footsteps, watching intently as though their captain was on the brink of some great discovery.

Harkly's performance was clearly enough of a distraction, for a moment later there was an angry squawk and a great deal of rustling before Karin emerged from the bushes, holding a struggling pirate in a great bear hug. "Bind her!" she growled, angrily. "She *bites*."

Only when the writhing woman had been securely tied at her wrists and ankles did Karin drop her roughly and step back, sneering. The lank-haired pirate glared balefully up at them, grumbling and cursing. "Ambush!" she spat. "Treason, to set about bold Captain Rooke in such a way. You're worse than the others!"

Karin tensed as if to deliver a kick, but Scraps waved her away and crouched down by Rooke, seemingly unconcerned by the wad of spittle that arced past his ear. "Others?" he prodded. "There was another crew here? Tell us!"

Rooke's demeanour changed in an instant, her struggling and epithets replaced by a knowing coyness. When she spoke next, her voice was like grease. "Maybe there was, maybe there wasn't…" she cooed. "Hard to remember, when I'm so hungry and my wrists hurt so…"

"We are not untying you," Karin said flatly, "Let's just go. Her mind's too rotted to speak the truth regardless."

"Wait!" Rooke wailed as the four pirates made to leave. "I remember now! I'd never forget their wicked faces, not when they were so cruel! The cheating crew of the *Morningstar*!"

"So there *was* a crew here, and you saw them," Scraps pressed. "What were they doing? Did they mention a destination?"

"Of course I saw them! That ugly bear figurehead and those silly starry sails! I chased them all the way here, to make things even when the time was right!" Spite was evident in her voice. "They never saw me hiding. Too busy with the wall of words."

Harkly let out a low rumble. "Release her," he commanded. "We're all on the same side here. But in return, *you*…" He pointed a gloved finger at Rooke, who stared at it as if mesmerised. "You're going to show us where they were poking around. If you try to trick us, we'll go back to being enemies." He loomed over her, adding, "I don't have many enemies. At least, not for very long."

Even Rooke could tell that Harkly meant every word of this, for she meekly allowed her bonds to be cut and then led the crew of the *Prideful Dawn* along the beach, stopping at the pile of rubble where the mural had been.

"Looks like a powderkeg went off here," Karin said, nudging the scorched sand with her boot. "They must have taken what they needed, and then..."

"Sensible. But unhelpful. Maybe they let something slip." Harkly turned to quiz Rooke, but the scrawny figure was down on her hands and knees, drawing symbols in the sand with a long stick. "What's all this?"

"The wall is gone, but the words live on," Rooke crooned. "There are three keys to the great weapon, the skinny one said. Here..." The stick prodded at the three symbols.

Scraps made an impatient gesture. "What use are symbols we can't understand? Whoever left that message must be long dead. This has all been a waste of..." He stopped and glared as Rooke began giggling. "You think this is funny?"

"I know more than you think, pretty boy!" she chortled. "Strange runes, yes, but not secret ones! Not to good friends of Graymarrow!"

"What's a Graym—" Jewels began, but Harkly waved her into silence.

"Are you saying you can read these symbols?" he challenged.

Rooke brushed a strand of thinning hair aside and looked up at him through half-lidded eyes, slyly. "You take wise

Captain Rooke to your ship, show me the map, I can point the way… and maybe eat a hot dinner?" she added hopefully.

To the obvious surprise of his crew, Harkly reached down with one hand and helped Rooke to her feet, allowing her to return with them to the *Prideful Dawn*. Once aboard, she eagerly gulped down the remaining contents of their cooking pot before scoring dark crosses on the ship's charts, muttering to herself as her gaze roved from island to island.

"You realise she's a liability," Karin murmured to Harkly as Rooke fussed and fidgeted at her work. "If she was willing to help us, there's no telling who else she might blab to. Here, or on the Ferry of the Damned," she added meaningfully. "I say we throw her in the brig."

"It's hard to sail silently when someone's raving in your hold," Harkly countered. "Let's leave her to take a little nap while we go about our business. When the time is right, I'll get word of her to Adara."

"You will?" Karin narrowed her eyes. "How, exactly?"

If Harkly was going to respond to her question, however, he never had the chance, for that was when Rooke sprang to her feet. "All done!" she announced, as if she were a child who'd cleaned their plate. "Now we can make sail, get our revenge, and I'll cut their—" Her sentence ended in a dull groan and a thud as Karin, ready for the moment, brought a stove pan down upon her head with just enough force to knock her senseless.

Once they had returned the stupefied Rooke to the shore and Devil's Ridge had receded into the mists of a new morning, Harkly summoned the crew back to the map table.

"So then, our target is a galleon named the *Morningstar*," he proclaimed. "If Rooke's telling the truth, we have a head-start, but we'd be fools to count on it. Safer to assume that we're on an even footing and seeking the same thing. Namely, the three keys to this 'great weapon', whatever it may be."

Harkly wiped a gloved hand across his brow to wipe away some sweat, and continued. "From what I know of the *Morningstar*'s captain, Slate, he's a good old boy who should be polishing his army boots rather than pretending he's a pirate. Men like that, they do things by the book. That means once he knows where the keys are hidden, this…" Harkly leaned forward and tapped the map, "…will be where they head first," he finished.

Karin nodded slowly. "Because it was the first location listed on the mural?"

"Right." Harkly's hand swept over the charts. "That's why we'll be sailing *here*, to take the second key for ourselves. Maybe prepare an ambush. Pry another key from their cold, dead hands if we get the chance."

"We're only one crew," Jewels cut in, sounding a little uncertain. "If we told Adara what we know, she could send some of Flameheart's ships to pin down the *Morningstar* and they wouldn't stand a chance."

Harkly gave a grim smile. "We won't impress Flameheart by letting another ship claim the greatest prize ever seen on the Sea of Thieves, even if we are on the same side. I say we find that weapon ourselves! Return with an offering that will really prove our worth, not just some mouldy flag." Still smiling, he stomped away and up the stairs to the top deck, leaving the others to ponder his words.

"You know…" Karin said conspiratorially, her voice low. "An oath is one thing, but it'll never make up for a strong crew. If this weapon really is powerful enough to defeat Flameheart, and if we take it for ourselves, we could be the ones giving the orders for once."

Scraps looked slightly discomfited at this. "You mean betray Harkly? He'd cut us down in a second if he suspected. But even if we succeeded, do you really think pirates stand a chance at challenging Captain Flameheart? A Skeleton Lord?"

"That's just a fancy name for an ambitious bag of bones," Karin declared. "And if you strike at the right place, at the right time… bones can be broken."

7

THE *MORNINGSTAR*

The *Morningstar* dropped anchor on the outskirts of Plunder Outpost as the sun was rising. Jill's spot in the crow's nest gave her an ideal vantage point to watch merchants, shopkeepers and many others scurry about preparing for a day of traffic and trade, for pirates were already arriving to hand over last night's ill-gotten gains. It also meant that she was assailed by the aromas of half-a-dozen campfires laden with bacon and eggs, and she descended to the deck in the hope that breakfast might be an imminent part of Slate's plan.

She found their captain standing on the pier, deep in conversation with a pirate whose sloop was docked nearby, for Plunder Outpost was one of the more recent settlements to be established and not even Slate could navigate his way around by heart. He seemed to be seeking directions, and a few gold coins changed hands before he turned to face the *Morningstar* and whistled shrilly for the rest of his crew to join him.

Dinger and Fontaine appeared in short order, hauling themselves over the railings and dropping onto the jetty with an unusual sense of purpose about them. The promise of a secret weapon seemed to have made both men more alert and attentive than usual; even Fontaine seemed uncharacteristically enthusiastic about their trip and what it might mean for their future.

"Our business here is with the Order of Souls," Slate said briskly, once the four of them were assembled. "Our experience with their members is somewhat limited, I must admit, but Jill, I believe one of their representatives has taken up residence at the outpost you call home?"

"Oh. Yes, er, Olive's her name," Jill said, slightly flustered by this unexpected interrogation and choosing not to mention that she'd nearly trampled the poor woman the last time they'd encountered one another. "We haven't really spoken, though. At least, she's never come to enquire about a ship and I've never seen her in the tavern. People say they're all a bit weird, honestly," she admitted. "I've seen pirates bringing them skulls and all sorts of other odd things."

"Aye, we've heard much the same," Dinger agreed cheerfully. "A bunch of soothsayers and palm-readers, by all accounts. Maybe I'll cross their palms with silver and treat Fontaine to a fortune-telling session."

"A fool and his money are soon parted," Fontaine shot back. "Tea leaves and tarot cards can tell us nothing of the future, and if they could, what would be the point of getting out of bed?"

"However dubious their qualifications may be, Mister Edmond and I cannot think of anyone else who might have a hope of explaining these symbols to us," Slate declared. "And I have it on good authority that Madame Olivia, who represents the Order at this outpost, is the most senior among their number." He sighed. "We are taking something of a gamble by speaking with her, but we appear to have little choice. Unless any of you can offer me an alternative?" He looked to the others, but they could offer nothing more substantial than a shrug from Fontaine. "The Order it must be, then."

Jill was surprised to see that Madame Olivia's residence was much the same as Olive's pavilion back at Sanctuary, the outpost she thought of as "home". Heavy purple fabric draped over and around the supports of a building neatly converted empty space into a snug nook, within which the Order could do their business. *Either the Order disdain material things*, she thought to herself, *or just really hate paying their rent*.

The pavilion lacked a door to knock upon, so Slate settled for a polite cough before peeling back the drapes and stepping into Madame Olivia's abode. The others squeezed themselves inside one at a time, for the tent was a cramped affair, largely filled with papers and boxes that rivalled the *Morningstar*'s overstuffed hold.

The strangeness of Olivia's dwelling paled into insignificance when compared with the countenance of the woman herself. Jill had been expecting the flowing dress and inky streaks that ringed Olivia's eyes and cascaded down her cheeks – the woman was dressed almost identically to her associate on Sanctuary Outpost – but it was clear that her stained face and elaborate attire had taken Slate and the others by surprise, almost as much as meeting Edmond for the first time.

Slate rallied almost immediately. "Good morning," he said, with the slightest bending of the waist. "I do hope I'm not disturbing you."

"Not at all, Captain," Madame Olivia replied, her voice low and melodious. "The day is still in its infancy, and you are my first visitors. Besides, your arrival was made known to me." Behind Jill, Fontaine made an audible scoffing sound, and she resisted the urge to kick him in the shin. Whether or not she spoke the truth, Olivia's presence was spellbinding.

"Indeed?" Slate kept his tone carefully neutral. "Perhaps, then, you will also be aware that I hope to avail myself of your knowledge and wisdom, qualities I'm told you possess in abundance." He reached inside the pocket of his uniform jacket. "I have recently come into possession of a most unusual—"

"Pray, allow me to save you both your time and your breath, Captain," Olivia interjected, holding up two ring-laden hands as if to ward off Slate's request. "I cannot help you. Or to be more precise, I *will* not help you. Not yet."

Slate bristled. "Hardly seems fair to turn a fellow away before you even know what he's asking for."

Olivia arched an eyebrow. "Allow me to clarify further. No matter what your request may be, whether it is in my power to assist you or not, I am forced to put you to a hard bargain, for which I apologise but do not relent."

"In other words, you want something from us before you'll even hear what we have to say." Dinger shook his head. "And I thought it was the Merchants who liked to haggle."

"Do not confuse my motives with those of base greed," Olivia said, a sharpness edging her voice for the first time. "I would not be so callous were my situation not so dire, forcing me into this mercenary frame of mind when I would prefer to be focused on more spiritual concerns."

"Perhaps if you told us what your problem is," Jill suggested, eager to try and defuse the brewing argument given everything that was at stake.

Olivia regarded Jill for a moment, dark eyes glittering in the candlelight, then began to speak more kindly. "You are aware, I should think, that our Order is relatively new to these waters," she began. "Nevertheless, we have flourished here, in part due to a mutually beneficial relationship with others at this outpost, and I have sent my sisters to establish ourselves across the Sea of Thieves."

Slate gave a non-committal grunt, which Olivia took as an invitation to continue. "Recently, I have been made aware that one of our number, Madame Omina, has begun to lose both the trust and the trade of those who came to Ancient Spire Outpost, where she has taken up residence in the Order's name. Upon investigating the matter, I have learned that a Gold Hoarder at the same outpost, a boor by the name of Hector, has indulged in a deceitful campaign of disinformation, besmirching Omina's credentials and leaving her a practical pariah!" Olivia's voice rose as she spoke, filling the tent with her obvious anger.

"So someone's been badmouthing your mates, aye?" Dinger cut in. "And what, you want us to go and rough them up a bit?" Even without looking in his direction, Jill could practically hear Fontaine's eyes rolling.

"Only if absolutely necessary," Olivia said. "I generally prefer pirates to save their strength for dealing with the skeletal sorts who persistently plague these seas. It may well be that this Hector is labouring under a misunderstanding, or has himself been deceived in some way. Cooler heads may yet prevail. I, however, cannot afford to leave my post here to attend to the matter, while you have a ship on which to sail and, more pertinently, something you need from me in return."

"I dislike having my crew's affairs dictated in this manner," Slate informed her, "but your concern for your friend seems genuine enough to me. I am forced to wonder, however, what happens if we manage to restore the good name of the Order at Ancient Spire and then find that, after all our hard work, you are still unable to help us with *our* dilemma?"

Olivia locked her dark, inky gaze with Slate's own. "Since you believe it impossible to divine the future, that is simply a risk you will have to take."

The sun was shining, the gulls were freewheeling overhead, and Hector the Hoarder had a chest full of somebody else's gold. It was, he reflected, shaping up to be a fine afternoon.

As was common practice for the Gold Hoarders, he glanced around suspiciously and drew the emerald-green flaps of his tent tightly shut before turning his attention to the chest. It was locked, of course – they almost always were, and there was no point in trying to force your way inside – but that was no problem for Hector, because Hector had the key.

He could feel it now, a slight coolness against his chest as his breathing quickened with the thrill of new treasure, and wasted no time in pinching the chain it was attached to, removing it from his neck and bringing the little key to the lock of the gilded box before him. He inserted the key and turned it in a smooth, well-practised motion, letting out an involuntary shudder of excitement at the *click*.

The chest was... serviceable, Hector decided. A fair number of coins, a single precious stone and an interesting medallion that might well be repurposed in some way. In line with proper protocol, he dutifully tallied the value of the box's contents, referring to his notes for the Gold Hoarder-approved worth of the more esoteric treasures. Next, he methodically removed his percentage of the loot, along with a second amount which would cover what he'd spent to acquire the box from a passing pirate.

He permitted himself one last look at what remained in the chest before reluctantly closing the lid. It would remain safely stored among his wares – or, if the day was kind and profits were high, hidden in the secret compartment beneath the carpet of his tent – until the others came to collect it. *Fine tribute for the Master*, he thought in satisfaction, and flung the tent's entrance back open in anticipation of whatever riches might await him next.

"Good afternoon," said Captain Eli Slate, roughly three inches in front of Hector's nose.

Hector yelped in surprise and took an involuntary step backwards, nearly tripping over the chest he'd just been admiring. "You scared me," he said accusingly. "And you don't seem to have any treasure," he added, recovering his composure and looking his visitor up and down. "Well, we can soon sort that. I've got a fine map here that'll send you out to the Wilds, there's—"

"I'm not here for a voyage, Sir," Slate interrupted. "And, as I have neither the time nor the desire for duplicity, I shall come to the point. I'm here to ask about your dispute with the Order of Souls and, if possible, resolve it."

Hector's expression clouded, first with disbelief and then with suspicion. "And just what business is it of yours, eh?" he thundered. "What sort of person sticks their nose into other people's private affairs?"

"I believe the word you're looking for there is 'pirate'," Slate replied.

"Yeah, well, the only pirates I care about are the ones fetching me my gold, and if that ain't you, Slate, you can stop wasting my time," Hector said hotly. "Oh yeah, I know who you are. You've done work for the Gold Hoarders in the past, aint'cha?"

"Quite so," said Slate, immobile as a rock in front of the tent, making quite certain the Gold Hoarder couldn't simply walk away from the conversation. "But while we have faithfully surrendered all kinds of treasures and trinkets to your Company over the years, I have never once seen anything that suggests your business could be threatened by one young lady, let alone why you would seek to turn the Outpost against her."

"Well, that shows what you know," Hector sneered, unable to resist bringing this supercilious captain down a peg or two. "That little witch had barely set up shop here before she came creeping around my tent, offering to sell me maps and riddles to all kinds of swanky swag!"

Slate raised an eyebrow. "And you refused her offer?"

Hector stared at Slate in disbelief, bewildered that anybody could say something that stupid. "Are you potty? I had the maps off her quick as you like, and they were some good hauls, too, proper plunder to be found. Business was booming!"

Slate took a deep breath. This situation was getting more confusing by the moment. "Forgive me, but it sounds to me as though this arrangement should have endeared the young woman to you, not given you cause to take offence."

"That just shows you ain't no businessman," Hector said smartly. "'Cos I gets to thinking, see, if she's got all these maps and charts to the best treasures, how long is it going to be before she realises she can cut the middle man, which is to say me, out of the equation? If she started selling the maps to pirates directly, I'd be ruined!"

"Maps to chests that only you Gold Hoarders have the ability to open," countered Slate. "I was there when they were first introduced to the Sea of Thieves. I've seen the power they contain."

"Yeah, for now." Hector looked grim. "But if anyone's gonna break through the voodoo that keeps 'em locked, it'll be that bunch of weirdos in the Order. Besides..." He lowered his voice, as if what he was about to say next was deeply confidential. "If the high-ups found out there was treasure coming to the Outpost that wasn't making its way to my doorstep, I'd be for it, make no mistake! So I takes a little wander over to Omina's place, and I tell her she's got to swear and sign a contract that she won't work with anyone who ain't a Gold Hoarder."

"The Order have affairs of their own," Slate pointed out, "I assume she wasn't exactly pleased by this demand?"

In response, Hector turned around and pulled aside his long, matted hair to reveal a sizeable bruise across his neck and shoulders that had bloomed into a sickly rainbow of purples and blues. "She hit me with one of those crystal ball things and then started lobbing actual skulls at me," he whined. "If I hadn't scarpered she might have turned me into a newt!"

Slate sighed. "So that's why you've decided to slander the poor woman? All because she wouldn't indulge your paranoia?"

"Well, she ain't exactly made many friends here anyway," Hector said smugly. "So all I had to do was suggest that maybe the Order of Souls is to blame for this Flameheart business." He sniffed. "It wouldn't surprise me if it were true an' all, what with all the hocus-pocus they get up to. I'm amazed we're not up to our necks in cursed captains. If you ask me..."

"Enough." Slate looked pained. "This situation is even more ridiculous than I imagined. You're to stop spreading these rumours and apologise to the young lady before her livelihood is completely ruined. If you sound sincere, she may continue to sell you those maps you're so fond of."

"No chance!" Hector snapped, stepping up to Slate so that their faces were once again mere inches apart. "Crews that don't want to work with the Order no more all come and see me instead. Business has never been better! And before you try and put the fear in me, Mister Big Scary Pirate," he added as Slate opened his mouth to argue, "don't even think about pulling a gun on me or anything like that, or I'll see you and your *Morningstar* never work for the Gold Hoarders again. I've a Master who doesn't care for his loyal employees being threatened."

Hector could tell that Slate took his meaning, for the pirate took a step back, anger visible on his face. "Perhaps we could find some other form of understanding," the pirate persisted. "There must be something my crew and I could do that would convince you to change your mind."

Hector had won, and he knew it. "It's like I told you at the start, Slate," he said loftily. "You ain't got nothing I need. Now if you don't mind, I've got coins to count. We're done." He half expected the obstinate captain to keep arguing, but Slate merely stalked away from the Gold Hoarder's tent in the direction of the docks, fuming with indignation at his defeat.

The argument left Hector feeling invigorated for the rest of the day. He beamed delightedly at any pirates who came his way with chests to sell, particularly those who'd barely escaped with their lives thanks to a run-in with skeleton ships loyal to Flameheart. These pirates were taken into the strictest confidence and warned to stay away from the highly suspicious new arrival in the purple tent…

Pirates could call upon the Gold Hoarders at any hour of the day or night, and the more successful Company Liaisons often worked long hours, making sure that any ship with treasure to sell could do so swiftly and easily, in case they changed their mind. Even so, when darkness fell Hector found himself casting his gaze up to the peak of Ancient Spire Outpost, and to the light spilling out of the Unicorn Tavern. He deserved a treat after today's endeavours, he decided. Maybe he'd be neighbourly and play the place a visit tonight – and maybe, there'd be some new arrivals who'd be willing to hear cautionary tales about the strange soothsayer who was definitely up to no good…

Having made up his mind, Hector took down the last of the day's takings in his ledger, piled the chests into the underground storeroom for safekeeping and fastened his tent closed to keep prying eyes away from his business. Sticking his hands in his pockets and whistling tunelessly, he began to climb the steep trail that would ultimately lead him to the Unicorn and an evening's entertainment. It was a long and winding path, one that spiralled around the towering central peak that gave the outpost its name, but it had been a long day and the chance to stretch his legs felt good.

Hector reached a makeshift rope bridge that connected the cliff to its neighbouring promontory and offered a path into a winding set of caves; puffing slightly from the exercise, he saw the tell-tale glint of treasure shining in the torchlight. He stopped, squinting, and sure enough there was some trinket or other lying just inside the cave mouth. Hector normally had little reason to cross to the northern half of the outpost since it was largely uninhabited, but if some careless visitor had dropped something shiny over there...

His curiosity piqued, Hector picked his way across the bridge, which creaked alarmingly in the wind but seemed solid enough underfoot, and crouched down to get a better look at the little object. It was a small brooch made of twisting silver chains, into which a single opal had been set. Though nothing particularly expensive, it was probably of great sentimental value to someone. But then, what would people think if they saw Gold Hoarders running around trying to return jewels? Better to add it to the pile when he got back to his tent.

Hector pocketed the little gewgaw with practised ease, and was about to turn on his heel and leave when some new strangeness gave him pause. It sounded like creaking – a rattling sort of hollowness that he couldn't immediately identify, but which seemed to be coming from further into the cave. He squinted into the darkness of the cavern, wondering if the brooch's owner might possibly be in the vicinity, searching for their missing trinket. "H-hello?" Hector called, feeling suddenly timid as the hairs on the back of his bruised neck began to rise.

There was another scraping sound in response, louder this time, or – a worrying possibility – perhaps just closer. As Hector's eyes adjusted to the gloom he realised that there *was* a figure stumbling about and heading unsteadily in his direction – an inebriated pirate, perhaps? Someone he knew? He took a hesitant step closer, and rasped a tongue across lips that were suddenly dry. "You okay there, pal?"

There was a rush of motion, and Hector got his answers in quick succession. He absolutely did not recognise the shambling figure, and they were definitely not okay. As his unexpected assailant lurched out of the darkness, Hector's raw instinct kicked in and propelled him backwards towards the mouth of the cave as fast as his trembling legs would carry him.

He almost made it, too, before the skeleton bore down upon him, wrapped two bony hands around Hector's neck and began to choke the terrified Gold Hoarder to death.

8

THE *PRIDEFUL DAWN*

Harry Harkly, Pirate King, roared with laughter. All around him, his loyal crews did the same, stamping their boots and hurling insults as the piles of tribute piled around Harkly's great throne began to topple and tumble in great glittering cascades. At Harkly's feet, the objects of their derision cowered and grovelled, begging for mercy.

Harkly looked first into the eyeless sockets of Captain Flameheart as the skeleton knelt before him, then at the terror-stricken face of the ghostly Pirate Lord beside him. Their war of attrition had been ended with a single decisive strike that neither had been expecting, and now the man who ruled the Sea of Thieves would cement his victory with one final act.

Harkly raised the weapon of the Ancients high over his head. It flowed and changed in his grasp from one moment to the next, first a gleaming sword, then a great poleaxe, and finally an immense hammer. With a great bellow of triumph, Harkly brought the weapon down upon his enemies, who both seemed to have dwindled to little more than part of a decorative frieze on the floor of the palace. His blow splintered and distorted the two pirates with a satisfying crunch.

The cracks continued to spread, twining and wrapping around the walls and pillars of the great hall. Thin licks of flame began to rise through the splintered floor, growing larger as more of the frieze fell away. Sweating in the unexpected heat and nervous about the destructive force of his blow, Harkly turned and strode swiftly towards the doors of his palace, seeking the fresh air and salty smell of the ocean water.

Here was a beach, just as he had expected, but he found no respite here, for the water before him hissed and bubbled as though the entire ocean was being boiled away by some great conflagration. There were fingers of rock jutting out of the water, but these glowed white with heat, and ships that struck them immediately went up like matchwood, their sails burning away to cinders as Harkly watched in horrified fascination.

He did not have time to watch for long. A huge hand clamped down on his right arm and twisted it behind his back, spinning him around with a deliberate roughness designed to make the boy squeal – Harkly was a boy again, he must be, for the figure that held him in a vice-like grip towered overhead. He always had done.

"'ARRY, YOU BLEEDIN' ROACH!" The words were

thick and ran together on breath sour with drink. "YOU BEEN BRUISIN' AGAIN? LIFTIN' AGAIN?"

"No, Da!" Harry insisted, pain lancing through his arm as he dangled in the behemoth's grip. "It was just a bit of fun! We didn't mean nothing by it! We was only playing!" He looked in mute, desperate appeal to the shadowy figure of his mother at the stove, but she said nothing, just continued to chop away at the dinner like always, each motion of the knife counting away the seconds and bringing Harry closer to his inevitable punishment. *Chop, chop, chop.*

Harry was being dragged by the titan now, his bare feet scraping uselessly on the rough flagstones of the kitchen, the beach and the burning ships replaced by the heat of the hearth – the great roaring fireplace of his home, magnified to an impossible size and burning brighter than perdition itself.

Chop...

Harry tried to explain, to shout, to wriggle free, but his voice had abandoned him to the flame. He was no longer being forced towards the fire by his father's grip; he himself was walking as if hypnotised, his legs betraying him as he teetered on the very precipice of the inferno...

Chop...

Harry's arm jerked outward of its own volition, fingers twitching as they inched towards the blazing brightness. He couldn't resist; there was no free will left in him as his hand began to blacken and crumble from the ashen wind of the roaring fire. He could only watch in unblinking dread as more of his arm gave way to the flame...

Chop...

The dream melted away, and the blinding fire became nothing more than a shaft of sunlight, slicing through the curtains of the Captain's Cabin to fall neatly onto the bed where Harkly was sprawled. For a moment he did not know where he was, and then reality rushed over him as he wiped away the clammy moisture that soaked his brow and collar. The agony inflicted upon his right arm remained all too real, however. It seemed that not even dreaming would disguise it.

Enough of weakness. Dreams could not hurt him, and if day had broken they must be nearing their destination.

Harkly strode from the cabin and mounted the steps to the ship's wheel two at a time to take the helm from Karin, eager to occupy his attention with anything other than the residual horror of his nightmare. The second of the three islands Rooke had marked upon their map loomed on the horizon. It was a sizeable landmass, and it was beginning to dawn on Harkly that they had no idea how to find the key they were seeking, or even what form it might take.

Jewels, who had been at the prow of the *Prideful Dawn* inspecting the horizon through the scope atop her Eye of Reach, trotted up the same steps a moment later. "The coast seems clear, but this is a big place," she reported. "I'd feel better if we could scout out the other side before we drop anchor."

"I could fire you out of a cannon for a better look," Karin offered, apparently in earnest.

Jewels blanched. She knew that skilled pirates really could – and occasionally did – cover great distances by squeezing themselves into a ship's guns and letting themselves be launched into the sky, but the thought of it made her stomach turn.

"We stick together," Harkly insisted. "Slate could be here at any moment." He span the wheel sharply, easing the *Prideful Dawn* towards a small beach from which a winding pathway snaked between two high cliffs and out of sight.

Scraps had prepared bundles for each of them, filled with provisions and useful supplies like sturdy lengths of rope and pouches of ammunition. They went ashore slowly, taking their time to check every suspicious crevice that might open out into a sizeable cave, always keeping watch for any tell-tale rock paintings to point the way. The thin gully they'd spied from the beach turned out to snake its way inland for a while before opening out onto a plateau, and it was here they first began to spot signs of civilisation. Carved pillars covered with moss and flagstones peeking out from the thick mud suggested that someone, presumably the Ancients, had settled here long ago.

It was when they heard cheerful singing that the crew of the *Prideful Dawn* realised that somebody had made this place their home in the here-and-now. A cooking fire had been set up under a thick canopy of trees near the centre of the plateau; as Harkly and the others watched intently from the shadows, weapons ready in their hands, the source of the off-key ballad soon presented itself.

Rather than a representative of some lost Ancient tribe, however, the man was clearly a pirate – the eyepatch and the tankard of grog in his hand were a dead giveaway. But it was Karin who confirmed the man's identity, stepping forward with an uncharacteristically startled look on her face. "M-Merry?" she called, uncertainly. "Is that you?"

The singing stopped abruptly, the tankard frozen halfway to its beard-lined destination. "Eh? Who's that?" the pirate demanded, looking around. "An' have you got any spuds?"

"It's him," Karin muttered, and stepped forward so that the perplexed pirate could see her clearly. "It's me, Merry. Karin, remember? From the *Golden Colt*? Everyone, this is 'Merry' Merrick. We go way back."

Recollection dawned on the pirate's weathered face. "Cor, I ain't thought about that ship in an age," he grinned. "These yer new shipmates then, eh? Shouldn't think there's much to plunder in a crumbly old place like this. Not even any 'sparagus, unless you've got some in them sacks of yours?"

"No, we don't have any asparagus, Merry," Karin said patiently. "No potatoes neither." She looked to the others, clearly uncomfortable at her past and present colliding in this unexpected meeting, and muttered, "Merrick's a bit of a fussy eater. Likes the posh stuff."

Scraps perked up at this. "Is that why you're out here, old-timer? Looking for ingredients? Because we're almost out of—"

"Nay, lad," Merrick announced, taking a deep swig of his grog and then gesturing grandly with the tankard, spilling quite a lot of what remained. "Y'could say I came to this old place looking for inspiration. A way to fill me noggin with thoughts of the old times and put them to parchment in a new song. Can't seem to find me muse anywhere else on the seas, but the legends and stories a temple like this can tell, well, it's bound to fire the imagination!"

"There's a temple?" Jewels pressed. "That sounds like the sort of place we might be looking for. Is it close by?"

Merrick chortled. "You might say that, aye, we're standing on the roof! The whole place is underground, y'see. There's a way in just over yonder, but it's dark and there ain't much what you'd call solid footing, so I've been 'appy to make camp up here and soak in me surroundings."

"Show me," Harkly demanded at once, and waited impatiently as the bemused pirate staggered over to a small stone circle which might once have been the start of a spiralling staircase leading down into the ground.

The others gathered around it, peering down into the gloom. Just as Merrick had said, much of the masonry had fallen away and the few steps that remained looked ready to crumble the instant anyone's boots so much as scraped the stone.

Scraps looked grim. "I could take the plunge," he said, not sounding too happy. "For all we know there's solid ground down there, just out of sight. Or water to land in, maybe."

"Even if there is, you'd have no way of getting back out," Jewels observed. "And if you die, you'll be stranded on the Ferry for who knows how long while we've got the *Morningstar* breathing down our necks."

Harkly gave a sudden bark of anger and flung a fallen coconut into the pit, where it struck an outcropping and exploded in a shower of milk and husk. "Damn it all. We'll have to go slowly – use our ropes, make some stakes for footholds, and be sure we've got a way out again."

"That'll cost us our lead—" Jewels began, but Harkly silenced her with a glare. Working as carefully as they could, they unpacked the ropes and braces from their belongings and secured them around the stoutest trees, knotting and looping the coils together until they had something sturdy to shimmy down into the abyss. Next, they each looped a length through the handles of their lanterns and around their shoulders and waists, strapping the lamps to their own chests so both hands would be free for their descent. Through it all, Merrick dozed by the fire, a grog-fuelled morning having caught up with the old salt at last.

When the time came to enter the hole, Harkly insisted on taking the lead, grasping the rope in both hands and feeling around for the first knot to use as a foothold. The stairway seemed to go down and down forever, but thanks to the light he was carrying, Harkly found the descent easy enough, moving gloves and boots carefully one knot at a time. It wasn't long until he spied solid ground below his feet, along with a hole in the rocky wall nearby.

"There's a passageway here," he called up, and allowed himself to drop the short distance onto a solid, sandy floor. Confident that the way ahead was safe, it was a simple matter to bring the others down one at a time with the same measured motions until at last all four pirates were standing, sweaty and dishevelled, at the entrance of the Ancient temple.

"You sure we can trust Merrick?" Scraps asked. "If we come back with the key and find that rope's been severed…"

"You can relax," Karin insisted. "Merrick's a drunk, and mostly cracked, but he's a solid ally. Besides, he knows what

I'd do to him if he tried to double-cross us. Let's see where this leads." They walked in single file into the darkness, but soon found that they no longer needed the lanterns to see. Before long there were fires to light the way, burning brightly after all these years without so much as a drop of oil – a sorcery for which they were all secretly grateful, as the temple had a rather ominous atmosphere. They couldn't quite shake the feeling that they weren't alone.

Eventually, the torch-lined corridor opened out into what could only have been the temple's main chamber. It was immense. An enormous circular room taller than any steeple, with a sloping floor that dropped away into a single central aperture filled with water. Beneath that, there was yet another great chamber below them, but since the hole was blocked by thick bars of polished obsidian, it was evident that they would not be going swimming any time soon.

"I feel like we're the last grains of sand in an hourglass," Scraps commented, tossing a single coin against the wall and watching it spin and tumble its way downwards until the curve of the floor carried it into the waterlogged hole with a tiny "plop".

"Yeah, and this place is a maze," Karin added. There were stone platforms and wooden walkways above and below them at different elevations; some were connected by handholds in the stone walls, while others served to create bridges between smaller antechambers filled with shrines, statues and other Ancient leftovers. "The key could be anywhere."

"Maybe…" Jewels was once again squinting down the scope of her Eye of Reach, surveying the temple in excruciating detail, "but if you ask me, what we're looking for's down there. See that alcove?" The others pulled out their own spyglasses and clustered together to spy what she could spy. Sure enough, there *was* an important-looking chamber far below them, one that contained a stone dais ringed with braziers – and atop it, a gilded box. It was unusually angular in its design, but any pirate worth their salt could tell a treasure chest when they saw one. The lid was embossed with the crude, golden shape of a man wielding a spear.

"I do see," Harkly said. "And I also see it's blocked off by more bars, which suggests whatever's inside is important."

"That might mean a box full of gold or gems," Karin said levelly. "Valuable to whoever built this place, but not what we're here to find. We should check out the other alcoves too, in case this key has been right under our noses all along. No point in being careless now."

"Fine," Harkly conceded. "We split up. Karin and I will make our way down to that treasure chest, Jewels and Scraps will scour the rest of this place so we don't miss anything."

Navigating the labyrinth of platforms proved easier said than done, however. Many of the criss-crossing ledges seemed to serve no purpose other than to baffle or infuriate intruders, and it wasn't long before Harkly and Karin found themselves staring at their destination from a high platform, lost and annoyed at the lack of any obvious way to reach it.

"This is stupid," Karin announced, and took a few steps back, making ready to leap – but Harkly threw a thick arm across her path. "If you drop down there, you may not find a way back up again," he warned.

"Good thing I've still got some rope left, then," Karin countered, dropping her bundle at Harkly's feet. "Take it, it'll only weigh me down." Without waiting for a response, she ducked under Harkly's outstretched hand and took a running jump, launching herself towards the ledge below and landing roughly, winded, colliding with the hard stone wall. She grunted, ignoring the grazes on her arms and hands and taking stock of the situation now that she could get a better look at the mysterious chest and the room where it was sealed away.

Peering through the obsidian columns, it was obvious – and rather aggravating – to confirm that there really was only one way in or out of the nook where the box resided, which meant that Karin was now stranded on a dead-end ledge in the lowest part of the chamber. She would worry about that once the chest was in her possession, however. Inspired by Scraps's earlier performance, she began to methodically check the bars to see if any had come loose, though they remained resolutely steadfast. Karin was next forced to examine every last brick and tile, hunting fruitlessly for a secret switch or mechanism that might open a path.

Having made their way to the highest reaches of the temple, Jewels and Scraps were similarly frustrated. There were plenty more alcoves that needed investigation, each containing a single object that might well have been an Ancient key of some sort – or, perhaps, only a decorative art piece from long ago. Stone totems, golden discs, strange necklaces… Scraps was methodically collecting them all, just in case.

The next alcove they checked had apparently fallen victim to some tremor or other, for a small rockfall had dislodged whatever had been displayed here from its plinth. Jewels found it lying nearby; a strange, cylindrical object that weighed less than she was expecting – a drum, she realised, giving it an experimental *rat-a-tat* with two fingers. This at least seemed safe enough to leave behind, so she placed it carefully back on the plinth before giving it one last absent-minded slap with her hand.

The thunderous boom that issued from beneath her palm startled her so much, Jewels almost tumbled off the ledge. A second, more cautious strike produced similarly magnified results – the shape of the alcove seemed designed to greatly amplify the beats of the drum when it was set in its proper place. Entranced, Jewels tapped the drum a third time.

"What the devil is that racket?!" Harkly bellowed, but this was intermingled with an even more distant shout from Karin. "The bars are moving!" she called out. "Whatever you're doing up there, keep doing it!"

Jewels needed no further encouragement and set about the drum with both hands. As she beat out a steady rhythm high above, Karin was satisfied to see the columns that had frustrated her slide smoothly into the floor of the alcove. Only when they had fully retracted did she utter a shrill whistle, signalling to Jewels that she could stop, the silence unnaturally oppressive after the last echoing drumbeat died away.

The instrument's tones were replaced by a low roar that echoed up from the very bottom of the chamber. Peering over the edge of their various platforms, the scattered pirates could see that the stone grating above the pool of water had also retracted, presumably thanks to Jewels's performance. As they stared down into the gloom, there was another great roar and a dark shape flitted past the aperture.

"What the hell's that?" Scraps called, the remaining treasures quite forgotten. "A shark? It must be the size of a galleon!"

"A guard dog, a pet... Who cares?" Harkly snapped. "Just don't fall in the hole. We've got a key to collect, remember?"

Mindful of the chest she'd come to retrieve, Karin dragged her attention away from the shadowy shape as it continued to fill the temple with angry noises. Stepping smartly into the room, she reached between the braziers, took the chest in both hands and prepared herself for what promised to be a long climb back to her crew. "If you've still got that rope, Harry, I could use a lift about now," she called, casting another glance down at the lurking beast – realising the full consequences of using the mysterious drum to unseal the temple's depths.

Slowly but inexorably, the water below was beginning to rise.

9

The *Morningstar*

It is said that when someone believes they are about to die, their life flashes before their eyes. Unfortunately for Hector the Gold Hoarder, he was being shaken back and forth so violently by skeletal hands that he was missing most of the best parts.

A rock, he thought feverishly. *I need to find a rock to hit this thing with. That's what people do in fights, isn't it?* Unfortunately, the landscape of Ancient Spire Outpost seemed to be cruelly devoid of any fist-sized rocks, stones or even a patch of gravel. Hector's fingers closed instead around a small, leafy branch, which he thrashed ineffectively against the skeleton's rib cage for a moment before it was knocked from his grip.

"Help me!" Hector wailed, his strangled voice sounding thin and reedy in the echoing cave. "Somebody, please!" He had assumed he was already at the peak of all possible terror, but felt his stomach lurch anew as he caught sight of a second silhouette, ambling with no particular haste up the same pathway from which the skeleton had emerged. Didn't these things like to travel in groups? "No…" he moaned, despair engulfing him like a cloud. "Somebody…"

"Somebody?" The voice was both familiar and impossibly calm. "Did you have anybody particular in mind?"

Hector tried to focus on the figure, which was tricky, given that he was still being shaken like a rag doll. "S-Slate?!" His eyes bulged. "Don't just stand there, man! I need you!"

"Really?" Slate raised his lantern, illuminating the scuffling pair, but made no other move. "It was only a few hours ago you told me that I had nothing that you needed. You were quite insistent on that point, as I recall."

"This ain't time to joke! I'm being murderised!" Hector pleaded. "How do I get this thing off me?!"

"Oh, your average skeleton's not so tough," Slate said blithely. "Give the thing a few swings of your sword and it'll… Oh dear." He paused, leaning forward with acute academic interest. "Of course, you fellows don't carry weapons, do you, because you're not… now what was your phrasing… big scary pirates?"

"Got… gold!" Hector wheezed, his feet kicking and scrabbling uselessly on the sand. "Will… give…"

Slate shook his head, slowly. "Believe it or not, Hector, this isn't about profit. This is about people. Specifically, the people at this outpost. If, and I really must stress that word, *if* I choose to help you, you're going to do exactly as I say. And I know the Gold Hoarders take their business arrangements very seriously, so let me ask you…" Slate came to a halt mere inches away from the skeleton, which seemed to be ignoring his presence entirely. "Do we have a deal?"

"D...Deal!" Hector was barely able to spit the word out; as soon as he had Slate sprang into action, pistol in his hand and ready to fire. The bullet struck the sand, but it was enough to cause the skeleton to reel backwards in alarm, releasing Hector from its clutches at once and dropping him to the ground. It hissed menacingly at Slate before turning and vanishing into the shadows.

Hector remained on the floor for a moment, rubbing his neck and glowering at Slate. "You missed."

"Didn't want to risk shooting you in the leg now that we're business partners," Slate replied. "Besides, it'll think twice before it sneaks onto an outpost again. You'll be quite safe now." He reached down and grabbed a fistful of the Gold Hoarder's jacket, hauling the man to his feet. "Now, why don't we finish your little jaunt to the tavern, eh? I dare say you could use a drink after all that, and you've still got a lot of apologising to do…"

Tears rolled down Dinger's cheeks and into his beard as he rocked back and forth against the railing of the speeding *Morningstar*, consumed by mirth. "Oh, that is priceless!" he roared. "You really marched that skinflint to the tavern and made him say sorry?"

"Let us just say our friend Hector has found a new and very public respect for the Order of Souls and Madame Omina in particular," Slate replied, straight-faced as ever.

"How fortunate that Fontaine had persuaded her to attend that evening so that Hector could apologise in person. A fine job – and to you, Mister Edmond, for playing your part."

"It was a cunning ruse," Edmond declared, "and far more exciting than waiting in the hold with nothing but a surly snake for company. I might have gotten slightly carried away with my performance."

"What's important is that we got you back aboard without being spotted," Jill pointed out, "but I still don't understand how Olivia intends to help us in return."

"A swift return to Plunder Outpost should see that question answered soon enough," Slate assured her. "And as the route is now somewhat familiar, I think it is time you took your turn at the helm…"

Jill felt somewhat uneasy about directing the *Morningstar* given the urgency of their mission, but the night was calm and the wind in their favour as they left Ancient Spire and the exhausted Hector behind. With Dinger and Fontaine managing the sails unsupervised, she was even able to bring the ship neatly alongside the jetty when they reached Plunder Outpost. She wished the Senior Trader, watching them guardedly from the stall of the Merchant Alliance, looked just a little more impressed at her accomplishment.

Madame Olivia greeted Slate and his crew far more warmly than before, looking as close to genuinely happy as they had ever seen her. "Your quest was a rousing success, as I knew it would be," she declared grandly.

Fontaine opened his mouth to protest this, for it should have been impossible for word of what had transpired to reach Plunder Outpost before the *Morningstar* itself had done, but Olivia gave him no chance to interrupt. "Each of these skulls," she continued, indicating four crusted craniums tinged with a ghostly green light, "are the result of bounties issued to brave pirate crews. They roamed far and wide, but they have one thing in common. They all served a Skeleton Lord named Graymarrow."

"Now there's a name I've not heard in a long time," Slate murmured.

Olivia gave him a sharp look and continued to speak, picking up the closest of the four skulls. "Graymarrow has long made use of an obscure set of runes – though the term glyphs would be more accurate, I feel – to communicate with his underlings. Unwittingly, his guile has revived a forgotten dialect of the Ancients."

Olivia reached into the folds of her dress and pulled forth a large tobacco pipe of the kind Fontaine occasionally used, upon which she began to puff industriously. As the bemused pirates watched, she brought the skull to her mouth as if to kiss it, only to exhale a large cloud of smoke straight into the cadaverous head. Almost immediately, the ghostly glow flared as bright as any lantern, and the skull reciprocated, sending a burst of ethereal vapour into Olivia's open mouth, seemingly with no ill effect. Once this was done, she allowed the skull to topple carelessly from her outstretched palm. It struck the floor and cracked, unheeded.

"Fragments of knowledge… A weak mind that remembers little of what it once knew…" Olivia said critically, as if she were a teacher scolding a child's poor arithmetic. "However, I believe I have sufficient samples for the task."

"If you're working to make me lose my appetite, you have already succeeded," Fontaine said weakly. Olivia ignored him and proceeded to repeat the ritual three times more, until the table before her was empty and the floor crunched underfoot.

"The knowledge of these runes has passed to me," Olivia declared matter-of-factly once the grisly affair was complete. "Your parchment, Captain?" Even Slate looked a little green around the gills, but handed Edmond's notes over with a grunt. Olivia picked up a quill, glanced up and down the strange symbols with as much confidence as if they were her own writings, and appended the document with three island names written in large, flowing letters.

"Well, would you look at that," Dinger breathed. "That's a trick I wouldn't mind learning."

"First we would have to teach you to read," Fontaine jibed, seemingly keen to dispel the mood of mysticism that had filled the tent. "Do we make sail, Captain?"

"No." This came not from Slate, but from Olivia, who still held a firm grip on the parchment, though she twisted it around to face the crew. "While it is not strictly part of our agreement, I have no wish to send honourable pirates to their doom. Do you recognise this first island, Captain Slate?"

"Only by name," Slate admitted. "Pretty desolate place, isn't it?"

"No longer," Olivia said, looking grim. She turned and moved to the rear of her tent, sifting through scores of bound parchments for a long moment until one was selected from the pile. This turned out to be a treasure map, presumably marked for sale to the Gold Hoarders, though the island it depicted looked like none the pirates had ever seen before.

"Under the auspices of Flameheart's Ashen Lords, this forsaken crag has been transformed into a mighty fortress," Madame Olivia intoned. "The memories from which this map was divined brought visions to the Order – barricades, watchtowers and many other armaments. The fortress itself is perched atop a high arch to which there is no natural pathway, and *that* is ringed by a sturdy palisade." She glanced at Dinger. "A big spiky wall, before you ask. Supplies and ammunition arrive by ship and are winched up to the keep overhead. It brings me no pleasure to tell you these things, Captain, but the *Morningstar* would not survive long enough to approach this place, let alone seize a treasure from its stronghold."

"Um. Sorry, but I don't think that's true. Or at least, it doesn't have to be." Jill had been studying the map intently without speaking. "I mean, there's a shipwright at this outpost, I assume?"

Slate stared at Jill. "Are you suggesting that we might be able to modify the *Morningstar* in some way?"

"Impossible," Fontaine cut in, bluntly. "Any ship with a hull strong enough to withstand fire from these fortifications would be so encumbered that manoeuvring through the outer barricades would take an age. And even then, we would still have no way to scale the cliffs and reach the fort itself."

Jill shook her head. "You're thinking like pirates. Sorry, but you are. Trying to expect the unexpected by being the biggest or the fastest because you're always dealing with the unknown. But this time..." She tapped the map. "We know exactly what we're up against. We don't have to reinforce the hull or add more cannons or anything like that if we have a plan and we stick to it." She looked up at Slate with bright eyes. "Weren't you a soldier once, Captain? There's a name for this sort of strategy, isn't there?"

"I believe you're referring to what we used to call a 'pre-emptive strike'," Slate replied. "It's an intriguing suggestion. We can't win in a fair fight, so we avoid it altogether and use knowledge of our enemies against them."

"Mad Frankie!" Dinger exclaimed. The others, even Madame Olivia, stared at him. "Oh, a lad I grew up with," he explained. "Scrawny wee nipper who got on the wrong side of one of the big lads, one who was famous for ending a fight with a great big kick in your..."

"Direction?"

"Aye, if you like. Anyway, Frankie knows what to expect, so the day before the fight, he sneaks to the kitchen and finds a set of scales, good solid iron ones, and Frankie takes one of the pans, y'see, and he hides it down his—"

Jill didn't need the clairvoyance of Madame Olivia to see where this anecdote was going. "It's *sort* of the same idea, Dinger, yes," she said kindly.

"We merely need to decide where we place our pans, so to speak," Fontaine mused, leaning in. "May we purchase this map, please?"

"You may take it with my blessing," Olivia said lightly, "so long as your friend promises not to finish his story. I bid you good day and good fortune, Captain." She ushered Slate and his crew out of her pavilion at this point, and only when she was quite certain that they were out of earshot did she allow herself to burst out laughing.

Madame Olivia had foreseen Slate's arrival at her door, not to mention his success at Ancient Spire, long before their first encounter had taken place. Even so, there was no amount of prognostication, no oneness with the spiritual planes she might strive for, that could ever have predicted Mad Frankie.

The rest of Jill's day was spent in hushed and hurried conversations with Sue, the local shipwright, who seemed bemused but willing to accommodate Jill's unusual requests. The supplies they would need proved harder to come by, but Fontaine and Dinger haggled, begged and occasionally slyly absconded with the raw materials the two shipwrights needed to renovate the *Morningstar*.

Jill could sense Slate's increasing impatience, but insisted on thoroughly testing each and every mechanism before they got underway, whether it was the large winch she'd acquired or the sturdiness of the box she'd added in the crow's nest. "We really don't want it spilling its contents," she explained to the others, who readily agreed with her. Even Edmond had played his part, although he was forced to spend much of his time lurking inside an innocuous barrel, since Sue had the run of the ship and would soon have noticed a skeleton roaming below decks.

Only when Jill's exacting standards had been met did the *Morningstar* finally sail away from Plunder Outpost.

Her course was somewhat erratic to begin with, as the crew struggled to compensate for the scores of tiny changes Jill had made. Under Slate's measured orders, however, the ship remained as reliable as ever as she ploughed across the waves, making for the unnamed waters where the different regions of the Sea of Thieves collided.

Their destination was not hard to spot, but the map Olivia had presented had done little to prepare Jill for the sheer scale of the rocky archway they were approaching. It dominated the horizon, far higher than the peak of Devil's Ridge, and by squinting through the spyglass Jill could make out the twisting and precarious pathways that had been laid down.

Just as Olivia had forewarned, the stronghold was fenced in by enormous wooden stakes that must surely have cost an entire island its forests, and four squat watchtowers lay inside the perimeter, peering over the spiky barrier with their cannons primed. It was towards this barrier that the *Morningstar* was accelerating, for the first part of their plan required considerable speed.

As expected, the rapid approach of a galleon did not go unnoticed for long. Beacons began to light around the fort, and a hail of cannon fire followed shortly after. Slate held their course steady, however, weathering the blows and sending the others below decks to patch the damage caused by any shots that made their mark upon the speeding ship.

When approaching any potentially hostile island, pirates were faced with something of a dilemma. If they raised their sails and slowed down enough to bring the ship in safely, they became an easy target. If they did not reduce their speed, while much harder to hit, they would more than likely crash headlong into their destination. That impact would do huge amounts of damage to the ship as a ripple of force was sent through the hull, proving just as destructive as cannon fire. Jill was fairly confident that she had a solution that would allow the *Morningstar* to reach the fort at speed, even if it would only work once. Even so, she found herself holding her breath as they sailed ever closer to a high-speed collision with a wall of wooden stakes.

Fifty feet. Forty. Twenty.

They were turning now, but too late. Nothing would stop the *Morningstar* from smashing into the wooden palisade.

Five feet.

No feet.

Jill would later ponder what the fort's undead denizens must have thought, watching the front of the *Morningstar* disintegrate. With Sue's help, she had removed the ship's figurehead, stowing it safely below deck. Next, she had made a series of deep cuts along the prow, transforming it from a rigid length of sturdy wood into a delicate latticework designed to crumple and collapse.

Just as she'd hoped, the modifications absorbed the full force of the collision, and while the shock was still enough to stagger the crew and obliterate what remained of the prow, the rest of the ship was still intact. More than that, she was now nestled snugly against the outer wall of the fort, close enough to be safe from any more incoming fire from the watchtowers. Their own cannons were also useless now, of course, able to target nothing but wood or water, but that was where the next phase of their plan began.

Keeping as close to the ring of wooden stakes as he could manage, Slate began to guide the *Morningstar* in a slow orbit around the fortress, which was Fontaine's signal to begin his role in their attack. They had been able to procure a small number of fragile glass spheres, which Edmond had filled with a peculiar mixture of chemicals drawn from his notes. He had called them "firebombs", a popular tool during his time serving Flameheart, and explained that they would be far more effective at sabotaging the fort's sturdy watchtowers than a volley of cannonballs.

A supply of these firebombs had already been loaded into the new box atop the crow's nest, and it was from here that Fontaine began to hurl them whenever Slate's methodical circuit brought one of the watchtowers into range. Should a firebomb hit home, tongues of orange flame would immediately spread, licking up and down the legs and ladders in a great conflagration.

One or two of the more intelligent skeletons attempted to take out their own weapons and aim at Fontaine, but they soon had to flee the flames he was spreading, diving into the murky waters beneath the fort to extinguish themselves. Flameheart's devotees they may have been, but fire was not their ally. Even better, one of the watchtowers had been stacked with a stash of black powder, and a well-aimed projectile from Fontaine brought the whole structure crashing down.

Jill and Dinger, meanwhile, stood on the balcony that ringed the Captain's Cabin, where they had faced Rooke just a few days earlier. It felt like a lifetime. Now they were each clutching gunpowder barrels like the one Slate had used to destroy the Ancient mural, counting steadily out loud in as close to unison as they could manage. "Seven... eight... nine..." On "ten", one of the pair would surrender their gunpowder to the sea at the aft of the ship, where it would come to rest, floating at the base of the palisade. Another ten seconds, another powderkeg.

When Slate saw the first of these bobbing gunpowder barrels coming up ahead, he broke course with a sharp tug on the wheel, sailing the *Morningstar* away from the fort and back onto open waters. He could do so safely, as Fontaine's efforts ensured that no cannoneers remained in the watchtowers to strike the ship as she moved to a safe distance.

Only when he was sure the *Morningstar* was out of harm's way did Slate spin the wheel once more, spinning the ship around so that her starboard side faced the fortress. He surrendered the helm briefly and selected one of the four cannons, loading in a heavy metal shot with a slight grunt of exertion.

The waters were choppy, but Slate had the steady hand of an experienced sailor. His aim was true and a single cannonball collided with the flimsy shell of the nearest powderkeg, igniting a blossoming flower of flame – an explosion that engulfed the bobbing barrels on either side, which reacted in kind, as did *their* neighbours... It was a magnificent chain reaction that circled the stronghold, tearing the wooden stakes to splinters and breaching the defences in a dozen places. Many of the gaps were wide enough to sail a galleon through, and this was precisely what Slate did next.

High overhead, Jill could just about make out skeletons scrambling to react to the devastation wrought by the

Morningstar. A few were trying to aim down at the ship with yet more cannons mounted high on the rocky peak, but these had never been intended to attack enemies within the fort's own perimeter and their shots whizzed uselessly into the sea. Slate ignored them, bringing the *Morningstar* to rest directly underneath the looming archway, and ordered that the anchor be lowered. It may not have been a conventional journey, but they had arrived.

"Well, we made it this far," Dinger said cheerfully as the crew regrouped, moving to the rear of the ship to begin the last stage of their assault. "That's got to count for something."

"This doesn't end until it ends, Mister Dinger," Slate said. "Weapons at the ready, all of you. It's high time we introduced ourselves in person."

10

THE *PRIDEFUL DAWN*

As the temple continued to flood with water, the great leviathan wasted no time squeezing its bulk into the underground chamber while Harkly and the others watched in horror. It most closely resembled a shark, a common enough sight on the Sea of Thieves, but this specimen was large enough that it could have swallowed one of the ash-grey predators without needing to chew. Its hide and fin were a rich blue, fading to a creamy white on the creature's underside. Its four emerald-green eyes roved hungrily around the chamber in search of prey.

Jewels, with the closest thing to a formal education, was able to name the beast. "A Megalodon…" she breathed. "It's beautiful!"

"It's a damn great fish that wants to eat us," Scraps hissed, scooping up his bundle. "We've got to get back down there and help the others!"

Jewels nodded, but when she turned back to recover her supplies from near the altar where she'd first found the drum, she felt the faintest of breezes on her cheek and realised that another alcove had opened behind them while they'd been distracted by the Megalodon. "There's another passageway up here!" she called. "I think it might lead outside!"

"Nobody leaves until we have that key!" Harkly insisted, picking his way own way across the expanse. "See if you can't lower a rope down to Karin." Following Harkly's order, however, first required the two pirates to take a circuitous path around the huge chamber, Scraps fussing with lengths of cord while Jewels took the lead and navigated the maze. By the time they could see Karin directly below them, the fin of the hunting Megalodon was almost brushing the ledge on which she was marooned.

The Megalodon itself patrolled the temple, moving in a lazy circle as it gradually rose higher. When it found its path blocked by the lowest of the wooden platforms it simply accelerated, smashing the walkway to pieces before continuing to swim as if it had all the time in the world. Judging from the number of scars and old wounds on its body, Karin supposed that might well be the case. The creature looked *old*.

Karin felt something brush her shoulder and realised that while she'd been staring, hypnotised, at the huge creature swimming closer and closer, Jewels and Scraps had managed to position themselves on a ledge overhead and lower their rope. She grasped it gratefully, looping it under her arms and around her waist to create a harness of sorts, before grabbing the chest in both hands. "Ready!" she bellowed, and felt the rope go taut as Jewels and Scraps began to heave upon it. A moment later, her booted feet left the floor.

Hauling Karin aloft was a painfully slow process, as she outsized both Jewels and Scraps, and there was nothing nearby to which they could secure the rope. The added weight of the chest only slowed them down more. "Can't you drop that thing?" Scraps called, panting from exertion. "We only need the key, not the box!"

"Oh, now why didn't I think of that?" Karin yelled back. "It's locked, you—" The rest of her insult was obscured by a loud smashing sound as the Megalodon obliterated yet another walkway. The straining pirates redoubled their efforts, but the rising water was outpacing Karin's lengthy ascent, and Harkly seemed no closer to finding his way up to them so that he could lend his considerable strength to the rescue effort. Confounded by the labyrinthine temple, he was now clambering up a ladder towards a nearby platform, roughly level with Karin, his brow furled in frustration.

Seeing him draw level gave Karin an idea. "This isn't working," she declared. "But if I can't go up, maybe I can go across!" She began to kick out with her legs, back and forth, building up a swinging motion that carried her and the chest closer and closer to Harkly.

The unexpected movement almost wrenched the rope from Jewels's grasp and caused Scraps to swear, but Karin kept swinging regardless, bending her knees and preparing to use the wall of the chamber as a springboard to propel herself in an even greater arc. She only half-heard Scraps's warning that the rope was beginning to fray. *Three more swings*, she thought. *Four at most, and I'll—*

The rope snapped.

Karin flung the chest aside instinctively, hurtling through the air towards the platform Harkly was making for, arms outstretched in desperation. The fingers of her left hand scraped across the ledge but found no purchase, though her right managed to get a tenuous grip on the walkway. Karin was left dangling, white-knuckled, the strength of five straining fingers all that stood between her and a plunge into the icy water where the Megalodon waited.

Harkly, who had at last hauled himself up onto the same ledge that Karin was now hanging from, saw all of this. He also saw the chest that Karin had cast aside, which had come to rest on the level below. It was momentarily safe, and he could see a way to reach it – but he would need to be fast, for the rising tide was about to consume it. Once the box was underwater, no-one would be able to retrieve it without becoming a tempting snack for the ravenous Megalodon. But if he acted quickly…

"Harry!" Karin called, her fear evident. "Get over here, I'm slipping!" Her voice was enough to snap Harkly out of his indecision – but he did not start in her direction. With a look of grim determination on his face, he instead swung his legs back down onto the ladder from which he'd just dismounted, ignoring her pleas and heading straight for the Ancient chest.

From their vantage point, Jewels and Scraps could see their captain abandon Karin to her fate and let out cries of anger and alarm, but these were drowned out by another cry. Karin's cry, as her grip on the platform gave way and she fell, howling, into the water.

She struck the surface of the pool gracelessly, painfully, and it forced the last of the breath from her lungs, causing her to thrash and kick among the fallen debris as she sought precious air. Had she stayed perfectly still, there might have been the slightest chance that the circling Megalodon would have ignored her, but her frantic motions as she broke the surface drew the creature's attention. It opened its mouth, revealing several rows of jagged teeth, and flicked its tail as it took a sharp turn in Karin's direction.

Karin also started to swim, striking out for the nearest platform, but her speed was no match for the Megalodon. It gave another mighty roar – and then spasmed as something hard and silver struck just below its emerald eye.

Lying on her front on the ledge high above, Jewels was sighting down the scope of her rifle, trying to distract the creature from its meal with the only tool she had at her disposal. It was working, too. The Megalodon clearly didn't understand why it was in pain, but its interest in Karin was momentarily forgotten as it twisted this way and that, trying to locate the source of its discomfort. Jewels now had only one shot left. By the time she could retrieve more ammunition, Karin would be halfway down the creature's gullet.

BOOM! The great thundering sound of the drum echoed down from overhead. Jewels hadn't even realised that Scraps had left her side, but he'd made it back up to the instrument and was using its percussive power to full effect. The Megalodon let out another great roar and dove deep, before leaping out of the water as high as it could with a deafening crash and a great surge of spray. It tried desperately to reach the source of the sound, the call of the drum commanding its attention once more. Unheeded for the moment, Karin managed to scramble out of the water and began a fresh ascent to safety.

Harkly, who remained dangerously close to the flood, was an arm's length away from the chest when the enraged Megalodon completed its jump and landed back in the water with an impact that sent an immense wave out in all directions. The water rose high enough to engulf the chest, sending the box tumbling from its resting place and down into the depths.

Harkly let out a roar of fury that rivalled the Megalodon. He was often angry, but this was something else entirely, burning within his chest so fiercely he thought he must surely be about to explode. In that moment, had the great beast been close enough, Harkly would have leapt down the creature's maw quite willingly if it meant a chance to tear the monster apart from the inside.

Karin ignored Harkly entirely, anger and adrenaline propelling her upwards through the temple until she reached the same platform as Jewels and Scraps, who was still clutching the drum. "Thanks," she said brusquely, before adding, "I didn't mean to drop the chest. It was just…"

"Forget all that," Jewels cut in. "How are we going to get it back out of the drink? Think the drum would keep that thing busy long enough for one of us to dive down and find it?"

"Somehow I don't think it's going to let us distract it from dinner a second time." Karin looked grim. "Maybe it'll leave eventually, but who knows how long it takes for something that big to lose interest in a meal?"

"If we can't get the key, the *Morningstar* can't either," Scraps pointed out. "Maybe the chest is better off left down there being guarded by that thing?"

"Do you want to be the one to stand before Captain Flameheart and tell him that yeah, there's a weapon that could turn the tide of war against him, but it's okay because the key's being looked after by an oversized halibut?" Jewels shuddered. "Anyway, I don't think Harkly's just going to let us walk away. He'll have us down here armed with harpoons before he gives up that chest." She paused, sensing that Karin had a lot to say about Harkly and his recent choices. "Where did he get to, anyway?"

The three pirates moved back to the edge of the platform they were standing on and peered into the chamber, which had become increasingly gloomy as the rising water extinguished torch after torch. They could just about make out Harkly's figure down below, but he was no longer making any effort to reunite with his crewmates.

From what they could make out, their captain appeared to be in distress, hunkered down on a large, circular platform and immobile, as if injured or exhausted. He did not respond to their calls, nor did he flee the rising water. It soon became obvious that something else was wrong.

"Is it me," Scraps commented as they stared, "or is it getting hotter in here?"

"I don't think it's you..." Jewels said slowly, once again bringing out her Eye of Reach to get a better look at the unresponsive Harkly. "I think... I think it might be *him*."

The water all around Harkly began to give off wisps of steam. Condensation trickled down the walls and pooled on the walkways, making them slick and treacherous underfoot. It was as if the entire temple had been transformed into an enormous kettle, and the pirates found themselves unable to get any closer to Harkly as the heat continued to rise. Fearful of being scalded by the rising steam, they had no choice but to make for the exit Jewels had spotted.

As uncomfortable as it was for the pirates, the unexplained heat was taking a much worse toll on the Megalodon. Though moments away from being able to crunch its great jaws down upon Harkly and the platform on which he was kneeling, the cold-blooded creature was swimming haphazardly, almost blindly, crashing and thrashing around the chamber in search of respite from the pain.

More by luck than judgement, its long fin brushed up against the rim of the hole through which it had entered, and the embattled behemoth gave one last wounded roar before slipping back into the depths of the temple, seeking a cooler climate far away from the morsels that had proven too much trouble to eat.

Once the bellowing of the Megalodon had died away, Harkly stood stiffly, as though he was a marionette moved by some unseen puppeteer. He stepped into the simmering water, and resurfaced moments later with the chest held in his hand, quite unharmed. The others, who had already retreated through the passageway that led to cool, fresh air, never saw this. Nor did they see Harry Harkly climbing as though hypnotised, eyes staring blankly ahead as he followed them back to the surface.

Only when a soft squall of rain touched his skin, for the weather had turned while the crew of the *Prideful Dawn* had been deep underground, did Harkly emerge from his trance. He stared around him in confusion, and then down to the chest in his hands. It took him a moment to banish the open bewilderment from his face, and only once he had resumed his usual scowl did he move through the jungle to locate the rest of his crew.

He found them collapsed around Merrick's campfire, soggy and exhausted as the old sailor bombarded them with questions about their ordeal, and the cause of the great crashing and banging he'd heard from up on the surface. They were in no mood to tell the story, and merely bade Scraps to toss their provisions into the cooking pot along with a less-than-healthy quantity of rum.

When Harkly stepped out of the undergrowth and dropped the chest to the ground with a loud thud, their demeanour changed instantly. Jewels's face was lined with concern, while Scraps showed just a hint of fear of his captain. Karin's expression, however, was one of cold fury. Only the presence of Merrick seemed to restrain an outburst, as she seemed unwilling to let the grizzled old sailor learn the truth of their misadventure. She glared daggers at the back of Harkly's head as he turned towards the chest, pointed a gloved finger and said, dully, "Somebody open this. I don't care how."

To Harkly's surprise, Merrick seemed to take the words as an invitation, crouching down on his hands and knees to get a better look at the Ancient casket. "Worr, this old thing?" he slurred. "Found a couple o' them boxes around these parts. Tough as nails, but they don't last long with a good set of picks in yer hand!" He began to cast around in his pockets, pulling out tiny fish bones, bits of string and other bric-a-brac before finally extracting a long, thin wire. The others, apart from Harkly, took it in turns to sup Scraps's thick stew from the cooking ladle of the pot, silently watching Merrick at work.

At last Merrick gave a satisfied sigh, though it ended up mostly as a belch, and the lid of the chest fell away. There was only one item inside the box – a large, triangular stone, the size of a dinner plate and as thick as a ship's logbook, with a spear-wielding figure engraved at each of the three points and a large, pale blue gem in its centre. Harkly, who was closest, reached inside mutely and held it up for the others to see.

"You have got to be *joking*!" Karin exploded, leaping to her feet and stamping around the camp. "We just went through hell and after all that, it wasn't even the chest with the key inside?!"

She froze as Merrick began to laugh, a hoarse, wheezing chuckle. "You always were a hot-head, Karin!" he chortled. "Course it's a key! Just not the usual sort. I seen plenty o' places where you could use it, usually down on the seabed, though I dunno how you'd find the right one. An' I tell you what…" he added, with a cunning glint in his eye. "If yer finished with that drum, Ol' Merrick will take it off your hands for free."

Scraps, who had all but forgotten he'd carried the instrument out of the temple, shrugged and tossed the drum to Merrick as he returned to the fire. It landed in his lap and the old pirate began to study it, playing some soft *rat-a-*

tat-raps. "Not bad..." he said, slowly. "Not bad at all... I can already feel me brain starting to fizz! This might be just what I need to get the ol' creative juices flowing!"

"Great," said Harkly, without a shred of sincerity. "We have what we came for. Let's get back to the ship." The others nodded and clambered wearily to their feet, though Merrick was so intent on beating out another rhythm on his new drum, he barely seemed to realise his guests were departing. Karin made as if to bid him farewell, then changed her mind, leaving the peculiar pirate off in a grog-fuelled world of his own.

Once they were back on the path to the shore, Jewels gave a small cough. "So, yeah, Harry... Do you see what I mean now? About my bad luck?" she added, sourly. "Leave it to Jewels to find the one magic drum that lets a bleedin' great shark out of its cage at the worst possible time. It's a curse, plain and simple."

Scraps rolled his eyes. "If you hadn't touched it, we'd have no key and would still have been staring at a set of bars when the *Morningstar* sailed in. You're just imagining things." He drew level with Karin. "Don't you think we should have warned your friend that the drum he's so fond of just so happens to summon a gigantic sea monster?" he asked. "It might get him into trouble one of these days."

Karin, however, was not paying the slightest bit of attention, nor had her previous explosion of anger abated. Her gaze was fixed on the back of Harkly's head, and she surged forward to give him a rough shove, staggering him. "You let me *fall*!" she hissed. "We're a crew, we're meant to look out for one another, and you let me drop onto a monster's dinner table because all you care about is finding that damn weapon!"

The others tensed, expecting Harkly to lash out with his signature bad temper. When he turned around, however, his face was a stony mask, as expressionless as if Karin had inquired about the weather. Somehow, this was much worse.

"I had a decision to make." The words were delivered without the slightest hint of remorse. "*If* the Megalodon had killed you, which it did not, then you... you would have arrived safely on the Ferry of the Damned. The key, on the other hand, might have been lost forever."

"I'd have arrived on the Ferry *because I'd have been eaten!*" Karin bellowed, crimson with fury. Now their captain did look angry – but it wasn't his usual innate aggression. Harkly smouldered with the righteous indignation of a scorned fanatic.

"Yes, you would have died!" he shouted. "Are you saying that you are not willing to sacrifice, not willing to suffer in the name of Captain Flameheart? If so, tell me now, and I'll do you the mercy of leaving you here with the old man so that you can rot yourself away with grog while the world ends."

"Listen to yourself, Harry!" Karin insisted, as the hulking pirate turned once more and began to stride across the beach towards the *Prideful Dawn*. "You used to say Flameheart was a means to an end! A chance for a fresh start, for pirates to wipe the slate clean. All this talk of suffering and sacrifice, it's... it's like I'm hearing someone else's voice in your mouth. What did they *do* to you in that dungeon?"

"Yeah, and what was that trick with the water, anyway?" Scraps chimed in. "I've never seen anything like it before."

"Power," said Harkly. "The might of the faithful. The sort of power that will be offered to us when we succeed – or turned against those who would betray their oath. Power," he added with a deadly certainty as he reached the ship's ladder, "that the crew of the *Morningstar* shall fear soon enough."

With precious few alternatives, the others boarded the *Prideful Dawn* with some reluctance, placing the Ancient chest and the key within it carefully in the hold. There was work to be done, for the brief storm had filled the lower deck with water to be bailed, and Scraps insisted on returning what was left of their supplies to the appropriate spots on the ship. Only then did they set sail for the third of the spots Rooke had marked on the *Prideful Dawn*'s map. Their captain once again retreated into his quarters, giving no new orders.

Harkly stood before a mirror, staring at his own fingers. He found that he could no longer remove the glove, but neither did he any longer feel the agonising burning sensation that had been building in his bones ever since they'd left Flameheart's shipwreck graveyard. The heat had poured out of him back in the temple, in the moment when he'd been paralysed by rage and helplessness. He hadn't thought, he'd just acted, placing his palm upon the stone and letting the white-hot fury pass into the icy water – water that should have boiled him like a lobster, but which had merely felt pleasantly warm.

"What's happening to me?" He hadn't meant to say the words out loud, nor had he expected a response. Nonetheless, one was provided.

Rebirth…

Harkly's head snapped around to the strange box that lay open atop his desk, one of the many that Adara's minions had brought aboard. He went to it immediately, kneeling before it as though in prayer. "My master, I... I did not know you were listening."

There is little that escapes my influence. Now tell me... What of the weapon?

"It... exists," Harkly admitted with some reluctance, "but will not pose a threat much longer. Thanks to the strength you have gifted to me, we have already secured one of the keys needed to claim it."

Excellent! There was no denying the glee in the disembodied voice. *I was not mistaken when I sensed potential in you. Secure the remaining keys at once, and I shall prepare to make sail.*

Harkly opened his mouth to acknowledge the order, but could sense that he was no longer being heard. Captain Flameheart had spoken to him somehow, departed, and now it was up to Harkly and the *Prideful Dawn* to obey him. And if any of the pirates aboard his ship were unwilling or unable to follow Flameheart's orders, well, he had been blessed with the strength to do something about it.

Harkly flexed his fingers, which were already starting to feel warm again, and grinned.

11

The *Morningstar*

Slate felt deeply uneasy about leaving the *Morningstar* unmanned – save for Edmond and Chomps, who would hardly be enough to save her from a serious attack – but so long as the ship remained snugly stationary underneath the high, vaulted arch upon which the fortress had been constructed, he supposed she would be safe. *We're the ones who are about to hurl ourselves into trouble*, he reminded himself as he clambered carefully into their rowboat.

Cramming all four crewmembers into one of the tiny craft, while technically possible, was always an exercise in contortion. Slate was glad that they would only be travelling a few yards – horizontally, at any rate – and that he had firmly ordered Edmond to stay aboard the ship, stating that anyone who had betrayed Flameheart would make a very tempting target for his loyal followers. Privately, while

Edmond had proven a reliable ally so far, Slate was not yet so trustful of their passenger that he would place a weapon in his skeletal hands and turn away.

Squinting into the ocean spray, Slate could just about make out the dangling wires that Flameheart's ships attached to treasure and supplies, allowing those above to winch them up into the fortress for safekeeping. Dinger was now easing them into position so that the rowboat, which Jill had modified with matching mechanisms at the front and rear, was seconds from gliding neatly between these wires.

Once they were in position, there were a few awkward moments involving far too many knees and elbows as Jill hooked the rowboat up to the cables, then began to turn a small crank, one not dissimilar to a capstan but barely the size of a stool. Slate felt the slight lurch as the rowboat left the sea and began to rise. "What's that, then?" Dinger asked curiously, momentarily forgetting the need for silence. "One of those blocky tackle contraptions, or—" He caught the scowls of the others and put his finger on his lips.

A wooden platform hung from the bottom of the fortress like a barnacle clinging to the hull of a ship. Once the rowboat was high enough, they stepped onto it one at a time, ascending a short set of iron rungs which led up to a wooden trap door. They had expected the entrance to be locked, or at least guarded, but when Fontaine eased it open ever-so-slightly and peeked inside for signs of patrolling guards, there were none to be found.

"Can they really not have worked out what we're doing?" Jill murmured, as loudly as she dared, once the four of them had crept into the very lowest levels of the fort.

"Flameheart has countless followers, but many are simple skeletons," Fontaine replied, *sotto voce*. "They have little brain left in what remains of their heads. Skeleton Captains are a different matter. More cunning, more memory of who they once were."

"We mustn't get complacent," Slate added. "Simple or not, they greatly outnumber us." Thus warned, they made their way carefully towards a curved wooden ramp that would bring them into the heart of the skeleton fort. They could hear shambling, scuffling sounds from overhead as distant skeletons milled around, clearly agitated but unsure what to do about the invading pirates now that their ship was no longer a target.

They emerged into a large cavern, vaguely circular, open to the elements on one side and offering a commanding view of the sea. More gangplanks and walkways had been affixed to the cliffside, providing a choice of several winding paths that doubtless led even higher up the exterior of the mammoth archway. On the opposing wall, numerous entrances peeled off into a warren of caves and passages. What drew the pirates' attention, however, was a large wooden keep that had been constructed within the centre of the cave, ringed with more walkways of its own.

Slate motioned them to come to a halt. "Stealth has carried us as far as it may," he muttered. "We still have the element of surprise, but only for one shot. Make it count. On three…"

Three seconds later, a shuffling skeleton who was morosely swapping ammunition from one cannon to another was reduced to a pile of bone meal by the business end of Dinger's blunderbuss. The crew of the *Morningstar* had begun the assault. Skeletons began to pour out of the keep, called into battle by the sound of gunfire.

"Spread out!" Slate ordered. "There's no sense in presenting a single target." His crew obeyed, finding what cover they could behind piles of barrels and old supply crates piled haphazardly in the gloomiest corners of the cavern.

They each fought in their own way. Dinger was as chatty as ever, calling out to lone skeletons with jibes and insults, goading them to come and find him as he lurked inside a labyrinth of boxes. One after another, hissing angrily, the lurching corpses took the bait, disappearing into the maze only to be struck down by the blow of Dinger's blade as they rounded the final corner.

Fontaine was far more cautious. He darted from cover to cover, using the gift of shadow to reload his pistol, taking his time before selecting his next target. Once prepared, he steadied his aim, sighting carefully before landing shots that first staggered and then scattered the bones of his foes.

Slate, Jill saw, was unorthodox in his movements. He traced a deliberate path around the edge of the cavern with his back to the wall, sword drawn, gradually herding a group of angry skeletons into a single group as they pursued him. He had fired only one shot so far, and that had seemingly missed its target, striking a cask of pomegranate wine and sending its contents spilling out across the floor of the fort. At last, he stood in the open, boldly facing down a pile of skeletons as they splashed through the sticky liquid, their bony arms outstretched as they advanced on Slate, eager to claw and slash at their elusive prey.

Slate's hand moved to his belt, and from a pouch at his side he drew another of the glass orbs Edmond had created, the glowing flame at its heart casting strange, flickering shadows across the cavern. He lobbed it forward with an easy grace, stepping back smartly as the skeletons stopped in their tracks, mesmerised by the light.

The firebomb landed among the skeletons and its fragile casing disintegrated, igniting the alcohol in which they were stood, filling the cave with a flash that caused Jill to instinctively shield her eyes. When she could see again, Slate had already moved on to new opponents, his luckless victims little more than smouldering bones lying on the scorched stone.

Jill herself swung clumsily at another of the skeletons, which had picked its way towards her while she'd been momentarily distracted by Slate's ploy. The blow of her cutlass sent it slamming into the cave wall and Jill followed this up with an angry punch level with its head. Its skull tumbled to the floor, reducing the rest of it to lifeless bones.

For a moment, it appeared as though that might be the last of the encroaching skeletons, but the victory was short-lived as a horn sounded from somewhere within the keep. It was answered by the distant cries of undead reinforcements – clearly, whatever reprieve the *Morningstar*'s crew had earned, it would be short-lived.

Jill, who was closest to the exterior walkways, glanced outside. To her dismay, she saw a veritable squadron of skeletons making their way towards her, their fleshless feet slipping slightly on the slick wooden ramps. She knew she didn't have the skill, let alone the ammunition, to pick them all off with an untested pistol before they overwhelmed her, but maybe there was another way…

Sheathing her sword, Jill moved quickly to a stack of barrels, scattering the trinkets atop them with one sweep of her arm, and grunted as she got the great container in a bear-hug. It was clearly full to the brim and extremely heavy, which was exactly what she wanted. Years of hefting huge masts and lugging ship parts into position had prepared her for this, and she focused on the lifting techniques Suki had taught her, bringing the barrel up first to her waist and then to her shoulder. *One step at a time*, she told herself firmly, *it's all about balance.*

Step by step, Jill made her way into the sunlight, standing at the top of the ramp and glowering at the ascending line of skeletons. She wasted no time taunting them, instead setting the barrel down on its side at the top of the ramp and planting a hard kick that sent it on its journey to make some new and unwitting friends. She watched with satisfaction as the barrel bowled through the skeletons, smashing some to pieces and sending others plummeting over the edge of the walkway to be dashed on the rocks beneath. She heard a few final hisses and then a loud smash from far below, but there was no sign of anyone else trying to climb up to attack her.

If she had been Dinger, Jill decided, she would probably have made a pun at this point. Something about having her opponents over a barrel, perhaps. Then again, jokes were for people who weren't gasping for breath in a fight for their lives. Satisfied that no more skeletons were going to sneak up behind them, she ducked back into the cave to help the others as best she could. Slate, Fontaine and Dinger were on the offensive now, moving into the central keep as a group, and Jill jogged over to join them.

The inside of the incongruous structure was filled with ragged banners crudely daubed with oversized symbols, presumably ones saluting Flameheart in some way, not to mention plenty of what could charitably be called "junk". Fontaine and Dinger wasted no time in ascending to the keep's higher level, in case any more skeletons were lurking in the rafters for an ambush, but no new threats seemed to present themselves.

"I don't like this," Jill said uneasily. "That can't be all of them. This doesn't feel like a win to me."

"Indeed not," Slate said, clearing his throat and striding towards the centre of the chamber. "But I suggest that we avail ourselves of the opportunity to—"

A thick wooden gate slammed down behind Jill, so close that she could feel the breeze on the back of her neck. Had she been lingering in the doorway it would surely have impaled her, but there was no time to worry about that now, for the floor underneath their feet was starting to come apart. Rotten planks splintered and the air filled with the smell of spores and mould as, one by one, skeletons began to dig themselves out of the ground, ripping away the driftwood that had concealed them in their slumber.

Even Slate seemed anxious as more and more grinning ghouls began to emerge from the floor, driving him back to the periphery of the chamber as they chuckled and chattered menacingly. Their leader was the last to appear, and there could be no mistaking him for anything else. He wore a long coat and a hat hooped with fusewire, both of which seemed to glow with an infernal heat of their own.

"Foolish fleshies," he rasped, in a voice far coarser and less practised than Jill was used to hearing from Edmond. "You thought to defy the will of Flameheart, and now you are trapped in the heart of his empire! Outnumbered, and sport for my troops. I have but to give the word and they shall cut you down like the dogs you are. What do you say to *that*?"

Slate considered this for a moment. "Now?" he suggested.

A moment later, Dinger dropped heavily from the rafters and planted his considerable bulk onto the shoulders of the Skeleton Captain, who was borne to the floor by the pirate's weight. Dinger grunted in pain as he thrust both hands into the mass of fizzling fuses, but held fast. A moment later, the skeleton's skull was wrenched free from his body with a loud popping sound that Jill doubted she'd be able to forget any time soon.

The effect on the rest of the skeletons was surprising and immediate. They began to collapse, crumbling away to bone and ash. It was as if their bodies no longer had a reason to hold themselves together, and by the time Dinger had gotten to his feet, sucking at his scorched fingers and grumbling that the fall had smashed his favourite compass, the pirates were alone in the bastion.

Jill and Fontaine hauled the gate back into a raised position while Slate reached into the Skeleton Captain's ragged coat and retrieved the fortress's stronghold key – which, to nobody's surprise, turned out to be shaped like a skull – and they climbed to the highest levels of the keep where the treasure awaited.

Slate inserted the key into the lock, which ground noiselessly aside. Ramshackle though the fortress might be, it was clear that its former occupants had taken the job of safeguarding Flameheart's treasures very seriously indeed. The place was piled high with all manner of chests, gemstones, crates of stolen merchant goods and a few trinkets that nobody in the crew could readily identify.

At the back of the room, unnoticed and unheeded, sat a small plinth clearly far older than anything else in the fort. It looked carved straight out of the cliff, and upon it rested a large, three-sided object with a jewelled centre. The same warrior figure that had adorned the mural was just about visible, daubed on the weathered stone.

"If that's not the key, nothing is," Slate asserted, reaching out with some trepidation, then claiming the prize once he was sure that taking it wouldn't bring the ceiling crashing down around their ears. "I'm sure Mister Edmond will be pleased."

"Aye, and when we get the rest of this hoard aboard, that's when Dinger will be pleased," Dinger declared. "I'll start loading up the rowboat with the smaller stuff."

"You'll do no such thing!" Slate barked, then softened his tone slightly at Dinger's hurt expression. "Time is of the essence, my lad. We have no time for treasures, tempting as they may be."

"Tempting does not begin to describe it," Fontaine interjected, moving to stand at Dinger's side. "Surely a single chest as a memento of our victory here, containing a few hand-picked items, is not too much to ask?"

Slate hesitated, and in the brief silence, they could hear

another sound. It was faint, barely audible above the wind and the gulls, but troublingly familiar. Forgetting the treasure, they raced out of the keep and onto the walkways overlooking the ocean, now able to clearly hear the source of the sound. Edmond was ringing the ship's bell of the *Morningstar* hard enough to wrench it from its hinges, and from up here it was easy to see why.

Another ship was bearing down upon the fortress, and its blood-red lanterns and ragged sails thrashing in the wind made its identity obvious. This was a skeleton galleon built by the notorious Ashen Lord, Old Horatio, packed to bursting with skeleton soldiers loyal to Captain Flameheart.

"Can we fight?" Fontaine asked, dubiously, the contents of the vault quite forgotten. "We have the fort's armaments at our disposal."

"And leave the *Morningstar* a stationary target?" Slate shook his head. "Our only chance is to set sail. We're not ready for another battle so soon, and we don't have the supplies to last. We'll have to make a run for it," he added grimly, though the words clearly left a sour taste in his mouth.

Jill, who had dashed along the walkways to the far side of the fort in case any more skeleton ships were on the horizon, gave a shrill and urgent whistle. "Another two galleons are heading straight towards us," she bellowed. "They don't look like Flameheart's ships, but what else would they be doing here?"

"Raiders, I'll be bound," Slate fumed. "They've been laying low while we did the dirty work and now they'll sink us and empty the vault for themselves. And we're so far from the blasted ship..." He stared at the water furiously, as if he were considering plunging himself over the edge in order to return to his precious *Morningstar*.

"We're not dead yet!" Dinger called from his own lookout point. "Those other galleons are veering away, see?" And indeed, the two vessels had angled themselves in a fearless attack formation aimed directly at the skeleton ship. More than that, the new arrivals took the time to raise long, thin pennants atop their central masts.

"An alliance…" Fontaine breathed. "They're trying to bring us into an—"

"*Get to the ship*," Slate thundered, spurring them into motion. They pelted back through the fort and practically flung themselves into the rowboat as the first sounds of cannon fire echoed back and forth. Jill winched them down as quickly as she dared, but Slate was unwilling to wait and made a great leap for the deck of the *Morningstar* as soon as they were close enough.

Fontaine scrambled up to the crow's nest once aboard, raising a pennant of their own in return to signal that yes, indeed, they were *extremely* eager to join the life-saving alliance. Once they had raised the ship's anchor, Slate eased them out of their hiding place, edging cautiously through the obstacles that remained and keeping a watchful eye for the skeletal galleon.

They needn't have worried. In the brief time it had taken them to leave the fortress, the two pirate galleons had executed an expert pincer manoeuvre that reduced Flameheart's followers to driftwood and a few floating skulls. Some of the skeletons' treasures bobbed in the water among the wreckage and a young, blond-haired pirate was out among them, gamely treading water and striving to gather them all up.

"Captain Slate, I presume?" The voice from the other vessel was unnaturally amplified, projected through a speaking trumpet. Slate cursed, for although he was sure there was a similar trumpet on board the *Morningstar* that he could use to reply, recent days had seen so much disruption he realised he had no idea where to find it. "I hope you don't mind if I invite myself aboard!"

There was a loud bang, a blur of motion, and suddenly a stranger was standing aboard the deck of their ship, brushing the soot off his sleeve as if launching oneself out of a cannon was a perfectly normal method of travel. He was tall, with a mane of dark hair and a wild beard, the unkemptness of which stood in stark contrast to his impeccable red and gold uniform, which was certainly tidier than any attire worn by the *Morningstar*'s crew after their battle.

"DeMarco Singh," the newcomer announced, delivering a sweeping bow. "I believe you're acquainted with my father."

"Hm?" Slate was momentarily taken aback, but recovered himself. "Oh. Ah, yes, you're Ramsey's lad. Not been sailing these waters for long but already making quite a name for yourself, so I hear. You and your sister both," he added, nodding at the other galleon pulling up alongside with a stoic, fierce-looking pirate at its helm. The rest of her crew were roving around the ship, patching and bailing to repair the damage they'd taken during the short-lived firefight.

"Too kind, I'm sure, especially coming from an experienced sea dog like yourself," DeMarco said smoothly, "and while I suspect us arriving when we did was rather fortuitous for you, it is dear Lesedi and I who owe you the debt of gratitude." He gestured expansively towards the looming fortress. "My comrades and I have had our eye on this place for quite some time now, eager to find a home so that we might establish a little venture of our own."

"And then Flameheart's lackeys moved in ahead of you?" Dinger chimed in, unable to help himself.

DeMarco gave a hearty laugh and slapped Dinger affably on the shoulder. "Quite so, friend, and more than a few rude words were uttered as a result, most of them by my charming sister. We've been keeping an eye on the place ever since, and when we saw you'd concocted a scheme to breach the palisade we decided to strike while the iron was hot, as they say."

"Ah." Slate was still trying to adjust to this sudden change of fortune. "Well, Mister Singh, there's a vault-load of treasure up there that should go some way towards financing whatever grand plans the two of you have in mind, and leaving it in your care seems like the least we can do by way of thanks. Getting that rat's nest shipshape is going to be quite the endeavour, mind you. Could take months."

"Oh, years, I'm sure!" DeMarco chuckled. "Still, the Trading Companies must have their uses. Once we have established a few new relationships, we shall be in fine shape to unveil…" He paused, and gave the crew a sly wink. "Ah, well, let's leave that a secret for now. My friends are on their way, and we have a fort to explore. Safe travels to you, Captain. You too, *Morningstar*!" He turned and took a mighty leap towards the deck of Lesedi's nearby galleon, landing with cat-like agility and striding towards the helm, already in animated conversation with his sibling as more allied ships appeared on the horizon.

Slate's head tilted in bemusement. "Curious fellow."

"That's one way of describing him," Jill said, weakly. *Those eyes...*

"I for one do not see the appeal," Fontaine sniffed. "It is one thing to strut about like a peacock, but what good is glamour when it comes to keeping your ship afloat, ah?" Even so, Fontaine disappeared shortly after, and the others couldn't help but notice that when he next appeared on deck, his own uniform was once more every bit as spick and span as the apparel of Captain DeMarco Singh.

So... You think that you have achieved a victory today? Fool! Already, you have been cast unwittingly into the endgame.

Edmond, who was lurking below deck and pondering DeMarco's conversation with Slate and the others, froze. If he'd still had blood in his veins, it would have run cold at the sound of that voice. This time there could be no other explanation – no chance of hallucination. The voice had come from a particular point somewhere in the hold. He began to creep through the piles of supplies, turning his head this way and that, hoping that Flameheart would continue his taunts.

You should have learned, after all this time, that there are no secrets kept from me. I know of your pathetic attempt to stand against me, and you are too late. Already, pirates loyal to my cause have claimed the second of the three keys you seek...

It's coming from the far corner, Edmond thought, *it has to be. But there's nothing there except…*

His eyeless gaze landed upon the unassuming box that had sat on his shelf for many years. A curio, a relic of his time at Flameheart's side, daubed with symbols and safeguarded for one very special purpose.

A box that, when it had been brought aboard the *Morningstar*, had had its lid knocked slightly ajar. *Oh, no…*

Now my armada will set sail. I shall see you soon, coward…

Edmond slammed the lid of the box closed and made for the steps that led above deck, taking them two at a time. He burst onto the deck of the *Morningstar*, not caring who might see him. The others, who were getting ready to set sail, reacted in surprise at his sudden appearance, but Edmond ignored them and raced into Slate's cabin, where the captain was washing his face in a bowl of cold water. "It's Flameheart," he blurted. "He knows what we're doing, and he already has one of the keys!"

This drew gasps from the rest of the crew, who had followed Edmond into Slate's cabin to see what all the fuss was about. "How could he possibly know?" Jill demanded. "We've been so careful!"

"He's been spying on us," Edmond said simply. "And taunting me. I thought I was imagining it, but I should have known there was more to that box than…" He waved a skeletal hand in exasperation. "What matters now is that there's another crew of pirates out there, and they have the second key!" He looked around, beseechingly, as if willing them to understand how desperate their situation had become. "They must be on their way to find the third."

"Perhaps they already have," Fontaine said pessimistically, but the skeleton shook his head. "If they had, Flameheart would not have been able to resist telling me as much. We have to hurry and reach the third hiding place before they do."

"On the contrary," Slate said evenly, drying his face with a small towel and moving to sit in the captain's chair. "That is what they will expect of us, and therefore precisely what we must not do. Having two keys out of three confers no particular advantage on us. First things first..." He leaned forward, fixing Edmond with a stern glare. "There are to be no more secrets between us, is that clear? To begin with, you can elaborate on how it is that Flameheart has been monitoring us for all this time..."

Once Edmond had answered Slate's questions to the best of his ability, the crew of the *Morningstar* gathered around the map table to decide upon their final gambit in what had become a race to find the weapon of the Ancients. Only Fontaine was absent, for Slate had instructed him to seek out the ship's speaking trumpet, decreeing that their business with the Singhs had not yet concluded. This time, it was Slate's turn to board DeMarco's galleon, taking with him an object that, he was keen to stress to the bemused siblings, would need to be kept safe at all costs.

Finally, once they all understood the plan, there was nothing left to do but set sail. As they made to leave, however, Edmond requested one more moment of their time. "You know me as Edmond," he began, uncomfortably, "but in truth, I have not used that name in many years. I told you before that Flameheart believes it is his right to rule the Sea of Thieves. To take his place as its king. It would please him to give his most trusted lieutenants regal-sounding titles – the four Ashen Lords, the Duchess, and so on. I was counted among their number and encouraged to adopt the name he chose for me. If there are to be no more secrets, I felt that you should know this."

"I see," Slate leaned forward, drumming his fingers lightly on the desk. "Then your preferred name is…?"

"Call me Duke," the skeleton replied.

12

THE *PRIDEFUL DAWN*

"What I still don't get," Jewels said as she struggled with the rigging, "is why we're in such a hurry." The ship's sails billowed as they hurtled across the Sea of Thieves towards their third and final destination, the galleon hard to control as the winds rocked her this way and that.

Scraps rolled his eyes, for this was their third time having the conversation. "We're in a hurry 'cause the captain told us we were, all right? What with Slate swiping a key while we were busy trying not to be fish food." Some time after they had gotten underway, Harkly had barged out of the Captain's Cabin and informed the crew of new orders, direct from Captain Flameheart. The *Morningstar*, he had explained with an air of obvious anticipation, had acquired one of the Ancient keys – but more than that, a scout had spotted Slate's ship making for the same island as the *Prideful Dawn*, providing an opportunity to intercept, attack and put the wretches to the sword.

"And Harkly knew that how, exactly?" Jewels pressed. "If you ask me, he's stringing us along. There's no way he's speaking with Flameheart all the way out here, not unless he's got some carrier pigeons we don't know about. Or a crystal ball." Harkly had given no inkling of how he'd come by the information, and had returned to his cabin without another word.

"I wouldn't put anything past him," Karin said, coldly. "Not anymore. Harkly's not the same man I met in that alliance. He's not going to let anyone else deliver the keys to Flameheart. This has turned into some kind of twisted display of devotion, and we're just along for the ride."

"You speak as though this doesn't benefit all of us in the end," Scraps snapped. "Whatever's happening to Harkly, he was right about why we came out here. Flameheart is our last, best chance to keep the seas free of the rule of merchants and lawmakers. I've never met this Slate, I don't know what kind of a man he is, but I know he's a fool if he thinks the weapon will bring peace to the seas."

"I think..." Jewels replied, "you might be able to ask him yourself, Scraps. On the horizon, there, see?" The others squinted and reached for their spyglasses to fill out the details only Jewels could see with the naked eye. There was indeed a ship ahead, half obscured by the outline of a large island where clumps of trees jostled for position atop rocky crags. She was adorned with white stars on her red sails and the figurehead of a roaring bear – just as Rooke had described the *Morningstar* to them.

"It must be them," Karin said warily, while Scraps gave the ship's bell two sharp clangs to gain Harkly's attention. "But that's not where the third key is supposed to be, is it? Unless Rooke steered us wrong somehow. She wasn't what I'd call right in the head."

"There are plenty of reasons to make land," Jewels pointed out. "Maybe they're just stopping for supplies. This could be our chance to overtake them."

"Or sink them." The voice was Harkly's, and he moved to the prow of the *Prideful Dawn*, brooding. "What are you up to, Slate?" he mused. As he stared at the distant ship, he caught a tell-tale glint in the sunlight, and smiled humourlessly. "Not to be taken unawares, then. They've seen us now, but they've no reason to suspect us of being anything more than another crew on the hunt for an adventure. Arm the cannons while I take us in closer, and we'll see what their game is."

Harkly took the helm from an unprotesting Karin, and the *Prideful Dawn* cut a sharp line through the waves under his command. They were close enough to make out individual pirates moving around the *Morningstar* through their spyglasses, though Slate and his crew seemed in no hurry, neither making preparations to sail nor turning the ship so that their cannons were ready to launch a salvo in the direction of the incoming galleon.

As they drew closer, they saw Slate move forward and raise a large, conical speaking trumpet, his voice carried on the wind as he addressed the speeding ship. "The *Prideful Dawn* was reported commandeered from the docks at Golden Sands several days ago by those expressing some…

unorthodox opinions," he called, without preamble. "And given your obvious interest in our affairs, I think it's safe to say we both know why we're out on the waves. I am therefore going to propose a parley."

"Raise the sails," Harkly ordered, though the others were so thunderstruck by the audacity of what they'd just heard that it took them a moment to respond. The headlong flight of the *Prideful Dawn* began to slow, and by the time the ship had come to rest, Harkly had emerged from the Captain's Cabin with a speaking trumpet of his own. "What is it that we would discuss at this parley?" he called. "The price of grog, perhaps? The best way to clean a capstan?"

"We are at an impasse," Slate retorted, ignoring the sarcasm. "Both sides have something the other wishes to possess, and I am an old man who would rather not spend his days locked in an endless tug-of-war over trinkets."

"You assume we'd be evenly matched," Harkly smirked, "but your idea amuses me. What do you suggest?"

"To begin with, we each show the other party that we still in fact possess one of the keys and have neither hidden nor destroyed them," Slate said, reaching into the coat of his uniform and pulling the triangular stone from his breast pocket. He held his prize up for all aboard the *Prideful Dawn* to see, and after a moment's consideration, Harkly did the same with the key they'd retrieved from the Megalodon's lair.

"Very well," Slate continued. "As you can see, our vessel is already moored alongside this peninsula. You should bring the *Prideful Dawn* to the other side. When we meet, you can sit facing your ship, and my crew shall sit facing ours."

Harkly grinned. "So we can all be sure that no allies

sail over to sink us while we raise a tankard on the beach. You have a suspicious mind, Captain. I can appreciate that. Weapons will be forbidden, of course."

Slate nodded. "Of course. And both keys should remain safely aboard our ships, too, so that nobody is encouraged to pick a pocket or, worse, start a scuffle."

"Then before I accept your offer of parley, Captain, I have one further condition," Harkly said, gesturing grandly at Scraps. "My crew and I are fair famished from our journey, and our cook here masters a stew pot like no other. Perhaps you would care to share a bite with us?"

"I look forward to it," Slate said lightly. "Let us meet at noon."

"Noon, aye," Harkly agreed. Lowering the speaking trumpet, he turned to find the others clustered behind him wearing expressions that ranged from suspicion to outright astonishment. "Get to it, then," he barked. "Moor us near the beach, nice and friendly."

Jewels and Karin reluctantly took their stations, but Scraps lingered a moment longer. "You've got something in mind, then?" he asked in a low, urgent voice. "We're not really planning to go breaking bread with that stuffed shirt?"

Harkly gave him a bare-toothed smile and placed a heavy hand on Scraps's arm. "Come down to the galley with me," he instructed. "It's time we talked about dinner…"

Once everything was prepared, Harkly commanded the crew to strip away all their weapons as agreed. Karin was particularly irritated by this, wanting to keep at least a dagger in her boot, but Harkly seemed to take a perverse kind of pleasure in attending the parley in good faith. Karin had never seen him so filled with guile, and surrendered the last of her knives with obvious reluctance.

As noon approached, Harkly was the first to hurl himself into the water, paddling towards the shoreline with his mystified crew in tow. They staggered onto the shoreline dripping wet, grateful for the strong sun and the heat of the cooking fire Slate had built to dry them out, and took their rest upon two large pieces of driftwood that had been dragged to face one another.

"Well, I know your name, so it seems only right that you should know mine," Harkly declared once they were seated. "Captain Harry Harkly, commander of the newly liberated *Prideful Dawn*. My comrades here – Karin, Jewels and Scraps." The others grunted in acknowledgement and Scraps began to lay out ingredients from a number of oilskin pouches.

"This is Dinger, Jill and Fontaine," Slate replied. "Two crews, each with four capable minds and a common purpose. To seek the keys that will unlock a great, and potentially very dangerous, power."

"Not so common as all that," Harkly pointed out. "I intend to claim the weapon in the name of Captain Flameheart."

At this, Dinger made a loud scoffing sound. "See, now, that's the part I don't believe no matter how many times I hear it. Flameheart wants to destroy pirates like us. Wipe us all off the map if he can! Why would you throw your lot in with someone like that?"

Karin leaned forward. "When I stare across this fire, I see a cocky lad in a starched uniform, who spends his days counting cargo crates for the Merchants and handing over plunder to those who lack the strength or the skill to find it themselves," she said accusingly. "Working for the weak. You may know how to sail a ship, but I can only see four pirates at this campfire. Why don't you scurry back to a Union port town to earn your coin, and leave these wild waters to those of us who still care?"

Slate scoffed at her words. "Speaking as one who has been sailing these wild waters, as you put it, since the founding of the first outposts, I can safely say that younger pirates' romantic notions of those early days are coated in a very sticky sugar indeed. We had freedom, yes. Huge hoards of treasure for the taking, yes, but we suffered and starved for them, scraping by with our supply barrels empty and no idea when we might next find safe harbour. The shipwrights, shopkeepers – yes, even the Merchants – would never have flourished out here if not for one simple truth: we needed them."

"And if you do not wish to make your coin hauling goods or pursuing bounties," Fontaine put in, "then why not aim your *Prideful Dawn* at the horizon and set sail? These last few days have reminded us all how much more there is that we have yet to discover. Riches beyond our wildest dreams, and much more besides."

"Hah!" Scraps was still stooped over the fire, but he glared daggers at the *Morningstar*'s crew. "That's all well and good until the day you check that horizon and see it's swarming with the merchant navy. And oh look, wouldn't you know it, here's Mister Grand Admiral on your ship, looking at your riches, only it seems as though they're not yours anymore because someone with medals on their chest stole the seas while you were busy playing pirate."

He began to stir the soup, so viciously that some spattered over the edge of the pot and started to bubble on the rocks of the campfire. "Nobody's born free. If you want the chance to live like us, like pirates, you've got to fight for it each and every day. And if you ain't fighting, you've already lost your freedom. You just don't know it yet."

"I didn't come here for riches beyond my wildest dreams, or to fight anyone, or to make big speeches about what it means to be a pirate," Jill said in a low voice. "I just don't want Flameheart to hurt my friends." She thought she heard the tiniest noise of affirmation from Jewels at this comment, but when she glanced up, the fair-haired pirate was staring fixedly into the flames, fiddling with a trinket on her wrist, and an awkward silence descended.

"Well," Harkly said, full of the same false camaraderie his crew had seen him employ when addressing Tom Toggs. "It seems we all have a lot to say, so it's time we filled our bellies before our jaws are too tired to chew. Then we can get down to business. Hand a bowl to Jewels or Karin if you please, Scraps."

"Eh?" Jewels came out of her reverie. "Why us? I thought we were all going to share?"

"Of course we are," Harkly said, a flicker of irritation creeping into his tone, "but I know that Captain Slate will want one of us to take the first bite, to prove it's not poisoned. Quite right, too."

Jewels shrugged, and accepted a helping from Scraps, swallowing a few spoons even though the heat and the spices made her eyes water. "You don't all need to gawp," she snapped, "I'm still here, aren't I?" Dinger, who had been staring at her most intently of all, blushed and looked away. Karin took her portion next, then Scraps served the *Morningstar*'s crew.

Seeing that Slate's mouth was full, Harkly began to speak once more. "Suppose the *Morningstar* were to find the weapon first. Use it themselves, naturally. Turn its power against Captain Flameheart and those loyal to him. Other pirates will hear about it. In time, so will the Grand Maritime Union, or others like them."

Harkly stood, setting down his untouched bowl, beginning to pace as he continued speaking. "Will you turn the weapon on them, too? Almost certainly, if the alternative is to be destroyed. So now here you are, the most powerful force on the Sea of Thieves, fighting an endless fight because the only alternative is to surrender to those who despise you. How, then, are you different to Captain Flameheart?"

Slate swallowed his mouthful before responding. For a moment he too made as if to stand, but then elected to remain seated. "Flameheart slaughters the innocent if they oppose him, or should happen to be in his way."

Harkly laughed at this. "Really? Do you imagine every last swabbie, cook and cabin boy aboard the ships you'd face would be fighting you by choice? You are not born for war, Slate. Surrender the weapon to someone who understands the price of wielding it."

"I think not," Slate yawned. "Which leaves us yet to find a way past this stalemate."

"You know as well as I do it is only a matter of time until Captain Flameheart finds you. If you hide the key, he'll make you talk sooner or later. If you destroy it, the last hope of the Pirate Lord will be lost forever. There is no stalemate," Harkly sneered. "Every minute we stand here in this ridiculous parley brings your ship closer to my master's clutches."

There was a light thud behind him as Jewels slumped to the ground, and Harkly moved to Slate's side, crouching next to him. "As for you? You can barely even hold yourself upright."

Slate tried to fix his stare on Harkly, but seemed to be having trouble focusing. "You'd poison… own crew… just to get…"

Harkly laughed again and gave Slate a shove, sending him toppling backwards onto the sand. "Poison? That would send you to the Ferry of the Damned, and who knows when and where you might pop up again? No, you and your crew are going to have a nice, long nap here while we go about our business. And if you're lucky…" He trailed off, realising that Slate was already unconscious. "Sleep, old man. While you have the chance."

Scraps, the only other pirate still standing, looked nervously at Jewels and Karin. "They're going to be furious when they wake up, you know," he said. "We *could* have told them about the sleeping draught."

"Then they might have hesitated, and given us away." Harkly reached down and picked Jewels up easily, slinging her limp body over his brawny shoulder. "Leave them to me. You get over to the *Morningstar* and find that key." Scraps nodded and began to make his way along the beach to Slate's helpless ship.

Harkly decided he'd found the whole affair quite invigorating. In fact he felt in fine fettle, and without thinking much about it, he reached down and grabbed the collar of Karin's coat, tugging her along with him as he waded into the shallows. It never occurred to him that, even for a man of his physical stature, swimming while carrying two of his crew was a feat he'd never normally have attempted. He climbed the ship's ladder to the top deck of the *Prideful Dawn* without much difficulty, dropped both women down on the deck with no particular care, and was about to begin preparations to get underway when he realised that something was very wrong with his ship.

The *Prideful Dawn* was dying.

As he swam towards the *Morningstar*, Scraps realised he was still angry. He'd tried to focus on preparing the food without drawing too much attention to himself, of course, peppering in innocent-looking herbs and disguising their taste with spices so that the oblivious *Morningstar* crew would stuff themselves into a stupor, but all he'd wanted to do was dash the pot over Slate's head for suggesting that pirates somehow *needed* the Companies. The self-righteous prigs might as well have been wearing GMU colours, as far as Scraps was concerned.

Deciding that relieving the *Morningstar* of its key would make him feel better, Scraps scrambled onto the deck and looked around, assessing all of the nooks and crannies the stone might have been concealed in and deciding to start with the Captain's Cabin. A close inspection of the room left Scraps scratching his head, however. While he had the impression that Slate liked to run a tight ship, he'd expected at least a few personal effects. There was nothing in this room to suggest so much as a shred of personality. No trinkets, no books or journals, not even – when he opened the captain's wardrobe and peered inside – a change of clothes.

This can't be right, Scraps thought uneasily. *They were all wearing those stupid uniforms, there has to be at least a storage chest around here somewhere.* He made his way down to the mid-deck, and then to the lowest level, only to find the ship similarly threadbare throughout. It was as though the *Morningstar* had been stripped of every last piece of its own history, and though he scoured the ship from end to end, Scraps could find no sign that Slate and his crew had ever made their mark on the vessel. More worryingly, he also couldn't find the key, though by rights the ship's sparse interior should have made that a simple task instead of this confounding waste of time. Eventually Scraps found himself back outside the Captain's Cabin, frustrated and empty-handed.

That was the moment he caught sight of the ship's nameplate, and everything fell into place with a dull thud.

This ship was not the *Morningstar*.

Swearing loudly and colourfully, Scraps tore headlong up the length of the deserted ship, diving into the water and swimming as fast he could back towards the island.

Trying to sprint when soaking wet was an exercise in frustration, but Scraps staggered along the sands towards the campsite as he made his way towards the *Prideful Dawn*, barely aware that a scene that should still have housed four slumbering pirates was now deserted. He plunged into the waves for a third time, eventually struggling aboard the deck of his own vessel sopping with seawater and in a singularly foul temper.

The ship, he realised with dismay, was a total shambles. The deck was scorched, the capstan stuck fast, and he could hear the familiar sound of creaking and groaning that let any pirate know the *Prideful Dawn* was taking on water. Had they not parked in the shallows near the parley, they might have sunk by now. Only the ship's masts had been left intact – their collapse would have been easy to spot from the campsite – but that was hardly consolation considering the full extent of the damage. He could hear someone, presumably Harkly, lumbering around down below making repairs, but this was a disaster that would take more than two pirates to avert.

Jewels and Karin were still lying sprawled on the deck, and Scraps stumbled past them, moving down to the mid-deck, where the cause of all the damage became obvious. The area all around the stove was charred and blackened, the cooking pot reduced to a hollow, melted mess. From there, the fire had crawled its way along the walls of the ship, twisting the hull from within as it feasted on cloths and tarpaulins that the galleon's former owners had left aboard. Harkly had already extinguished the flames, but the damage was done.

Scraps moved swiftly to the sack containing his belongings, which had been tucked away under the stairs and was only slightly singed. He rummaged around until he found a little glass bottle, mercifully intact, and clutched it tightly as he bolted back above deck, tipping a portion of its contents down the gullets of the two sleeping pirates. As he'd hoped, their eyelids began to flutter, and a moment or two later Jewels sat up with a groan that rivalled the creaking of the ailing *Prideful Dawn*.

Karin's unfocused gaze settled on Scraps, and her eyes narrowed. "You!" she hissed. "I'm going to wring your scrawny little—"

"Later!" Scraps snarled, anger overriding his fear that Karin was likely furious enough to follow through on her threats. "The ship's been wrecked, we'll sink if we don't do something!" The signs of sabotage all around were enough to convince Karin of the need to act, and she helped Jewels to her feet before making for the supply barrels – which were empty, their contents cast overboard.

With no lengths of wood to board up breaches or fix the damaged wheel, the crew had no choice but to use the *Prideful Dawn* herself to make repairs. Harkly's bed, the map table, even the empty barrels themselves were torn apart for raw materials. Judging from the banging and crashing from the lowest deck, their captain was doing the same. They lost all track of time as they laboured but, now that they were working in unison, they were able to haul the *Prideful Dawn* back from the brink of destruction.

Finally, when the last of the holes had been plugged and the three exhausted pirates stood around the space where the map table had been, Harkly appeared on the mid-deck, but he did not look pleased to see them. He was moving with the glacial speed and purpose of a predator preparing to strike. "You did this," he said, tonelessly, gesturing at the scorched stove as he moved towards Scraps. "You left food to burn while we were away."

Scraps had had enough. "I'm not an idiot, Harkly!" he hissed. "I've cooked a thousand meals on ships from here to the Shroud and I've never once been so careless. Whatever happened here, it had nothing to do with me!"

"*Liar!*" Harkly roared. "But are you lying because you're a careless idiot, or…" He paused, as if some dark new notion had just occurred to him. "Or were you sent here to betray us? A spy from the very beginning!" He advanced on Scraps, looming over him. "All that talk about the Companies was very convincing, but I see it now. You just wanted a way to earn our trust! What's Slate paying you, eh?"

Jewels and Karin shared an alarmed glance. They too were still angry with Scraps, but neither of them considered him anything like a traitor.

"Nothing!" Scraps shouted, his hands balling into fists as he squared off against his captain. "Because I'm *on your side!*"

"Then prove it!" Harkly demanded, thrusting out a hand. "Give me Slate's key."

"I don't have it!" Scraps blurted, realising immediately that this admission was not going to do him any favours. "That ship, it, it wasn't the *Morningstar*! It looks the same, but inside, there wasn't any… And the nameplate, it's a different—"

Harkly began to chuckle, then burst into a low, wild laugh, striding over to the Ancient chest, which had proven sturdy enough to withstand the flames. He yanked the lid back savagely, spinning around to show the others that the box had been emptied of its key, then held it aloft in one hand while his other lashed out, grasping Scraps by the neck and lifting him effortlessly off the floor.

"You've betrayed us," Harkly growled, oblivious to the rain of kicks and punches a terrified Scraps was unleashing upon him. "Worse, you have betrayed your oath. Betrayed your *king*. As captain, the responsibility of punishment falls upon me."

"Harry!" Karin snapped. "Enough. Let him go!" She stepped forward, but suddenly Harkly was surrounded by a roaring wind that burned her skin like sandpaper. Jewels and Karin were forced to retreat to the stairs, shrieking for Harkly to stop, as the impossible maelstrom below deck swung the lanterns wildly and sent supplies this way and that.

Scraps was also screaming now, and from his open mouth emerged swirls of green light that danced in the air for a moment before vanishing into the Ancient chest. It was eerily similar to the extraction rituals practised by the Order of Souls, Jewels realised, except it was happening to their crewmate right in front of them, and there was nothing they could do to stop it.

As quickly as it had flared up, the vicious wind dwindled to nothing. The lid of the box snapped shut. Scraps's lifeless body hit the deck, and Harkly dropped the chest alongside it with a satisfied grunt.

Jewels's voice was hoarse from screaming into the wind and from holding back tears. "What... What did you do to him?"

"Confinement," Harkly muttered in a low monotone. "For the soul. The Ferryman does not deserve to waste his time on traitors. Another gift for my continued fealty to King Flameheart." Kicking the chest into a distant corner, Harkly stamped past the two horrified pirates towards the stairs, and as he ascended they saw that the arm he'd kept covered since Adara had released them was covered no more. The cloth had burned away during Scraps's execution, and they could see that what had once been Harkly's healthy human arm was now laid bare as nothing but ash-coloured bone.

The price of loyalty.

13

The Morningstar

"How long was I out?" Slate demanded the instant his eyes snapped open. He suppressed the involuntary twitch of revulsion at the sight of Duke's skull looming over him, though he doubted he'd ever get completely used to the notion of a skeletal shipmate. *All it takes is to touch the wrong treasure*, he reminded himself. *That could be the face staring back at you in the mirror, one day. The risk of the pirate's life...*

"A few hours," Duke replied, moving back so that Slate could sit upright. "The others woke up a little while ago and we've been making good time."

Slate rubbed his eyes wearily and then hauled himself off of the captain's bed where he'd been lying. "I think you'd better fill me in on exactly what happened. The four of us taking a nap wasn't part of the plan."

Duke nodded and perched on the edge of the mattress Slate had just vacated. "To begin with, everything went just as we'd discussed. Once I was sure that Harkly and the others believed the ship they'd seen to be the *Morningstar* rather than our decoy, I slipped overboard with our key and down onto the seabed."

"I hope that 'decoy', as you put it, is still in one piece," Slate interjected. "Persuading Mister Singh to lend us one of his galleons was no mean feat, let alone dressing her to resemble the *Morningstar*. Her crew will expect her returned safely, or I'll be paying for the repairs."

"If we're able to stop Flameheart, I should think the Pirate Lord himself will settle your debts," Duke replied. "Regardless, I was able to take a short jaunt across the ocean floor and use the *Prideful Dawn*'s anchor to board her without ever being spotted. The sharks, mercifully, showed little interest in me. Once aboard, I retrieved their Ancient key easily enough – they'd made no effort to hide it – but sabotaging the ship was another matter." Duke paused. "That was when I remembered the old banana-on-the-stove trick…"

To Duke's surprise, Slate uttered a short burst of laughter. "Pirates were pulling that prank back in my day, too. It's a pity Harkly and his crew don't care to listen to their elders."

"Well, once I'd made as much of a mess as I dared, I hopped back overboard," Duke continued, "and came directly to the island only to find you all asleep on the beach alongside two of Harkly's own. Since we had concealed the rowboat nearby, I was able to bring you all back to where we'd hidden the *actual* Morningstar and get us underway."

Duke decided not to mention the undignified fashion in which the unconscious crew had been crammed into the little boat for the return journey. He doubted even Dinger would see the funny side.

"Quite honestly, I did not anticipate poison," Slate admitted. "An outright attack on the ship seemed more likely, hence our subterfuge. There's some aspect to Harkly, something twisting up inside him that I can't quite put my finger on…"

Slate settled into his seat behind the captain's table, twining his fingers as he brooded. "Whether or not the *Prideful Dawn* can be salvaged, Harkly let slip that Flameheart is on the move, and almost certainly knows our heading. I'm not at all confident we'll be able to find the key before our foes arrive, given that we have no idea where to start looking."

"Ah!" Duke jumped to his feet. "That brings me to the one piece of good news. Quite by accident, young Dinger reminded me of a rather remarkable discovery…"

"So what happened was, here I am with a singed shirt and a broken compass from all that skeleton business," Dinger explained, relishing a captive audience as they clustered together below decks. "So I'm down here to find replacements, I'm looking for something in my size, and I see the box where Duke had stashed the keys, aye? Well, them being so shiny, I can't help but pull them out for a little look, just to see, ye ken? So I set them down on the table, and that's when I notice something's gone wrong with north."

"I appreciate your love of a good yarn, Mister Dinger," Slate warned, "but time is of the essence. Get to the point."

"It was the compass," Dinger insisted. "My new one, I mean. It wasn't pointing north anymore, it was pointing right at the keys. The only way I could fix it was to stow 'em away again, but Duke knew what was happening."

"Actually, it's a technique I was taught by Flameheart himself, back when he still had a care for amassing wealth," Duke interjected. "With a few adjustments, an ordinary compass can be made to point towards treasuries of the Ancients, as surely as it once found north. Wayfinders, we used to call them. Fontaine managed to find me the tools I needed, and so…" Duke leaned forward and placed a number of silver compasses upon the map table. "If the final key is in an Ancient vault of some kind, these will point the way – once we get close enough, that is. Their range is rather limited."

Slate picked up one of the curious compasses and examined it critically. "I'm not certain I understand the science of it all, assuming there is such a thing, but if you say these contrivances might give us a fighting chance at finding the key before Flameheart finds us, that's good enough for me. Are any of you familiar with dowsing?"

Dinger blinked. "Well, I've put out a few fires in my time. We found this old haystack once, and—"

"Much as I would enjoy luxuriating in the hot bath of your endless ignorance, the captain is referring to water divining," Fontaine informed him. "The arcane art of waving a stick around, in other words, though some do believe that strange forces will drag the rod in the direction of underground springs as you approach."

"Precisely." Slate slapped the table. "Well, thanks to Mister Duke, we now have the means to go dowsing for Ancient vaults. Each of you, take a compass. Once we make land, we'll have a lot of ground to cover…"

Jill had heard a hundred stories from pirates who had trekked into the Wilds, and almost all of them mentioned Kraken's Fall at some point during their tale. Seeing the island for herself was another thing entirely; the huge bones she had heard described were even larger than she had imagined.

She couldn't help but wonder what had happened to end the life of the immense leviathan whose remains gave the island its name. The idea that it was only an infant and that other, larger specimens still roamed below the waves made her shiver. *Slate fought a kraken*, she reminded herself. *Once this is all over, that's a story I want to hear.*

Jill dragged her gaze reluctantly away from the monster's remains and forced herself to focus on the spinning needle of her compass. Was it just a trick of the light, or was it swaying less erratically than it had been while she'd made her way up the beach? Spotting Duke moving slowly in her direction, absorbed in divinations of his own, suggested that she was on the right track.

The pair arrived at the island's eastern shore at more or less the same time, at which point their compasses began to spin themselves into a frenzy, both needles whirling in an endless, dizzying dance. "Something tells me we've come to the right place," Jill said dryly.

"Indeed," Duke agreed. "Nice to know I haven't lost my touch. If an old pirate trick of Flameheart's helps bring about his downfall in some way, so much the better."

Jill considered this. "Do you miss it?" she inquired. "Being a pirate, I mean?"

It was impossible for a skeleton to look wistful, but something about the way Duke's shoulders slumped certainly gave Jill that impression. "Every day," he admitted. "Every moment. Not finding treasure or brawling in a tavern or having too much grog. That's what a pirate does, but it's not what a pirate *is*. When I can't pick a spot on the horizon and sail there to do just as I please, or when I feel that thrill of adventure and know I have to turn away, that's when I feel the part that's missing from me and remember that I'm not a pirate anymore."

Jill took a deep breath, then blurted, "Once this is over, you should ask Slate to join his crew. He could get you a... a disguise, or something. Nobody would need to know."

Duke chuckled a little. "Even if Slate agreed, I would always feel like an imposter. And besides, the *Morningstar* has already found its fourth crewmember, even if she doesn't quite believe it yet."

Jill opened her mouth to protest, but was interrupted by the arrival of Fontaine, jogging across the sand towards them with his own Wayfinder in hand.

While they waited for Slate and Dinger to arrive, the trio began to look around for signs of the Ancients' influence. "Remember, what we are looking for may not be as simple as a lever or a keyhole," Duke informed Jill. "The Ancients had many ways to hide their treasures. Sometimes, even shining a lantern's light in the correct place can reveal a secret."

"I don't see anything around here to shine a light onto," Jill pointed out. "But maybe there was once, a long time ago."

"I wonder…" Fontaine gripped the shovel that was slung across his back and struck the ground experimentally. He was rewarded with a loud *clunk* as the tool's blade collided with something hard, and the three dropped to their hands and knees, clearing away the dirt and sand that had built up over countless decades. Eventually, they had exposed a large stone circle, wide enough in diameter that they could all fit comfortably inside it with room to spare.

"There's something else here," Jill said slowly, examining a smaller hole at the centre of the circle, squinting at it from all angles and then poking one very cautious finger inside. "Funny. The thing it reminds me most of is the shank for a ship's capstan."

"If you are about to suggest dismantling more of the *Morningstar* to fill this hole," Slate said, striding up in time to catch the end of the conversation with Dinger hot on his heels, "I'm afraid I must refuse. My poor ship has suffered enough indignities for one voyage."

Jill laughed, "I shouldn't think we need go that far, Sir. A capstan's really just a fancy handle, when you think about it. Tell me, did any of you pass any shipwrecks on your way here?"

Dinger nodded, and Jill insisted on being led there at once.

It took a lot of strain and sweat, and more than a few whacks with her sword, but she was soon able to gather the parts she needed from the shipwreck's carcass, slotting a metal spar into the hole and substituting a ship's wheel for the spokes of a traditional capstan. It wasn't pretty, and Suki would never have approved the tatty old rope holding it all together, but Jill decided it would do at a pinch.

The *Morningstar*'s crew clustered together around the makeshift device, grasping at the handles and moving in step with practised ease, though none of them were sure what would be gained by working the Ancient mechanism. True to form, Dinger was the first to comment on the situation. "Is it me," he asked, "or am I getting taller?"

Fontaine took his hands off the wheel long enough to peer over the edge of the stone circle. "What we're standing on would appear to be some sort of platform or podium," he announced, "and it is currently being raised from the ground by our actions."

"I suppose a simple door would be too much to hope for," Slate remarked. "Put your backs into it, everyone, let's find out what this contraption is for." The muggy air of the Wilds combined with the physical exertion soon had them fatigued, and they were grateful when a final *clunk* suggested that the circle had risen as far as it would go, leaving them eight feet in the air.

Clambering back down to the ground revealed that the sides of the platform were decorated with a series of stone carvings. Having spent time in Duke's company in the hold, Jill thought she recognised several strings of symbols from his journals. Clearly, being concealed underground had protected them from the ravages of time.

"Incredible... And useful, I think." Duke walked around

the platform, trying to take it all in at once. "I wish I had my books…"

Jill was also staring at the stone, for there was one panel in particular that stood out to her as odd, and after a moment she realised why. She'd seen the disparity every day while adding new parts to old ships. "This one's different," she called out. "It's too… clean, like it was removed or replaced at some point."

"Perhaps," Slate replied, after studying the stonework himself for a moment. "But I believe the explanation may be more functional than aesthetic. Upon closer inspection…" He reached forward, bracing his hand against the mysterious frieze, and pushed.

There was a click and the entire panel slid smoothly aside, creating an opening to a hollow chamber inside the platform. Jill stared. "Did you know that would happen?"

"After so many years exploring these kinds of places you develop something of a sixth sense for hidden switches," Slate replied, raising his lantern so that he could peer inside the chamber. "Perhaps we should see where this leads us."

"A moment, Captain, please!" Duke pleaded. "I'm sure these carvings are more than a means to disguise a doorway. If I'm right, they point to a spot where the Ancient keys are supposed to be used."

"Information that's of little use until the third key presents itself," Slate pointed out. "But we are pressed for time, so let us divide our efforts. Get your books and anything else you need to make sense of this from the *Morningstar*. The rest of us will press onwards." Duke nodded and began to lope back across the rocky landscape of Kraken's Fall towards the ship, leaving the others to step warily through the entrance Slate had revealed.

The interior of the chamber, however, proved to be free of anything noteworthy – no treasures, and certainly no Ancient key – only a large, empty, circular room. Unlike the surfaces that had Duke so intrigued, the walls here were smooth stone, free of any interesting murals or paintings that might have offered a clue about what to do next.

"Perhaps someone has to remain above to turn the capstan," Jill suggested. "That would make the platform sink back into the ground again, wouldn't it? Maybe then it connects to another passage or something."

"Or it might simply serve to entomb whoever remains inside," Fontaine said, not looking happy at the prospect. "This chamber could have had many uses – storing materials, curing meats, fermenting wine…"

"Don't forget, the compasses led us here," Dinger persisted. "And Duke's sure the carvings are important. There's something special about this place, we just need to work out what it is." He moved forward to the centre of the chamber, and as he did so, his booted foot struck a raised flagstone at the very heart of the room. It dropped into the floor with a loud grinding noise, and then there was a lurch that sent them all staggering. "We're falling!" Dinger called, rather unnecessarily.

"Descending, certainly," Slate said, "but calm yourself, Mister Dinger, this is hardly a free-fall." He stared upward at the receding ceiling and the distant shaft of light from the doorway. "There was an old mineshaft in the town where

I grew up which had a cage for transporting goods and people. Doubtless this conveyance is something similar."

"It upsets my stomach," Fontaine muttered. "I think I would have preferred to take the stairs. And how are we supposed to make this confounded thing take us back up again?"

Before anyone could answer, there was a low rumble and the platform ground to a halt, at which point another section of wall slid quietly aside, much as the doorway on the surface had done, to reveal a passageway. Slate took the lead, moving cautiously but steadily across the uneven floor, raising an eyebrow at the torches still burning merrily after so many years.

"Be careful not to touch anything until we know it's safe," Slate warned as they emerged into a large, central chamber. "Or tread on anything, for that matter," he added. Dinger flushed.

The room itself had a high, vaulted ceiling that receded into a darkness too absolute for their lanterns to dispel. At its centre sat a plinth with a brazier on each corner, a strange glass-like surface and a large stone button on one side. Four columns had been placed evenly around the room, and these were adorned with strange patterns of glittering gems.

"I'm pretty sure this panel can retract," Jill called, standing between the strange pillars, having followed her compass in a slow tour of the vault. "There's no mortar around the stone, see? I think these columns can be moved around, too."

"And I'll bet this fancy table has something to do with

it," Dinger said. "What do you say, skipper? We've come this far."

Slate considered and then gave a curt nod. "Very well. Light the lamps, Mister Dinger, and we'll see what the Ancients have in store for us next." Dinger did as he'd been instructed, bringing his lantern to each of the four braziers that marked the corners of the peculiar plinth.

As the last of the braziers flared, the chamber door closed with a low rumble, sealing the four pirates inside the vault. The four columns likewise came to life; each of them glowed with strange lines of light, connecting some of the gemstones together in intricate patterns. The most startling change of all, however, was the appearance of an image on the glassy surface of the plinth, which had previously been featureless.

"Would you look at this," Dinger called, excitedly. "It's a painting like the one back on Devil's Ridge. It's even got the same bloke in it, see?"

"Why's he attacking a tortoise?" Jill asked, and this certainly seemed to be the case. The figure depicted in the plinth's display had swapped his spear for a hunting bow, aiming down towards a creature that, while crudely drawn, was unmistakably some kind of reptile.

"I haven't the slightest idea," Slate admitted, "but I suspect we'll need to understand all this before we get that door open again, let alone find the key."

There was another low grinding sound as Fontaine, who had been staring at the pillars as if hypnotised, began to grapple with the closest. As Jill had suspected, the stone column could be rotated quite readily, and each of its four sides revealed a different set of lines and stones as it turned.

"I thought so," Fontaine said triumphantly. "And if these are that, then the other must be…"

Dinger stared at him. "It's finally happened, then? His brain's exploded. I always said it'd happen if he kept thinking so much."

"Surely even you, having made a lifelong, studied practice of ignorance, cannot fail to recognise these?" Fontaine retorted, moving to another of the pillars.

"Well, I don't see the pattern either," Jill said shortly, "so why don't you explain it to *me*?"

"Constellations!" Fontaine said with obvious excitement. "These markings represent the night sky of the Sea of Thieves. The gems are stars, and each side of the pillar depicts a pairing, do you see? Here are Counting Crab and Proud Eagle, for example."

"If that's true, then I suppose these two figures are supposed to represent the Warrior and Turtle constellations," Slate said, jerking a thumb in the direction of the plinth. "But why would they be fighting?"

"Hmm…" Fontaine closed his eyes and stood deep in concentration for a few moments, as the others watched impatiently. "There is something, though I struggle to recall it precisely. There were many stories I was told by an old eccentric with a love of the stars. They were fables, perhaps of his own devising, though he claimed they were tales that the Ancients themselves used to tell, and that he had merely translated them."

Jill blinked. "Stories about stars? Not the usual kind of thing you'd expect a warrior to tell. Or a pirate, for that matter."

"Oh, it is quite common for heroes and other legends to be immortalised in the heavens," Fontaine assured her. "But I can only think of one where these two characters were in opposition." He paced slowly around the room, reciting in a slow, low voice as if reading a bedtime story out loud. "There was once a Great Warrior who wielded a mighty bow, a bow that fired an Obsidian Arrow fletched with the feather of an eagle…" He stopped at the farthest pillar and began to turn it, scouring the stones for confirmation. "Hah! Look, on this side, the Warrior and the Arrow are shown together."

"You think those pillars are a way to tell the story? Huh." Dinger looked at the columns suspiciously. "What happened next?"

Fontaine nodded swiftly. "If properly arranged, perhaps. As to the story – Great Warrior fires his arrow to show his clan how strong he is, and the arrow soars into the sea, where it accidentally strikes Patient Turtle and cracks his shell wide open. Turtle blames Warrior for this, of course, but Warrior will accept no blame. Instead, Turtle visits Sleeping Bear, wisest of all the animals, to pass judgement."

Slate had moved to the second pillar and was examining each of the glowing constellations in turn. "Turtle and eagle, no… Ah, here we are, turtle and bear paired together." Starting to understand what was required, the others moved to examine the remaining columns.

Fontaine continued to recite the tale as best he could. "Sleeping Bear summoned the Warrior and ordered him to fetch a new shell for Patient Turtle, to replace the one that he had destroyed. So the Warrior set out in a tar-pitch boat he had fashioned, using two trees as oars to make his way across the ocean. But although he searched far and wide, he could not find a shell of the size and lustre to match that which he had broken." Jill was unfamiliar with the constellations, but the boat Fontaine had mentioned was easy enough to spot – a simple bowl shape above a zig-zagging wave. Upon finding it paired with the Warrior, she set her pillar in place and backed away.

"Eventually," Fontaine concluded, "the Warrior made his way back to Patient Turtle, empty-handed – or so he thought. 'Oh,' cried Patient Turtle upon seeing the tar-pitch boat, 'Such a fine new home you have brought me!' He crawled underneath the boat at once, and dove back into the water, happy with his new tar-pitch shell. The warrior gave a great laugh, for he was relieved to have completed his task – but then he remembered that he would have to swim home…"

It took Dinger a few moments to wrestle the final pillar to the point where the constellations of the turtle and the boat could be seen from the central plinth, for the latter constellation was depicted upside-down, befitting the shell it had become. The key, however, failed to present itself and he looked scathingly at Fontaine. "Nothing's happening! You must have told the story wrong."

"I think," Jill interjected before the pair could begin bickering, "that we just haven't submitted our answer yet. Otherwise you could just keep spinning the pillars until you got it right." She moved to the plinth and placed her hand over the large button on its side. "We're all sure this is the right combination? We might not get a second chance at this."

"Self-doubt is a pirate's worst enemy," Slate informed her.

"We are the crew of the *Morningstar*. Whether we're right or wrong, we'll be right or wrong together." Jill thought those sounded worryingly like famous last words, but there was no going back now.

She pressed the switch.

The braziers snuffed themselves out immediately, the vision of the Warrior sparring with the Turtle vanished as swiftly as it had manifested, and – much to everyone's relief – the chamber door slid open a moment later. So too did the suspicious panel Jill had identified earlier, vanishing into the masonry to reveal the third key, safe and sound in a secret compartment behind it.

"Let it never again be said by the woefully uninformed among our number that reading is a waste of time," Fontaine said smugly. "Although I believe I owe Sudds a drink next time our paths cross."

Slate briskly retrieved the key from its resting place and they made haste down the passageway, finding with some relief that the central flagstone of the circular platform had returned to a raised position, as if waiting to be pressed. Dinger did the honours, and soon they were being carried up towards the surface on the column of stone, Slate looking over their prize with a discerning eye.

Even the murky sunlight of the Wilds seemed overpowering after so long underground, and the pirates were forced to shield their eyes as they stepped out under the open sky. Once they could see well enough to discern the sails on the horizon, though, their hearts sank in unison.

The livery of the *Burning Blade* was unmistakable even at a distance. Captain Flameheart had found them.

"We have to get back to the ship," Dinger gasped. "We can still make a run for it!"

"Correction, Mister Dinger," Slate said grimly. "Along with Duke, the three of you will make a run for it. I will remain here and stall Flameheart's forces for as long as I can."

Jill couldn't help but let out a horrified gasp at the prospect. "That's suicide!"

Slate looked at her sternly. "To be clear, crewman, that was what we captains generally refer to as 'an order'. Before we part ways, however, there are two more things I require…"

14

THE *BURNING BLADE*

Captain Flameheart could no longer hear the words of the *Morningstar*.

This displeased him greatly, for he had hoped to drink in their terror; bathe in the blind panic that would doubtless ensue when they saw him approach – particularly the traitor, Duke. He would hide his fear better than others, the loathsome turncoat always had, but he would be well aware of the fate that awaited him once he was captured.

Oh, at first it had amused Flameheart to think of the wretch in exile, squandering eternity in hiding, despised by pirates and skeletons alike. Yes, an infinity of hours for his disgraced Duke to reflect upon the day he had dared stand against his captain. Against his *king*, all in pathetic defence of those too weak to fight for themselves.

Flameheart stood, suddenly eager to begin the hunt, and

threw open the door of his cabin to take in the horizon. He needed no map to divine their arrival at Kraken's Fall, for a lifetime scouring the Sea of Thieves for adversaries worthy of his attention meant that he could recognise any island at a glance. Indeed, back before the skeletal curse had claimed the flesh from his body, he had often been able to navigate at night purely by the sounds and even the scents of the terrain around him. Not that Flameheart considered his condition to be a curse – rather, he had welcomed the transformation. Flesh was weak, and fire was strong.

That was why he had begun to experiment with his Ashen Lords; a chance to see how far their new forms could carry them, and examine possibilities of growing stronger still. Strong enough, perhaps, to augment their cursed bodies with artefacts that would make them unstoppable in combat, whether on land or at sea. What fool would deny themselves such advantages purely for the sake of vanity?

The Pirate Lord, for one. There had been a time, though he could remember it only vaguely, where Flameheart had spoken of the man with some respect – even told his boy tales of the grand adventures undertaken by the first rogue to chart the Sea of Thieves. Ultimately, though? Ramsey had squandered ownership of his domain, allowing the place to fall into the ruinous clutches of commerce and cooperation. Flameheart would not make the same mistake.

Flameheart cast an approving gaze along the deck of the *Burning Blade*, noting that each and every cannon had a skeletal crewman standing ready. Another advantage of their so-called curse, he knew, was that space that had once been wasted by the need for food or bedding could now be used to house additional ammunition. Soldiers, too. Were his ship to ever be boarded – not that anyone would have the audacity to do so – a crew of pirates would be easily outnumbered.

Captain Adara, who was at the wheel of the *Burning Blade* by Flameheart's express command, bowed slightly as her king approached. "Our scouts reported sighting the *Morningstar* a short time ago," she reported, speaking in the skeleton tongue. "If they are in the area, we shall find them soon enough. The *Prideful Dawn* has yet to make its rendezvous, however."

"Regrettable, but expected," Flameheart stated, placing two bony hands on the ship's railing as he stared out to sea. "You admitted yourself that they were a crew who lacked real conviction. Driven to our doorstep as outcasts, as if we would ever welcome waifs and strays into our fold! Oh, it was advantageous to have disposable pirates at our bidding, but the *Prideful Dawn* has long since outlived its usefulness to me."

"And what of her captain?" Adara asked, curious. "The ritual must surely have taken hold by now."

"Harkly..." Flameheart mused, tightening his grip slightly. "Yes, there is potential in him. A natural instinct for cruelty. It smoulders in his soul like a blade fresh from the forge. Ready to be honed."

Adara knew she was speaking out of turn, but they were possibly moments away from sailing into battle, and uncertainty lingered. "And what of this Ancient weapon?" she pressed. "If the *Prideful Dawn* has been destroyed, the pirates may well have—"

Flameheart turned towards her, slowly. "*If* those fools have found some trinket that gives them the courage to face me, then I gladly await their approach. It will make their annihilation all the more glorious – the first great victory in our war to free the Sea of Thieves! And if anyone aboard—" He stopped, suddenly, and light flared in his eye sockets as he snapped around in alarm. "We are under attack!"

A moment later, a cannonball struck the main deck, splintering an unfortunate skeleton and leaving a deep gash in the dark oak planks. The crew chattered uneasily, looking around for the ship that had dared to launch a sneak attack, but Flameheart's practised gaze followed the fading trail of smoke back to its source. The shot had been fired not from a vessel, but from an old cannon atop one of the many peaks that gave Kraken's Fall its distinctive shape. Momentarily, a huge brazier sputtered into life, sending a plume of dark smoke high into the air for all to see. Battle had been declared.

"Should we alter course, my king?" Adara queried. "We cannot readily return fire, and this is likely a diversion meant to distract us from pursuit of the *Morningstar*…"

"*Diversion?!*" Flameheart roared, drawing his sword and gesturing at the approaching island. "What you consider a mere distraction, I declare to be nothing less than a challenge. A challenge that shall be answered by a hundred blows of my blade!"

"But the *Morningstar*—" Adara reeled backwards as Flameheart struck her. She did not fall, but dropped to one knee nonetheless. "I apologise, my king, I spoke out of turn. I am merely… eager… to end the chase."

"My hold upon the Sea of Thieves increases by the hour," Flameheart hissed. "Soon there shall be no safe port for the *Morningstar*. Let them run, let them cower, and see how long they can escape my fury!" He took the wheel of the *Burning Blade* himself, as if urging her onward ever faster, and Adara moved meekly to replace the crewmember who had fallen in the attack.

Atop the craggy peak, Slate manhandled another volley into the mouth of the cannon he was using to torment the *Burning Blade*, though his next shot went wide of its mark as the vessel began to accelerate towards him. Satisfied that he now had Flameheart's full attention, he cast one final glance over his shoulder at the retreating *Morningstar* before clambering quickly down the rocky slope, ready to enact the next part of his plan.

Slate had exchanged his flintlock pistol for an Eye of Reach during his brief time aboard the *Morningstar*, and lay himself down atop an overhang, sighting along the weapon's length to make sure he had clear shots at the beach nearest to the *Burning Blade*. He waited, as still and as steady as the stone he was named for, until a gangplank had been extended and the first of Flameheart's skeletons, fizzing with fire and ash, stepped onto the sands. Then he fired, and reduced the crew complement of the *Burning Blade* by one.

A second shot dispatched another who had made the mistake of wandering close to an abandoned gunpowder barrel, but Slate knew better than to chance his luck, and was already on the move by the time the group of skeletons spotted the glint of his scope and began to amble in his direction. He paused only to scoop a few additional rounds out of an old ammunition crate as he made his way along the coast, being sure to leave just enough footsteps and make just enough noise that his pursuers did not lose track of him.

He crouched in the shadow of yet more kraken bones to fire a third shot, then broke into a sprint once more. Through the gun's sights, he could make out what he assumed must be Captain Flameheart, silently barking orders and laughing disdainfully whenever one of his skeletons fell to Slate's bullets. Clearly, he considered the chase to be marvellous sport.

Finally, Slate reached his destination, hauling himself atop the large stone chamber he and his crew had raised from the sand. He lay down flat once more, aiming along the length of the beach as Flameheart and his remaining troops approached. Once again, Slate's marksmanship demolished another skeletal crewmember, but the would-be king continued to stroll towards him as if he were out for an afternoon walk.

For a moment, Slate was tempted to adjust his aim and try to wipe the skeletal grin off Flameheart's face with his final shot, but he resisted the urge. *If Flameheart were that easy to kill*, he reasoned, *someone would have done it long ago. Keeping him occupied is what's important.*

Seeing that Slate was not about to flee further along the shoreline, Flameheart seemed to sense that this part of the game was over. He raised a hand to the sky, and the ground all around Slate's sniper's nest churned alarmingly. A moment later, three more skeletons had emerged from the soil, scrabbling up the sides of the platform to clutch and claw at Slate, dragging him roughly down to ground level and holding him still for their master's approach. *No wonder he didn't mind losing a few shipmates*, Slate thought, choosing not to waste his energy struggling. *He's got spares.*

Since he could do little else, Slate seized the opportunity to take his first real look at Captain Flameheart. Considering the Skeleton Lord's legendary reputation, he was surprised to face someone who, in life, would have been rather unremarkable. He was tall, but not extraordinarily so, and though the crimson coat and bone-laced tricorn hat he favoured were in excellent condition, it was an outfit no more ostentatious than the uniform Slate himself preferred. Like many who had fallen victim to curses on the Sea of Thieves, Flameheart had even managed to retain some of his human features – in this case, his large and bushy beard, which looked rather unsettling on top of his skinless face.

No, what made Captain Flameheart imposing was the fiery cauldron of fury that boiled within what was left of his ribcage; power that made his eyes glow with inscrutable rage. The conflagration was bright enough and hot enough that Slate could feel the warmth as he was hauled to his feet.

"At last," Flameheart sneered, halting just a few feet away and pointing his unsheathed sword directly at his opponent's chest. "The lackey of the Pirate Lord reveals himself. Captain Eli Slate!"

"In the flesh," Slate replied. "No offence."

"Your words cannot wound me," Flameheart retorted, "I consider my rebirth to be a great gift. Confirmation of my destiny to cast off mortal concerns and usher in my rule.

I wonder how you bear it, old man, to see your youth and relevance fade a little each day."

"If you think me so frail as all that," Slate asked, moustache twitching as he forced an unamused grin, "then why did you accept my challenge?"

Flameheart scoffed. "You consider that little game of cat-and-mouse to be a challenge?"

"No, merely the invitation," Slate countered. "The challenge will be the duel between you and I. You already have your sword drawn, which I take as acceptance, although I'm sure none of your followers would think any less of you if should you wish to withdraw rather than face a real pirate, bereft of cursed cannonballs and ashen armies to do your dirty work."

The skeletons surrounding their captain hissed and chattered angrily at this insolence, but Flameheart threw his head back and laughed so long and so hard, cinders actually erupted from his open mouth. "Oh, this is *wonderful*," he guffawed. "Such undeserved arrogance, just waiting to be cleaved away. I do indeed agree to your duel, Eli Slate, if only to watch as you choke on your own hubris. Release him!"

The skeletons holding Slate did as they were ordered, albeit with obvious reluctance, and the pirate shook the feeling back into his hands before drawing his own cutlass. "Getting on a bit now, this blade," he commented. "I'll probably never scrub away all the kraken ink from her hilt… Oh, but I'm forgetting, that business at Golden Sands was all before your time, eh? We had some fun in those days, I can tell you."

"And yet, for all your reverence of former glories, that

kraken did not destroy the famous vessel of the Pirate Lord," Flameheart sneered. "I did. Just as I shall destroy the *Morningstar*. And perhaps Golden Sands itself, one day, should I wish to see it burn."

"One day, perhaps," Slate admitted. "But not, I think, today." He lunged forward with his sword raised, sparks flying as he brought the blade down to collide with Flameheart's own. The two began to spar, exchanging easy blows as they took the measure of one another's strength. Flameheart's jibing aside, Slate knew that this was not a battle he would win – not with a weapon, at least. What mattered now was a convincing performance.

Slate began to inch backwards with each blow he deflected, slowly surrendering ground. As he'd hoped, Flameheart pressed his advantage, sticking close as their swords clashed over and over. Slate was no actor, but fortunately the sweat on his brow was very real thanks to the heat radiating from his opponent. The next part of his plan, however, would be decidedly trickier to execute – execution likely being the operative word if his scheme were to fail.

He lured Flameheart in a slow circle around the platform, noting with some dismay that the blows were becoming more rapid and harder to deflect. *Now's the time*, he decided. *Let's see how dishonourable Flameheart really is.*

Slate swept his blade in a high, horizontal arc designed to block an overhead swing from his adversary. Had the two been fighting fairly using only their swords, this move would have thrown Flameheart off balance and brought Slate a little time to back away and recover – but then, pirates so rarely stuck to the rules.

Just as Slate had hoped, Flameheart seized the opportunity to fight dirty and lashed out with a kick to his opponent's exposed stomach, giving Slate the excuse he needed to stagger backwards as if winded, toppling through the open door of the elevator that served as a gateway to the Ancient vault. He could see Flameheart outlined in the doorway and, pressing what he perceived as an advantage, the Skeleton Lord chose to follow him inside, bringing his sword down with a great stabbing motion that aimed to pierce Slate's midriff.

The tip of the blade sparked as it struck the floor, for Slate had already rolled aside, pressing his free hand down firmly on the central flagstone, activating the mechanism just as Dinger had done. The sudden lurch as their descent began was enough to make Flameheart pause in confusion, giving Slate enough time to get to his feet and resume a defensive stance.

So far, so good, Slate thought. *He's been separated from his crew. Unfortunately, I'm now trapped in the dark with a homicidal, sword-wielding warmonger.*

That darkness, Slate realised suddenly, could work in his favour, for Flameheart was now the only source of light in the chamber. If he stuck to the shadows, he would be able to see his adversary quite clearly, while Flameheart would struggle to detect Slate's movements and respond accordingly.

It was a fine plan, and had Slate been facing a flesh-and-blood opponent, it might even have worked. But whatever fell curse had afflicted Flameheart all those years ago seemed to have bestowed an excellent sense of night vision, and Slate was forced to duck as Flameheart made a precise jab into the darkness where he was lurking.

"You think you can hide from me? Amusing, but futile!" Flameheart goaded, bringing his blade around for another strike. "How long, I wonder, until your arms begin to tire? Until your knees begin to shake?"

Annoying as it was to acknowledge his growing fatigue, Slate had to admit Flameheart had a point – but then, he reminded himself, his goal in this fight was to delay, not to defeat. To that end, he backed towards the perimeter of the chamber, desperately parrying a rain of rapid sword-strikes, no longer wasting energy on attacks of his own. *Can't this contraption go any faster?*

His defensive stance seemed to aggravate Flameheart, who clearly felt he was being deprived of an entertaining fight, but Slate didn't care. As soon as the platform finished its descent, he abandoned the battle and dashed into the rocky tunnel that served as entrance to the Ancient vault, stumbling a little. His outstretched sword struck the wall and was wrenched from his grip as it rebounded, but Slate let it fall behind.

"So!" Flameheart bellowed behind him, "The coward reveals his true colours!" Slate ignored the insult, hurtling into the interior of the vault and racing straight for the pillars, spinning them this way and that as quickly as he could manage to disguise the sequence of images, well aware that his foe would only be a few seconds behind him.

When Flameheart charged into the vault, Slate was standing by the plinth with his lantern held high, three of the four torches once more ablaze. The Skeleton Lord cast a look around the room and let out a low, unkind laugh. "You have nowhere left to run, fool! All you have accomplished is dying in a different place." Flameheart stepped into the room with his weapon overhead, readying to deliver one last blow that would cut Slate down where he stood.

Slate was faster, and brought his lantern to the fourth and final brazier with such speed, the glass actually shattered against the stone. Just like before, as the last flame ignited, the room began to fill with glittering constellations, and the heavy chamber door slammed down, trapping the two pirates in the vault.

"What treachery is this?!" Flameheart bellowed, pounding his fist on the stone that had entombed them both. "You think this trick will save your life?!"

"Not trickery," Slate replied calmly as the skeleton advanced. "Tactics. I very much doubt your crew will be willing to leave their captain trapped down here, and while I'm certain they'll find a way to free you eventually, my ship will be a long way from here by then." He spread his arms wide. "I concede the duel to you, Flameheart. You may deliver the coup-de-grace." Flameheart lunged forward, sword raised high into the air – and brought the hilt down atop Slate's head like a cudgel, sending him sprawling. Stars danced in Slate's vision as he forced himself onto his hands and knees.

"If I killed you now," Flameheart hissed, "your spirit would certainly travel to the Ferry of the Damned. From there you would be able to return to your precious *Morningstar*. But for as long as you remain alive, in my clutches, there will be no way for you to help them. You will not even be certain whether they are dead or alive… So no, Eli Slate, I shall not kill you. But make no mistake – you *will* suffer by my hand…"

Groggily, Slate forced himself into a sitting position and began to fumble with his sleeve. "I did rather suspect you'd take that approach," he admitted gamely, tearing away the sleeve of his jacket to reveal a writhing mass underneath – a squirming, coiled shape strapped securely to the length of his arm. "Fortunately, I had just enough time to devise a plan."

Flameheart stared, incredulous. "What is this? A creature? Some kind of *pet*?"

"This is Chomps," Slate replied. "As you can imagine, having been trapped inside my coat all this time, he's absolutely furious right now." He tugged away the strap, allowing Chomps to rear up, its jaw opening with a vindictive hiss as the creature realised it could move freely at last. Fast as he was, Flameheart could not hope to match the reptile's speed. The incensed Chomps struck out at the pirate who had abused it so, sinking two sharp fangs deep into Slate's exposed arm.

Slate slumped backwards against the plinth as his life began to ebb away, snake venom coursing through his veins. "Furious…" he said, dreamily, "And altogether deadly…" He closed his eyes, ignoring Flameheart's threats of retribution and infuriated howls of rage. Chomps uncoiled easily as the pirate's body began to glow with a ghostly light, becoming insubstantial, and slithered across the floor to explore its new home. By the time the snake had glided past the raging skeleton and into a crack in the stone, the body of Eli Slate had disappeared entirely.

Slate was a cautious man by nature, and old enough to remember a time before the Ferry of the Damned had begun its work. He normally preferred to treat death as a permanent prospect, as it was for those in the wider world beyond the Devil's Shroud – besides, the Ferryman was a wild, unpredictable figure. Stories abounded of the luckless pirates who had been refused passage…

Even so, a life of adventure upon the Sea of Thieves had seen Slate make a handful of unintended trips on the Ferry over the years. Not that pirates ever remembered boarding her; new arrivals found themselves coming to on the deck of the Ferryman's vessel while its journey was underway, as if they had sleepwalked aboard. When Slate opened his eyes, he was already standing near a shattered railing, staring out at the endless, roiling fog that masked the true nature of the sea on which they now sailed.

Something was different this time, however. The doorway where the Captain's Cabin would be on a more traditional galleon – which housed the portal through which the Ferry's passengers ultimately disembarked – was shut tight, offering Slate no way off the ship. He waited patiently, though he could not say exactly for how long, but there was no sign that the threshold was going to open any time soon. Eventually, Slate approached the door and examined it, but this proved to be a fruitless exercise, for the handle on the door was frozen in place.

Uncertain about interrogating the Ferryman, but extremely eager to get back to his crew, Slate moved away from the door and ascended the steps to where the spectral visage stood at the helm – no, Slate noted, not quite *stood*.

The phantom's feet were floating slightly above the ground, as if the ghostly figure was clinging to the wheel to avoid being ripped away in a tornado.

Slate cleared his throat. "Sorry to disturb you," he began. "I was just wondering—"

"No," the Ferryman stated bluntly, his voice savage and raw. "My portal shall not open for you this day, Eli Slate of the *Morningstar*, for your destiny lies elsewhere. Events are now in motion, and so we must chart a new course upon these unending waves!" The Ferryman gave the wheel a sharp turn, and Slate put one hand on the railing to steady himself as the deck of the Ferry heaved beneath his feet. He didn't want to think what fate might befall anyone who tumbled overboard, not out here in this strange nothingness.

"Now hold your tongue," the Ferryman continued. "I require concentration, for these are unfamiliar waters even to me. If we should fail to find our way, there shall be a heavy price to pay."

"Price?" Slate was starting to feel irritated by the Ferryman's enigmatic tone. "What kind of a price?"

"The promise of four lost souls, Captain," the Ferryman informed him, gravely. "The lives of those aboard the *Morningstar*."

15

The Morningstar

As per Slate's final orders, the *Morningstar* fled from Kraken's Fall at full billow. Only when they were quite certain that the horizon was free of Flameheart and his scouts did her crew judge it safe to ease off the sails and take stock of their situation. Jill and Dinger joined Duke and Fontaine around the map table, which was once again covered in Duke's books, for he had spent the time during their wild flight away seeking the last piece of the puzzle – namely, where the keys they had collected were ultimately to be used.

"Any luck?" Jill asked, sinking gratefully onto the bench and resting her heavy head in her hands, for the last few hours had left them all in need of rest.

"Only the bad kind," Duke replied, gloomily. "I'm no Madame Olivia, of course, but based on her writings I have what should be a rough translation of the message. The problem is, it doesn't make one jot of sense to me."

"Well don't be shy," Dinger said, as cheerfully as he could manage through his own haze of exhaustion. "We're all in this together. What's the riddle?"

"Bring the three keys to the heart of the key," Duke recited. "Whatever that means."

Fontaine looked thoughtfully at the three keys. "Each possesses a different precious stone at its core, yes? Perhaps that is the 'heart' of the key?" He picked up one of the artefacts at random, poking at the ruby held inside it, turning it this way and that in the lamplight and even using his lantern to shine a shimmering red pattern onto the map in case some new truth revealed itself, all to no avail. "First it was constellations," he complained, "and now another sort of puzzle."

"Unless…" Jill said slowly, uncertainty evident in her voice as the tiny sapling of an idea began to form. "What if it isn't a different kind of puzzle at all? The constellations were just points connected by lines, right?" She picked up a quill and made a neat mark on the map. "We found the first key here, then the second at Kraken's Fall *here*…" She traced a line between them as neatly as she could.

"Actually, that was the third key," Duke pointed out. "The *Prideful Dawn* would have found the second here, according to the mural…" Jill followed his outstretched finger to the Ancient Isles and made a third circle, then connected the remaining lines. They all stared at the result.

"I may not have had much in the way of schooling,"

Dinger said, thoughtfully, "but even I can recognise an equestriatical triangle when I see one."

"The shape does closely resemble the keys themselves," Duke noted. "And if we are to assume that the 'heart of the key' is the centre of the triangle, that would put our final destination here…"

"In the middle of the ocean?" Jill looked crestfallen. "Aw. I really thought I was on to something."

"Oh, you've still a bit to learn about treasure hunts." Dinger, who had perked up, drew a slow circle around the seemingly empty spot. "Not every island on these waters finds itself chained to the map…"

Dinger's instincts were proven correct shortly after the *Morningstar* arrived at the centre of the triangle Jill had divined. There was land here, though not much of it; a few sandbars and coral reefs that they might well have sailed past without comment on any other day. There was at least one wrecked ship in the shallows, though; a broken galleon with a tiger figurehead that looked to have met its end many years ago.

"I can see why nobody bothered to chart this place," Fontaine said, hands on his hips as he stared down at the sea. "What a waste of ink it would be."

"Well, maybe that means no-one's bothered to scout around and we'll be the first to find something," Dinger retorted. "This is the last place anyone would look for a secret weapon."

"A very small secret weapon, perhaps." Fontaine rolled his eyes. "If you ask me, we should set sail at once, take the keys to the Pirate Lord and let his legendary pirates find the answers."

"Hey!" Jill had been scouring the island from up in the crow's nest. "I think there is something here after all. There's a gap between two of those rocks that looks to go pretty deep. Worth a look?"

Dinger began to struggle out of his jacket. "We've come this far, and I could use a good swim after that dusty vault." He lumbered up to the broken prow of the *Morningstar* and took a graceless leap into the sea, hitting the water with a heavy splash and diving out of sight.

Jill moved to stand by Fontaine on the deck of the galleon while they waited. The ship suddenly felt much larger and lonelier without Dinger's chatter and Slate's barked orders to provide a comforting consistency.

"Captain Slate will be all right, won't he?" she said at last, voicing a concern that had been preying on her mind since the *Morningstar* had abandoned Kraken's Fall. "I really didn't like leaving him behind."

"The captain is a capable fighter with many years of experience," Fontaine replied, without meeting her gaze. "Even so, Flameheart has a formidable reputation. But it is best not to dwell on the unknown, I think. 'We suffer more often in imagination than in reality', so it is said."

Jill wanted to retort that dwelling on the unknown was how philosophers like Fontaine were supposed to spend their time, but was distracted by Dinger's head emerging from the water nearby. "Aye, there's a tunnel down here all right, but it's a fair way down!" he called. "Not sure how safe it'll be for anyone who can't float."

"Then you'll just have to carry me back," Duke replied from directly behind the two pirates, causing both Jill and Fontaine to jump, startled. "My life's work has been leading to this, I'm not about to wait behind."

"We need to put a bell on him," Fontaine murmured, stripping off his coat and draping it over the nearest cannon. "Let's empty our pockets. There's no sense in taking more than we need." Jill nodded, and together they removed the bulkiest parts of their uniforms, though Fontaine insisted they brought their weapons along in case sharks or other predators had taken up residence in the waterways below the nameless island. He placed the Ancient keys carefully in a thick knapsack, which he slung over his shoulder before diving into the sea to join Dinger. Jill drew a deep breath, took one last lingering look at the *Morningstar*, then flung herself over the side of the ship. As she swam towards the sunken passage, she could just about make out Duke as he scrambled over the coral to join them.

The flooded tunnels went every bit as deep as Dinger had reported, and were rather too cramped for Jill's tastes. There were delicate, glowing plants that offered just enough light to see by, however, and occasional pockets of air where they could catch their breath. After descending for what felt like an age, the passageway finally started to angle upwards, allowing their heads to break the surface of the water and, at last, to wade out into the middle of a large cavern.

This was no Ancient treasure vault, but their influence could be seen throughout the cave regardless, most notably in the high, square archway that dominated the scene. Smaller pillars and statues were dotted around here and there, yet it was the carved table in the centre of the cave that commanded their attention, for its topmost surface contained three large, triangular indentations.

"These would appear to be our keyholes," Fontaine observed, his voice sounding tinny and unnatural in the echoing cave. "Though I've yet to see anything that looks like a weapon in here."

"I've seen enough moving platforms and secret passages today to believe that anything's possible once the keys are in place," Jill replied, tipping the seawater out of her boots. "We just have to trust that we're on the right track."

"Agreed." Fontaine shrugged off the knapsack he was carrying and began to fish around for the keys, handing one to Dinger and one to Jill. "Three keys, three pirates," he explained. "It seems appropriate that we should finish this together."

"I'll try not to take that personally," Duke deadpanned, emerging from the tunnel behind them. "There are some other chambers further ahead, including one containing a rather oversized head. I'd wager this place was important to the Ancients in more ways than one. Shall we begin?" The others nodded, and Fontaine stepped up to the platform, placing his key in the leftmost slot with an obvious sense of trepidation.

Given all that they'd experienced over the past few days, Jill thought she was ready for anything, but the burst of light that issued forth from the stone at the centre of the key caught them all by surprise. The initial flare eased off after a moment, though the gem still pulsed as if the key's heart had started beating. Even more surprising was the archway that lay before them, for the same kind of light was now creeping and crackling around the stony framework.

The air tasted faintly of copper, and maybe it was Jill's imagination, but she felt like she could feel a distant thrumming beneath her feet, as if a great army were marching far below. Even so, they didn't seem to be in any immediate danger, so she moved to stand beside Fontaine, raising her own key and placing it in the second of the three triangular indentations.

They knew enough to shield their eyes from the burst of light this time around, but now there was no mistaking the low rumbling that filled the cave. The archway was more alive than ever, too, dancing with ghostly energy. More worryingly, streams of stone and sand were starting to pour down from overhead. Age, and the pressure of the sea overhead, had taken its toll on this extraordinary, secret place, and it was reacting badly to being disturbed.

Wanting to waste no more time, Dinger took a deep breath and put the third and final key into position. This time, the burst of light from the key was accompanied by another, even brighter flare from the archway before them. As their vision cleared, they found themselves gazing upon the impossible. At first, Jill assumed she was looking at another image, like the vision of the Warrior that had been projected in the Ancient vault. As she moved closer, however, the perspective changed and shifted to accommodate her.

"Oh," said Dinger, flatly. "A magic door." And indeed, Jill could think of no better description. Rather than the far wall of the cave, peering through the archway revealed the interior of a corridor that was unmistakably Ancient in design, though it seemed far less weathered than the ruins they'd visited so far.

"Impossible!" Fontaine scoffed. "It can only be a very convincing illusion, perhaps showing us the location of the weapon." In response, Duke picked up a stone, more of which littered the floor with each passing second, and tossed it straight into the heart of the archway. It rebounded off one of the Ancient statues and came to rest on the flagstones, now drenched in the same sallow green hue as everything else in the scene.

"See?" Dinger said, triumphantly. "Magic door!"

Jill moved to the gateway, poking a cautious finger across the threshold, which turned out to be as easy as reaching through an open window. "Should we go through?" she asked. "What if there's no way back?" Suddenly, there was another large crashing sound from above and water began to pour into the cave. The tremors caused by the awakening of the gateway had taken too much of a toll, and now the entire ruin was threatening to come down around their ears.

"I don't think we've got much of a choice!" Duke yelled over the sudden roar. For once, Fontaine and Dinger looked to be in mutual agreement, and together they moved to the very edge of the strange portal, hesitating only slightly before stepping through into the unknown.

They emerged into the new corridor through a second archway, which looked identical to the first in its design. It offered them a view of the crumbling cavern they had just departed, but not for long. There was a thunderous commotion within the cave and a huge boulder crashed into the plinth where they had placed the keys. The portal vanished instantly, and the archway fell dormant once more.

"So much for our way home," Dinger lamented. "At least we know Harkly and his cronies can't follow us now."

"How comforting," Fontaine deadpanned. "Now, we can either stand here for the rest of our lives or see where this corridor takes us." With their swords drawn, they moved cautiously along the corridor and down a wide set of stone steps, entering a large room with a high-domed ceiling. The centre of this great hall was dominated by a massive, water-filled pool with a deep central shaft, the side of which was engraved with designs similar to Ancient cave paintings depicting merfolk and creatures of the sea.

All around were low stone benches arranged in clusters, along with a handful of wooden stalls that seemed to offer everything from painted clay pots to ornate golden daggers. Everywhere was neat, everywhere was tidy, and everywhere was utterly deserted.

"This is creepy," Dinger declared, his voice sounding even louder than usual in the silence. "I feel like we're being watched by people we can't see."

"This place," Jill said thoughtfully, "reminds me of the indoor market back at home. I suppose even Ancients needed to buy food and other everyday things."

"The question is," replied Fontaine as they made their way towards an exit at the far end of the silent room, "how has a structure this enormous gone undiscovered until now?

If it were to be colonised by pirates, it would surely become the finest outpost on the Sea of Thieves."

A moment later, the pirates stepped outside and understood.

"This," Duke said, finding his voice after a moment, "is not the Sea of Thieves. At least, it is not *our* Sea of Thieves." An unfamiliar sky was dominated by a sickly-looking sun blotted out by a perpetual solar eclipse, casting the world around them into perpetual twilight.

On the ground, at least, things were a bit more familiar. The deserted marketplace was tucked snugly up against a dense jungle of strange, purple plants and twisting vines, opening out onto a large port. There were woven sacks and great wooden casks discarded here and there, and even a couple of empty treasure chests lying around. Were it not for the foreboding sky overhead and the curious absence of life, the place could have passed for any Mediterranean port town.

"Well, that's definitely an ocean, right enough," Dinger stated as he gazed out across the murky water. "You can tell by how big and wet it is. Which raises the question of where, exactly, that godforsaken gateway has sent us."

"That, Mister Dinger," Captain Slate called out as he strode along the jetty towards his crew, "may take some explaining. Welcome to the Sea of the Damned."

Jill didn't think she'd ever moved so fast as when the crew of the *Morningstar* hurtled across the jetty to their captain, clustering around Slate and filling the air with a thousand questions. When able to get a word in edgeways, Slate urged peace and composure, promising to explain everything if they would only let him speak.

"As you have no doubt realised by now," Slate began once calm had re-established itself, "certain Ancients had the power to move between the Sea of Thieves and the Sea of the Damned without first ending their lives, much as you did when you came through the gateway. You can think of this place as a kind of... after-image, a memory of Ancient civilisation, carried into the Sea of the Damned by those who visited its strange shores."

Dinger couldn't hold his tongue any longer. "Feels pretty solid for a memory!" he began, but hushed when Jill's elbow found its way to his ribs.

"As you can see," Slate patiently continued, "the Ancients were master builders and craftsmen, though much of what they created has, of course, been lost to time. One of their achievements was a weapon so mighty, its creator chose to hide it away." He looked around at the others. "As we have seen, even knowing such a weapon exists can provoke confrontation. Better, then, to stow it safely in the Sea of the Damned until a time when it was truly needed."

Duke, who had been silently contemplating the landscape during the crew's reunion, spoke at last. "If this is an Ancient outpost – or at least a memory of one – where are all the Ancients?"

Slate smiled very slightly, and raised his lantern – no, they realised, this lantern must belong to another. It was shaped like a great hourglass and filled with the same green, ghostly light that had wreathed the Ancient portal. "This was a gift from the Ferryman," he explained, "to help us understand the truth."

Slate stood, holding the lantern high over his head, and Fontaine bolted to his feet upon realising that he wasn't the only occupant of the bench he'd chosen. He'd found himself seated next to an old man, face barely visible under a large, broad-brimmed hat as he dozed in the sunshine, oblivious to the pirates' presence.

Jill backed away slowly as two children ran past, swatting playfully at one another with crude wooden swords. "Are these ghosts, like the Pirate Lord?"

"Mere memories," Slate reassured her. "They pose no threat, nor will they stop us retrieving what we came for. Let us press onward and finish our mission, hmm?"

There was plenty more that Jill wanted to ask, including the details of Slate's encounter with Flameheart and how he'd come to be with them here in the Sea of the Damned, but she sensed that their captain was in a hurry to depart. He led them at a brisk pace along the jetty, turning a sharp corner to follow the contours of the cliffs that towered high overhead; all around them the Ancient outpost bustled with visions of the past.

Despite Slate's insistence that they were surrounded by little more than echoes, Jill was convinced that one woman – a priestess, she supposed, clad in heavy, crimson robes and strange adornments that hid most of her face – froze at the entrance to a nearby altar and turned to watch them, glaring intently at the *Morningstar*'s crew until she was finally out of sight. *How long would we have to linger here,* she wondered with a sudden chill, *until we became part of the picture?* As quickly as the thought had arisen, it fled from Jill's mind a second later. They had reached the weapon of the Ancients.

She was incredible. She was intimidating. She...

"She's gorgeous!" Jill gasped in delight, racing along the shoreline to the bay where a ship bobbed gently on the tide. This majestic vessel was longer and sleeker than the galleons and brigantines she was used to, with a hull that jutted proudly out where it met the sea, and a prow that curved so sharply it seemed to be reaching for the heavens. She sat low in the water, and Jill was reminded of the triremes and other antique sailing ships she'd studied in secret back home.

Though Jill had only known of the Ancients for a few short days, the ship was unmistakably their creation. Her sails shone gold and green, perfectly matching the Ancient decorations they'd seen on their journey, and her imposing frame was trimmed with rubies and emeralds wherever there was room. Even her flag carried a simple ship design that mimicked the rock paintings they'd encountered.

Despite being unattended for so many years, she looked so immaculate that Jill half-expected the paint on the ship's hull to be wet to the touch. "How long has she been here, I wonder?"

"Ever since she was sailed into the Sea of the Damned, one supposes," Fontaine replied. "I had wondered why we were at a seaport, of all places, but where better to hide such a magnificent vessel? I can see why she would be so feared." The warship was not too much larger than the galleons they were used to seeing across the Sea of Thieves, but she was clearly heavily armoured and bristling with weapons of all kinds. Squinting upwards, Jill thought she could even make out some kind of armament mounted upon the central mast.

"All that heft means she'll be slower than the *Morningstar*," Slate said, a touch defensively. "Clumsier, too. But if there's any ship afloat that can outmatch the *Burning Blade*, it'll be her."

As they approached, Slate's lantern illuminated another phantom figure making his way down the broad gangplank that bridged the topmost deck of the warship. He was bare from the waist up, and as he turned, they saw the great spear depicted in the mural slung across his Olympian shoulders. His muscles jockeyed for position as he took one last look at the ship.

The warrior held a strange totem in his hand, and this was placed with some reverence inside a large stone box on the quayside. Apparently satisfied that all was in place, the figure wavered and vanished.

The stone box, though, was still in place after all this time, and a cursory examination revealed that the totem also remained inside it. Dinger lifted it out slowly, uncertain as to its purpose, and carried it carefully aboard.

"I see much here that is unfamiliar," Slate said, casting a critical eye over the array of weapons and other devices that covered the warship from stem to stern. "Jill, I would like you to complete a full inspection of the ship. Work out what these strange devices are and how they might be used to our advantage in the battle to come. The rest of us will try to get underway as swiftly as we can. I can recognise a capstan when I see one, at least."

"Hold on, skipper," Dinger said, sounding a little plaintive. "We can't set sail on a ship with no name. That'd be bad luck for sure, and the last thing we need right now."

Slate looked a little exasperated. "Our time grows short, Mister Dinger, so what exactly would you suggest?"

Dinger looked thoughtful. "*Flameheart's Folly*? *Ramsey's Revenge*? *Skelly Smasher*?"

"*Ophelia*," Fontaine said, quietly.

Jill found herself surrounded by an unexpected and awkward silence, glancing uncomfortably at the others and trying to understand why. After a moment, Slate placed a gentle hand on Fontaine's shoulder. "I think," he said softly, "that is a most appropriate suggestion. *Ophelia* it shall be." Glad that the moment seemed to be over, Jill ducked below decks and began the examination she'd been ordered to make.

To Slate's chagrin, getting underway took considerably longer than expected, for the anchor seemed to be frozen in place, leaving them unable to set sail. Finally, it was Duke who solved the mystery by setting the totem they'd retrieved into a similarly shaped indentation atop the capstan. Only with the figurine snugly in place was the mechanism moveable, though it still took considerable might to do so. "A strange precaution," Fontaine panted as they weighed anchor.

Duke nodded. "Perhaps a protective measure to avoid thieves making off with the ship?"

"Maybe it's the other way around, and that Ancient bloke didn't want us leaving without his wee statue?" Dinger suggested.

"There are many things about this ship that are peculiar," Slate interjected, "but unusual as she may be, I do know that she won't be going anywhere unless we get to work on these sails." As with the capstan, unfurling the great folds of cloth took all the strength they could muster. Even with Duke's help, the *Ophelia* was every bit as exhausting to sail as Slate had predicted.

"Well, we've got a fair wind, all right, but what about our heading?" Dinger asked, as the four of them heaved and strained against the silvered ropes that served as the *Ophelia*'s rigging. "How are we supposed to find our way out of the afterlife?"

In response, Slate moved to the front of the ship, waving his eerie lantern this way and that as if to send a signal. A few moments later there came the tolling of a great bell, and the prow of another vessel emerged from behind the high cliffside. Even though none of the pirates had ever seen her from afar, there was no mistaking the dark sails or the gnarled figurehead that pulled up alongside them as anything other than the Ferry of the Damned.

True to his duty, the Ferryman had arrived to guide them home.

16

The Ophelia

In the days to come, no-one aboard the *Ophelia* could agree on the moment they returned to the Sea of Thieves, nor the precise nature of the crossing. Dinger insisted that there was a bright swirling maelstrom all around them, while Jill was adamant that the fog bank through which they had sailed had been parted by the sun to reveal familiar horizons. Fontaine, meanwhile, insisted that there was no one single instant of the transition, but that the landscape had slowly built itself around them as the swirling mists had taken shape, as when familiar objects can be glimpsed forming in the clouds.

Whatever course the Ferryman had set for them, they arrived back at the unnamed sandbanks where the Ancient archway had been discovered. The sight of the *Morningstar* on the horizon was a bittersweet one, for she was barely recognisable with a broken prow and borrowed sails. Seeing her in such disarray while he stood at the wheel of another ship gave Slate an uncomfortably disloyal feeling deep in his gut, and he hardened his resolve to see her restored as soon as their business aboard the *Ophelia* was done. Majestic though the Ancient vessel was, she would never be his home.

Far less welcome was the unfamiliar sloop parked in the *Morningstar*'s shadow. The pennant of an offered alliance fluttered in the breeze atop her central mast, but she appeared to be unoccupied, and Slate's brow furrowed at the prospect of uninvited guests ransacking his ship.

"I see movement, skipper," Dinger said in what he considered to be a low voice, which meant the rest of the crew could hear him easily. "Two aboard, I think, lurking in your cabin."

"Caught red-handed, eh?" Slate growled. "Flameheart be damned, I'm not about to leave my ship to the mercy of raiders."

Not without difficulty, he managed to wrestle the *Ophelia* into doing his bidding, bringing her alongside the *Morningstar*'s starboard while Dinger and Fontaine prepared the gangplank. They crossed swiftly, weapons at the ready, intending to fan out and conduct a thorough search for stowaways.

"We know you're here so there's no point in playing hide-and-seek," Slate called. "Whoever's aboard, they'd be wise to show... themselves..." He trailed off as two familiar forms emerged from the gloom of the cabin, for though they had met only briefly, there was no mistaking Karin's imposing frame as she squeezed herself through the doorway with Jewels in her wake.

"Well," Slate said after a moment's stunned silence. "I must say, you've both got quite some gall to show your faces again. If you came to take your key back, I'm afraid you're a little tardy."

"Please just hear us out," Jewels blurted, sensing Karin's irritation at being addressed like a wayward schoolgirl and eager to defuse any quarrel before it could begin. "We didn't come here to steal anything; we were looking for you, we wanted to explain—"

"Then start by explaining how you found us so quickly," Slate cut in. "The seas are vast, our location unmarked, and we were absent for but a few hours."

Karin stared at him, dumbfounded at this statement. "Hours? Wherever you've been, you were gone for *days*." She shoved her pocket-watch under Slate's nose to prove this point – sure enough, the little ticker that counted days suggested that almost a full week had passed in the time it had taken them to claim the *Ophelia*. Clearly, time ran wild in the Sea of the Damned.

"If we hadn't stopped for grub and heard about an abandoned galleon in the middle of nowhere, we might never have found you," Jewels interjected. "When we climbed aboard and saw the state of the place, we were sure Flameheart had already taken over the ship and offed the lot of you."

"Which would have made your life easier, I'm sure," Fontaine put in.

Jewels glowered at him. "D'you think we'd still be standing here if we were on Flameheart's side? Whatever the skellies did to Harkly, he ain't human anymore. He killed Scraps!"

"Worse than killed," Karin snarled. "Pulled his soul right out of his body and shoved it into a box, like it was some sort of trophy!"

"Yeah, and we weren't about to stick around and wait for him to try the same thing on us," Jewels added. "As soon as Harkly turned his back, we were over the side and into the sea, quick as you like. Lucky for us the merfolk arrived before the sharks did."

"And being honourable creatures, they returned you to your original sloop rather than the galleon you'd stolen," Slate surmised. "At which point you could have travelled almost anywhere in the world. Why come to us?"

Karin snorted. "Isn't it obvious? We want to help stop Flameheart."

"I've heard some whoppers in my time," Dinger exclaimed, "but that's a doozy of a pork pie and no mistake. Who sets out all pally with Captain Flameheart and suddenly realises they're on the wrong side?"

"Me," Duke flatly informed him, moving down the length of the gangplank to join them. Jewels and Karin looked momentarily taken aback by the sight of a skeleton among Slate's ranks, but both stood silent and firm before the *Morningstar*'s crew. "Understand, Dinger, that while Flameheart himself is a monster, the *promise* of Flameheart, the freedom that he represents, is and always has been alluring to many.

"This ship, this *Morningstar*, is unusual in many ways. You wear uniforms. You follow orders as promptly as if you were part of the merchant navy. You yourselves do not behave as many others on the Sea of Thieves do – but you still consider yourselves pirates, and you would be correct to do so. The ways of the Pirate Lord are not the only ways, and they never have been."

"Ramsey never tried to destroy people if they disagreed with him," Slate remarked, "but I suppose he must have seemed like quite the tyrant even so."

"I don't know about any of that," Karin stated, "I just know someone needs to pay for what happened to Scraps. If you don't want my help, fine. I'll take my sloop, set it on fire and crash it straight into Flameheart's flagship if that's what it takes to hurt him."

"We know you probably hate us," Jewels added, "and you definitely don't trust us. But we stand a better chance together."

"Hatred has no place on the deck of my ship," Slate replied. "It clouds the mind and will see you sunk more often than not." He stood stock-still for a moment, which his crew knew meant he was thinking furiously. "The 'weapon' we've been feuding over requires no small amount of manpower to operate at full efficiency. More pirates means more loaded cannons, and more bailed water should the need arise." He looked sternly from Jewels to Karin. "You are to be supervised, however. Mister Duke will be watching you like a hawk. Understood?"

Karin looked like she was about to snap back at Slate, but Duke gave them no time to argue. "You can count on me, Captain," he affirmed, "but isn't it about time they saw the ship we're going to be sailing on?"

"A point well made." Slate gestured towards the Ancient warship. "This vessel is our best chance at routing Flameheart once and for all, and Jill has been assessing her capabilities." That was all the encouragement Jill needed to take the bemused pirates on a whirlwind tour of the *Ophelia*, showing off the harpoons mounted on either side that could pluck supplies and treasure from the water as the ship passed by, the small raft to the rear of the ship that took the place of a traditional rowboat, the gun atop the crow's nest, the shining plates of unknown metals lining the interior hull that provided resistance to cannon fire...

Slate was most impressed by the map table on the ship's middle deck. Rather than a simple scroll held in place with pins, the Ancient warrior had charted his paths using something very similar to the plinth they had discovered underneath Kraken's Fall. When this was operated, a ghostly white image of their current position swam into being on the shiny, smooth surface that served as a tabletop. It showed not just their own position, but that of the nearby *Morningstar* and sloop, and a seasoned tactician like Slate could immediately see the value in being able to assess any battle with a bird's-eye view.

Finally, Jill took the crew to the bottom deck to show them the racks of ammunition at their disposal. They were loaded with cannonballs, or something very much like them, but each orb was filled with vibrant, swirling energies that swathed the ship in hues of pale green and vibrant orange. "I have absolutely no idea what these things do," Jill confessed.

"Likewise," Karin replied, "but I can't wait to try them out."

"Shame there's no stove," Dinger lamented. "I'm fair starving for a meal that doesn't knock me out."

"The only bit you haven't explained," Jewels said to Jill, pointedly ignoring Dinger's jibe, "is the name. Why *Ophelia*?"

"I..." Jill looked helplessly to the others.

It was Dinger who answered, not looking happy about it. "Ophelia was the name of our fourth crewmember. When all this Flameheart business started getting properly grim, she went to Captain Slate. Tried to convince him to take a more active role in stopping the skellies before it was too late."

There was a low cough from behind them. Fontaine was framed in the doorway. "My sister always preferred to let her heart rule her head. When Slate refused to escalate the conflict, she left the *Morningstar* to strike out on her own. I have not seen her, nor had any contact with her, since then. I had wondered if she had been captured, but now, having heard tell of this binding magic..." He trailed off, and a hush descended upon the room – but only for a moment, as a call from above roused the crew from their mournful reveries.

"It is time for us to be underway," Slate said when they emerged upon the top deck, gesturing towards a large, ominous, galleon-shaped cloud that hung stubbornly in place despite the strong winds of the open sea. "Flameheart is summoning his forces to battle, and unless my old eyes deceive me, I see the sails of Ramsey's ships on the horizon. In our absence, his Pirate Legends have finally made their move."

"Are we really leaving the *Morningstar* undefended?" Jill asked. "We could... Oh, I don't know, take her in tow or something."

Slate shook his head. "The *Ophelia* is cumbersome enough without more weight to bog her down. I suspect that the *Morningstar* will be safe here in our absence, so long as we can command Flameheart's attention." He made for the helm, but Karin interposed herself between Slate and the wheel. "Let me steer," she insisted.

Slate bristled. "I hardly think—"

"You said it yourself: this ship needs a firm hand, and I'm the strongest person here," Karin stated. "Unless you want to arm-wrestle?"

"That won't be necessary," Slate said dryly. "Besides, I was rather hoping to try out one of those special cannonballs myself." Relieved of his spot at the wheel, he continued to bark orders as the *Ophelia* got underway. She proved far more manageable with a crew of seven working with united purpose, and soon the ship was speeding towards the glowing galleon in the sky, cannons armed and ready, the unattended *Morningstar* reduced to a distant dot. They were ready to fight for the future of the Sea of Thieves.

High atop a rocky archway, overlooking the shattered remains of a skeleton barricade, DeMarco Singh stood with his spyglass in one hand and a speaking trumpet in the other, staring at the galleon-shaped cloud in the distance. "I suppose that's as good a signal as any," he muttered, before raising the trumpet to his lips. "Eyes up, you scurvy sea dogs!" he thundered down to the crews below. "Time to look lively! That powder's not going to carry itself…"

The results of Flameheart's wrath were evident long before the *Ophelia* reached his armada, for the sea was littered with wreckage and ruin. Broken flags, many carrying the distinctive emblem of the Pirate Lord's finest, bobbed here and there among the waves. As they stared down into the water they could see swarms of silver shapes darting back and forth – the merfolk were here in force, whisking away survivors and returning them safely to shore.

Staring at the carnage, Jill couldn't help but imagine the same devastation befalling Sanctuary Outpost. She saw Suki's stall smashed apart, with ships that never had their chance to set sail burning among the ruins. *Not while I'm here*, she told herself forcefully, tightening her grip on the cannon Slate had assigned her. *Not while I'm a pirate.*

Fontaine, who was positioned opposite Jill on the ship's starboard side, gave a sharp cry of alarm as the water behind them began to bubble and ripple. A moment later, the prow of a galleon erupted from the water; a ship full of skeletons jeering and hissing as their vessel broached the waves and drew level with the *Ophelia*. Jill supposed that not needing to breathe gave Flameheart's fleet the element of surprise, and resolved to fill their galleon's hull with enough holes to ensure its next trip to the seabed was a permanent one.

"*Fire!*" Slate roared, and the guns of the *Ophelia* sang out – or more accurately, they screamed. Jill had loaded every cannon with the ghostly ammunition the ship possessed in abundance, but hadn't been expecting them to unleash what she could only think of as a vengeful, screeching spirit towards the skeletons' ship. As intangible as the spectre appeared, it struck the hull of the enemy galleon with as much force as any flesh-and-blood projectile, splintering the barnacled hull and causing several of its crew to dive below decks to repair the damage.

Dinger and Fontaine gave them no respite, peppering the galleon with more of the howling phantoms, pounding the hull relentlessly. One of the more enterprising skeletons tried to fire back, but its shot went wide as the ship was rocked by yet more incoming wraiths. The ship's captain spun the wheel wildly, attempting to veer out of range, but a final, lucky shot from Fontaine tipped the scales, sending the ship and those aboard her back to the ocean floor.

"SO, THE COWARD RETURNS TO STAND AGAINST ME..." Flameheart's voice boomed across the waves with a power that far eclipsed any speaking trumpet the pirates possessed. Slate wasn't sure how their foe had magnified his words to such an extent, but he wasn't about to waste his own breath trading barbs. Flameheart, however, had much more to say. "GIVEN COURAGE BY A CRAFT OF THE ANCIENTS," he sneered. "A RELIC FROM A DEAD RACE. ITS FLAG SHALL MAKE A FINE TROPHY FOR MY NEW EMPIRE!"

"Has Flameheart always been so verbose?" Fontaine inquired. "When it comes to obnoxious prattle, I feel Dinger might actually have a competitor."

"He's trying to distract us," Duke replied, preparing a new volley from his own station. "And to buy time while he tests the strength of this ship. The quicker we reach the *Burning Blade*, the sooner this will all be over. What worries me is how many of his ships might have cursed cannonballs aboard."

As he spoke, two more skeleton ships burst from beneath the waves, catching the *Ophelia* in a calculating pincer movement. Taken by surprise, Jill's shot struck the deck of the ship flanking their port side rather than the water line, sending the crew scattering as the fiery phantom she'd launched exploded in a plume of flame. Jewels, who had taken her place at a cannon with extreme reluctance, was less successful, and swore in frustration as her shot missed its target by mere inches. "I knew it!" she moaned. "My bad luck strikes again."

Given a window of opportunity to return fire, one of the skeleton gunners decided to brave the flames long enough to load an ominous-looking violet cannonball, which Jill suspected must be one of the cursed variety. She fumbled with her own cannon, but wasn't fast enough to prevent them taking their first hit.

The skeleton aimed. The skeleton fired.

The cursed cannonball struck the side of the *Ophelia*, sending out a cloud of purple smoke that washed over the ship. Instantly, the strange totem Dinger had placed atop the capstan unleashed a pulse of energy, causing a sudden gust of wind. At the same moment, Jewels yelped in pain and stumbled backwards, clutching at her arm.

"Amazing..." Duke breathed, moving at once to the capstan. "It completely undid the effects of the cannonball's curse. No damage whatsoever!"

"Speak for yourself!" Jewels snapped, tugging the bracelet off her wrist and hurling it savagely to the deck. "When that thing went off it was like my arm caught fire."

"Cursed jewellery, I shouldn't wonder," Duke said, not all that sympathetically. "You found it in a cave or temple and snagged it for yourself without thinking, I imagine. What did you say about a run of bad luck?"

Jewels stared at him, the colour draining from her cheeks. "Are you seriously telling me that all this time... All the accidents, the missed shots, the bleedin' Megalodon... I really *was* cursed?"

Scowling, Jewels whirled around, pulling her Eye of Reach from her back as she turned to face the burning skeleton ship. She didn't bother with the scope, instead letting her natural experience guide her aim. One after another, skeletons fell as Jewels's shots found their targets with pinpoint accuracy. With no crew left to extinguish the flames, another of Flameheart's galleons soon found itself returning to the depths. Jewels let out a deep sigh of satisfaction and returned to her cannon, her jaw set with newfound determination.

Spurred on by Jewels's return to form, the crew urged the *Ophelia* forward. More skeleton-crewed galleons rose from the water all around them, volleys of cursed cannonballs at the ready, but whenever one so much as scratched the hull of the Ancient warship, the totem dispersed whatever ill effects might have befallen the *Ophelia* or her crew.

Before long, word seemed to have spread among the skeletal fleet that Flameheart's most infamous weapons were no use against this new threat. Instead, his ships concentrated on more traditional rounds of iron shot, aiming far higher than expected. One broadside sent Dinger stumbling away from the cannon he'd been loading, and he would have been flung overboard had Slate not been on hand to catch him. A moment later, Slate himself had to drop to the deck to avoid another shot whizzing overhead.

"Flameheart's doing this deliberately," Slate grumbled, clambering back to his feet with Dinger's help. "The *Ophelia* may be armoured, but its crew aren't. If he can send a few of us to the Ferry, he'll gain the upper hand. Jill, see if you can't make yourself a harder target." Jill nodded and scrambled up the ladder to the crow's nest, seized the swivel gun mounted there, and started to fire rapidly and unpredictably at any skeleton ship in range. As Slate had predicted, the skeletons attempted to strike the crow's nest and knock Jill from her perch, but the small size of her station, coupled with Karin's deft manoeuvres, saw their shots sail harmlessly past to land in the sea.

More colours appeared on the horizon as the battle continued, but these were a far more welcome sight. With Flameheart's armada focused on the *Ophelia*, the scattered survivors of the first, failed assault had begun to rally, sailing back into the fight with newfound determination. It wasn't long before the beleaguered skeletons were under attack from multiple directions at once, and whenever they tore their attention away from the *Ophelia* to retaliate against these new aggressors, Slate seized his chance and sent more screaming phantoms to tear their hulls apart.

Not all pirates who joined the fray did so in the name of the Pirate Lord, however. A dozen ships – crewed by cutthroats, outcasts and renegades who had already pledged their swords to Flameheart – followed in the wake of the skeleton fleet, and proved themselves just as cunning as their undead allies.

One enterprising assassin used the cannon of her sloop to launch herself aboard the deck of the *Ophelia*, and came close to cutting down an unwary Fontaine as he emerged from below decks with more ammunition in his arms. She was felled from behind with a heavy storage crate swung like a club by Karin, her prone form tossed overboard to the whims of the waves.

Had other crews tried similar tricks, the *Ophelia* might soon have been overrun with hostile pirates, but the beleaguered vessel found herself surrounded by a formation of yet more ships proudly bearing liveries of the Order of Souls and Merchant Alliance, and they even spotted a couple of Gold Hoarder emblems in the throng. Even the Trading Companies could see that the time had come to surrender their gold to willing pirates, in exchange for securing their freedom tomorrow. Keeping the *Ophelia* safely surrounded with their angled sails, these new arrivals ensured there would be no more unexpected boarders from above.

With the tide of battle now in their favour, Ramsey's Pirate Legends began to act more daringly, leaping from their sloops and galleons to scrabble up the sides of Flameheart's ships. Their swords danced and pistols flared, keeping their enemies distracted as they bought their allies time to patch holes or grab a bucket to bail away seawater. Most were soon overwhelmed, their bodies spirited away to the Sea of the Damned, but more pirates arrived to take their place. Through it all, Flameheart hurled insults and threats, promising dire retribution for those skeletons who failed him and even worse fates for the living that opposed him once his inevitable conquest was complete.

Finally, Slate decided, the time had come for the *Ophelia* to begin a direct assault on the *Burning Blade*, for the formation that had protected her had either been drawn away by attacks from other vessels or scuttled entirely. "Bring us around," he called to Karin, "and set a course for Flameheart's flagship. It's about time we showed him who—"

The rest of Slate's sentence was drowned out in a sudden commotion as the water in front of the *Ophelia* began to churn. They watched another vessel rise from the sea, but this was no galleon filled with chattering skeletons. Her hull badly scorched, and drenched with slime from her trip beneath the waves, there was no mistaking the tattered livery of the *Prideful Dawn* – now on a collision course with the *Ophelia*.

Karin gave a huge heave and span the wheel with all her might, but there was no escape. The two ships smashed into one another at a dizzying speed that knocked them all off their feet; the Ancient armour that had served the *Ophelia* so well until now buckled beneath the blow, but there was no time to even think about assessing the damage. A hulking figure sped across the deck of the *Prideful Dawn*, racing towards Slate and his crew.

With a mighty leap and a growl of triumph, the Ashen Lord that had once been Harry Harkly hurtled into the fight.

17

THE *OPHELIA*

Eight feet tall with his fleshless skull wreathed in fire, his distinctive shock of red hair now fused and twisted into something akin to glass, Harry Harkly's transformation into the latest of Flameheart's lieutenants was complete. His exposed bones were blood-red, and tongues of flame licked all along his exposed right arm as he turned in a slow circle, facing each of his adversaries.

If Flameheart was a furnace, Harkly was a wildfire. Had it not been for the remains of his outfit, which was now little more than a few smouldering rags, not even his former shipmates would have recognised him. Harkly's bony jaw split in a satisfied sigh at their presence. "I'd expected you traitors to have fled the Sea of Thieves by now," he rasped. "How kind to bring all my enemies together in one place!"

"You still insist upon this madness?" Slate challenged. "Look at yourself, Harkly! See what Flameheart has done to you for his own ends. There is no place for a pirate, any creed of pirate, in the world he seeks to create."

"Don't waste your breath!" Karin surrendered the wheel, striding down to the main deck with her weapon in her hand. "There's nothing left to reason with, Slate. Your pretty speeches won't make it through that thick skull. Harkly's dead. This thing killed him, just like it killed Scraps. And I'm going to make it pay for both."

Harkly threw back his head and laughed uproariously at this. "I always admired your spirit!" he roared. "But I haven't even begun to—"

Karin brought the muzzle of her blunderbuss point blank against Harkly's grinning visage, and fired.

The second shot was Dinger's; it struck a moment later, followed by a third from Fontaine. Harkly staggered this way and that under the sheer force of the blows, but stagger was all he did. He didn't even stop laughing as he balled up a fiery fist and struck Karin with such force that she hurtled backwards across the deck, smashing into the central mast with a wince-inducing crunch. She shook her head blearily for a moment, then scrambled back to her feet with a feral snarl to re-join the fight.

Though Harkly was outnumbered, the deck of the *Ophelia* made for a cramped and difficult battleground. Slate and the others jostled for space as they lined up yet more shots, and Fontaine came close to striking Dinger with a badly timed swing of his cutlass. Harkly seemed to relish having so many targets in proximity, lashing out this way and that as if swatting flies. He carried no weapon, but his raw strength was dangerous enough, and a glancing blow from one flame-coated arm set Dinger's jacket ablaze, forcing the yelping youth to drop to the deck and roll around until he could extinguish himself.

Inch by inch, Slate and his crew lost ground as Harkly advanced mercilessly across the deck of the unsteered ship, which was starting to veer erratically. He raised two fists over his head to deliver a double-handed strike on Karin – but toppled forward as cannon fire buckled the deck beneath his feet, knocking him off balance before he could deliver his deadly blow and giving the crew chance to regroup.

Slate looked around wildly, trying to determine the source of the shot as a second volley struck Harkly squarely in his exposed back. Glancing upwards to the crow's nest, Slate could just about make out Jill, who had angled the swivel gun to point at the deck of her own ship – the only weapon aboard, it seemed, with enough brute force to topple an Ashen Lord. She sank round after round into Harkly's prone form, oblivious to the damage done to the *Ophelia* itself.

Fearful that the ship would run aground or strike one of their allies if its headlong flight wasn't halted, Jewels seized her chance and made a leap for the capstan at the centre of the deck, shoving it as hard as she could to lower the anchor. She could barely hear the clanking of the chain under the cacophony Jill was making, but a moment later the *Ophelia* gave a huge lurch and came to a halt on the outskirts of the ongoing battle. Jewels turned, and caught something sparkling out of the corner of her eye…

Besieged by the gunfire raining down from overhead, Harkly grunted and executed a graceless sideways roll. Jill's next shot missed, and the confusion gave him enough time to get to his feet. Ignoring his foes, Harkly lumbered towards the central mast and drew in a deep breath before exhaling fiercely, his jaw lolling as a great jet of flame shot from his open mouth.

A few short seconds later, the mast of the *Ophelia* was alight, and the flames licked their way up higher and higher towards Jill's position. Spinning around to face the pirates behind him, Harkly inhaled for a second time and prepared to unleash another scorching inferno that would roast his enemies where they stood.

Slate steeled himself for the fatal firestorm, but the assault never came. A burst of light came from Jewels's hand as she struck the totem atop the capstan, her bad luck bracelet clutched in her fist. With each blow the totem sent out a wave of power designed to dispel the effects of any curse – including the kind that might transform a pirate into one of Flameheart's minions. Each pulse of energy wracked the Ashen Lord with fresh paroxysms of pain.

Harkly sank to his knees as the fire within him began to flicker and fade. He placed his hands down to steady himself – but his hands came to rest not on the wooden deck of a ship, but on the familiar flagstones of the family hearth.

Chop…

Cast into nightmare, the sound of his mother's knife in the kitchen as she toiled.

Chop…

The flames before him dwindled to mere embers as he

watched, horrified. The cold and gloom gnawed at his bones as he trembled, feeling weak – weaker than he'd ever felt.

Chop...

The fireplace was his responsibility, it always had been, to fetch the logs so that the house was fit for his father's return. In the gathering twilight, he could sense his mother's fear at what would happen to young Harry next.

Chop, chop, chop...

"HARRY, YOU LITTLE WRETCH! I WARNED YOU WHAT WOULD HAPPEN IF YOU LET THAT FIRE DIE..."

The voice was his father's... no, it was Flameheart's! Or was it perhaps neither. Both? It didn't matter. Either way, Harry Harkly's world was about to become an eternal night of cold, dark and suffering. He had failed to be strong enough...

...But this was a dream. And he could still wake up.

Still on his hands and knees, Harkly gave a wail of mindless, wordless fury. With the last of his strength he sprang forward like a cat pouncing on its prey and brought his fists together, smashing the capstan apart and sending fragments skittering across the deck as Jewels fell back in alarm. One last beam of light shot from the totem into the sky like a beacon, and then it began to sputter and die as it lay on the deck, nothing more than a broken curio from a bygone age.

"Close," Harkly said thickly as the spiteful fire within him began to rekindle. "But not close enough." He placed one hand on the ruined capstan, getting slowly to his feet and turning to face the pirates who had come so close to casting him into the dark. "You should have killed me when you had the chance," he informed Slate. "Because now?

Now, you wretched old fossil, you and this ship are going to burn."

High in the crow's nest of the *Burning Blade*, Captain Adara hissed in satisfaction and lowered her spyglass before dropping nimbly down to the deck to make her way swiftly towards the Captain's Cabin. She had seen all that she wished to see, and now she needed to take action.

The interior of Flameheart's quarters had once been among the most opulent of any vessel, but much of their former glory had been stripped away as his curse had taken hold. He had ordered the bed destroyed, replaced with a plain cabinet which housed weapons from foes dispatched over the years, while less valuable mementos of his time on the sea hung here and there, wherever there was space.

The only furnishings Flameheart insisted on keeping in pristine condition were a large lockbox that was opened only when he was in private, and an enormous captain's chair, the size of a throne, in which he would seat himself with a regal bearing while listening to reports from his subordinates. Even the trinkets on the captain's table were largely forgotten – a faded journal, a simple grog tankard, and a dusty chessboard next to a half-burned candle, remnants of a game abandoned many years ago.

Flameheart was meticulously sharpening the blade that had been dulled during his prolonged battle with Slate. His fury after that fateful encounter had been terrifying, even for those like Adara who knew him best. She had arrived in time to witness the destruction Flameheart had wrought on the Ancient vault that had entombed him, ripping the chamber apart bare-handed until the masonry gave way and he was free to seek his revenge, starting with the luckless skeletons who had failed to free him. Their bones now littered the ground of Kraken's Fall. Since then, Flameheart had waited impatiently for some new glimpse of Slate or his ship, but his scouts could find no trace of either. Infuriated, he had eventually announced that it was time for their conquest to commence.

Flameheart's foul temper improved when the first of the Pirate Lord's allies had the impertinence to intercept the *Burning Blade*. Ramsey's so-called 'Pirate Legends' were dressed in the finery of Athena's Fortune and wielded weapons that must have cost each of them a lifetime of loot. Nonetheless, their ships were ripped to matchwood by Flameheart's superior firepower as they approached, enticed by the galleon-shaped cloud Adara had summoned, caught neatly in an ambush as skeletal reinforcements emerged from under the sea.

Had it been up to Adara, she would have blasted the merfolk out of the water when they arrived, quashing their attempts to snatch up pirates and carry them to safety. Flameheart paid them little heed, however, for he was fixated on his human opponents. He reminded Adara that each scuttled galleon the Pirate Lord sent his way was another prize for his shipwreck graveyard – once the pirates aboard it had been exterminated, at least.

News from their skeletal scouts, heralding the arrival of a mighty new galleon that matched nothing the pirates had sent their way before, had delighted Flameheart as much as it had alarmed Adara. Even more serious was the revelation that some devious Ancient trickery protected the ship from her master's cursed cannonballs. Flameheart had kept the *Burning Blade* at the rear of his fleet as it approached, offering ample opportunity to observe the warship in combat before he chose to pit the might of his flagship against it. Since then, they had spent their time dispatching any pirates who thought to chance their arm against the might of a Skeleton Lord.

Harkly's arrival, while unexpected, had provided Flameheart with yet another stratagem. His skeletons had stumbled upon the crippled *Prideful Dawn* while answering Flameheart's rallying call and, with their assistance, the vengeful Ashen Lord had managed to get the vessel underway and reunite with the armada. Harkly had been relishing the opportunity to strike down Slate and his treacherous crew, but Flameheart's orders had been clear: Harkly was to find a way to destroy whatever source of power gave the ship the strength to resist Flameheart's dark influences.

With the Ancient artefact now in scattered pieces, Adara was concerned that Harkly might run amok, like a rabid bulldog let off its leash. If Flameheart did not take control of his newest Ashen Lord soon, there might be nothing left of the warship for them to claim.

Once inside the cabin, Adara bowed but did not wait for permission to speak. "Harkly appears to have succeeded, my king. The ship of the Ancients should be vulnerable to any curse you wish to inflict upon them."

"Excellent!" Flameheart exulted, sheathing his newly honed sword at once. "The moment of my triumph has finally arrived. Make sail immediately, sink all who would stand in our way, and we shall make an example – not just of Eli Slate, but of all those who refuse to accept the inevitable." Adara nodded, backing out of the cabin, eager to obey her king at once.

This left Flameheart to revel in his own anticipated glory. Now that the time was right, they would seize the Ancient warship and bring it into their own armada, taking its wraith-born weapons for themselves and turning them on the very pirates who had fought so pointlessly to acquire them.

Then, Flameheart decided, he would sail to the nearest outpost, reducing settlement after settlement to ash and rubble. This would continue until, at last, the terrified townsfolk finally agreed to surrender the location of the Pirate Lord and his allies, and then... Well, Flameheart knew much about dealing with troublesome spirits. Death would be no escape, not for anyone who dared oppose him.

For all the excitement and anticipation, there was one tiny shard of ice somewhere within the fire that filled his chest – a cold sliver of doubt that somehow persisted deep within him. Ever since he had learned that there were weapons on the Sea of Thieves beyond his understanding, that shard had turned colder still. Victory was his destiny. To acknowledge the possibility of defeat... It was madness. Weakness. Unthinkable.

And yet...

That was why Captain Flameheart, on the eve before this war he had chosen to wage, had summoned his Ashen Lords and Captain Adara to his chambers, and explained to them precisely what would happen to them if he lost.

As the crew of the *Ophelia* watched helplessly, Harkly dropped to his knees once again, but this was no act of supplication. More flames spewed forth from his open mouth, forcing everyone back towards the galleon's prow. Clouds were starting to form overhead, sparks of crimson lightning dancing among them. The *Ophelia* was swiftly finding herself at the heart of her own private thunderstorm.

Moments later, chunks of flaming rock plunged from the heavens, smacking into the ship and ricocheting into the water all around them, which was already starting to boil. Harkly's anger was superheating the world around him, just as it had back in the Ancient temple. Slate and the others dove for cover, but the exposed deck of the warship offered precious little protection. One lucky strike could end their lives at any moment, and there was no hope of making it past the scorching flames to find safety down below.

Jill watched all of this from the crow's nest, shifting uncomfortably as fire crawled closer along the mast Harkly had ignited. She doubted that she could dive into the sea from here, and even if she could make the leap, the bubbling ocean would hardly be an improvement. *But maybe*, she thought desperately, *I don't have to make it as far as the sea...*

Jill lifted one leg over the railing that surrounded the crow's nest, then the other, balancing precariously on the rim while she prepared herself. Fortunately, the *Ophelia*'s central mast had three large sails just as a pirate galleon did, which meant that the highest point of the rigging was only a few feet below. *You've done this sort of thing a thousand times on ships you've made*, she told herself sternly. *Of course, they weren't on fire, but that's just more reason not to miss. Three... Two...*

Before Jill could get to *One*, one of Harkly's flaming boulders smashed into the crow's nest. The impact pitched her forward to land roughly atop the smouldering sail, clinging tightly to the wooden spar from which it hung – so tightly, she wondered if she'd ever be able to let go again. Only when she dared to glance down towards the deck did she find the resolve to keep moving, for Harkly was advancing on Slate, who had been knocked back against what remained of the capstan and now lay in a crumpled heap.

"You escaped my king last time," Harkly crowed. "But I have no intention of letting the Ferryman claim you now. All I need to bind your soul is a suitable trinket..."

He's going to do to the captain what he did to Scraps, thought Jill, feeling the cold dread of panic despite the intense heat of the rising flames. She reached for her cutlass.

"Or perhaps the figurehead of this vessel would be more fitting," Harkly gloated, his fingers now inches away from Slate's throat. "I'm sure you believe the captain should go down with his ship."

Jill knew all too well that the rigging of any vessel, least of all a warship fashioned hundreds of years ago, was a mammoth tangle of supports and wires that might take even seasoned pirates hours to repair. Learning to recognise the single knot, the one vital length of rope that would cause everything else to unravel, could take a lifetime of study. But if fashioned correctly, there always *was* one knot...

Thank you, Suki, for all the times you scolded me. Jill drew back her arm. If this was a fine ship, built with no mistakes, there was only one possible choice. How could it not be so?

The blade of her sword sliced through the rigging, and the great sail began to descend as its supports released it from their clutches. Heavy fabric engulfed Harkly from on high, swaddling him in great folds of flame.

"YOU. LET. ME. *FALL!*"

Only Karin had the raw strength, never mind the vengeful fury, to tackle a creature of Harkly's size, so that was precisely what she chose to do. She rammed into the struggling skeleton shoulder-first, embracing him in a great bear-hug that sent the two of them, along with the burning sail, overboard with a mighty crash. Jewels gave a cry of alarm and ran to the railings, scanning the surface for any sign of her friend among the chaos and debris.

Jill thudded noisily onto the deck by clutching a spool of rope as it uncoiled, moving to Slate's side at once. "Captain! Captain Slate? *Dammit, Eli, don't be dead!*"

Slate was as still as the grave for a long, agonising moment, then gave a great, racking cough and opened his eyes. "My soul," he said weakly, "appears to still be here with my crew, where it belongs."

There was a whooshing sound and a shout of triumph from Jewels. Helping Slate to his feet, Jill saw that the fair-haired pirate had found an ingenious way to retrieve her friend from the water. Karin dangled by her belt from one of the ship's harpoons with a mixture of relief and anger on her face, caught on the line like a landed fish that had been scalded by the boiling sea. Dinger and Fontaine moved to help her aboard, but she brushed them away as soon as her feet hit wood. "Harkly's gone," she announced. "I watched him sink like a stone. One good turn," she added with a smirk.

"Good riddance," Fontaine said bluntly. "Orders, Captain? Should we bail? Try to fight the flames? We might still be able to raise the anchor if Jill can—"

"I think not," Slate said, suddenly seeming much older. "Our hull is breached, the mast an inferno. Doubtless we are half-filled with water by now. More than that…" He gestured towards the horizon. "The *Burning Blade* is almost upon us, and I fear we have lost our immunity to whatever cursed cannonballs Flameheart might choose to torment us with. I would sooner see the *Ophelia* burn to ashes than allow him time to discover her secrets. Therefore," he turned to face the others. "My final order is that we abandon ship."

The others nodded glumly and settled into a single-file procession behind Slate as he picked his way through the fires that now engulfed much of the *Ophelia*. Yet upon reaching the rear of the ship where the raft had been docked, they soon realised that not only had their single means of escape vanished during the confusion, but so too had one of their number.

Duke was gone.

18

THE *BURNING BLADE*

It was time. Flameheart could sense the proximity of his prey, which meant that the moment had arrived to take the wheel of the *Burning Blade* and put an end to the battle once and for all. As he made to leave his cabin, though, the sudden lurch of a lowered anchor gave him pause. Why had they stopped? Had he not commanded a direct course straight towards the Ancient ship? Biting down on his anger, he became aware of some commotion outside his door and paused, waiting to see what could possibly have torn his crew away from their duties.

Captain Adara entered without knocking, which was unusual, though the reason for her impertinence became apparent soon enough. There, held firmly in the clutches of two skeletal crewmen but doing his best to stand proud, was his Duke.

"Well, well..." Pleasure dripped from Flameheart's voice as he rubbed his beard thoughtfully. "In the final hour, the traitor returns to the fold." The conquest of the warship could wait. This was a moment that Flameheart intended to savour. "Release him!"

The skeletons obliged, rather more roughly than necessary, leaving Duke in a heap at Flameheart's feet. Flameheart moved to sit behind his desk, reclining in the captain's chair and motioning that Adara should leave the two of them alone. Once the cabin door had clicked shut, he leaned forward, staring down at the sprawled skeleton. "Did you expect that I would forgive your treachery? Allow you to return to my side now that my victory is absolute?"

Duke stood, slowly, and looked around the cabin with interest. "All these years and you haven't changed a thing. It's just as it was the last time I stood here. Including our final game, I see," he added, pointing to the chessboard. "It was my move, I believe. May I?"

Flameheart clearly found this request highly amusing, for he allowed Duke to light the candle that served as the game's timer. Duke eased away the dollop of wax used to keep the pieces in place during storms, separated his white knight from the board and blew the dust off before setting it into its new position – the first move any of the pieces had made in years.

"I left this game untouched as a reminder," Flameheart told him, selecting a bishop and using it to remove one of Duke's pawns from the board. "That friendships are folly, for even your closest comrades can abandon you when it suits their need. I will not make that mistake again."

"It was because I considered you a friend that I tried to steer you down a different path," Duke replied, sending his remaining rook in a bold sweep across the board. "There was a time when I really did think the world of you, you know?"

"You have always been drawn to those with a greater sense of destiny than yourself," Flameheart stated. "For all your talk of freedom, I know that you have come to understand the truth of this supposed pirate life." He leaned closer. "To be truly free, to exist unchained, one must cast aside their dependence on others. To live in the moment means believing in nothing, building nothing, trusting nothing, and still finding purpose. You, my Duke, do not possess strength enough for that, much as you may wish it. You will always have a need to *belong*."

"And what of your purpose?" Duke challenged. "To revel in destruction for destruction's sake? To bathe in the fires of war for all eternity?"

Flameheart laughed. "I *am* the fire of war. How fearful you must have been, to hear my voice again after all these years."

"Oh, yes," Duke agreed. "I had quite forgotten the boxes you created. One for each of your most faithful lieutenants. Remarkable objects, hand-crafted from arcana that none of us really understood." He began to pace back and forth as he continued to speak, the chessboard momentarily unheeded. "They became one of the most sought-after treasures on the Sea of Thieves, as I recall. Pirates named them 'Boxes of Wondrous Secrets', even though few people understood their true purpose…"

"Communication." Flameheart gestured towards the great chest behind Duke. "No matter what the distance. As simple as placing new orders inside my Captain's Lockbox, here on the *Burning Blade*."

Duke nodded. "And no matter where we were in the world, we could open *our* boxes and retrieve whatever was inside. A wondrous secret, indeed. I kept my chest safe, of course. At first I hoped I might intercept your messages even while I was in exile. Time passed and the scheme slipped from my mind. But you had anticipated that, hadn't you?" He brought a lone pawn forward, placing it carefully down next to Flameheart's castled king.

Flameheart nodded, never one to resist gloating over a victory. "That which gives can also receive. I began using the boxes to receive tribute from those worthy of serving me, accepting relics from all across the seas so long as the power they contained could further my ambitions. Over time, I realised that while the lid of a box was open, I could hear whatever was being said nearby, as surely as if I were standing there myself. And so, when your belongings were brought aboard the *Morningstar*, so too was my secret advantage."

"An advantage you surrendered when you revealed yourself to me," Duke pointed out. "It was only a matter of time until I figured out how you were doing it." He indicated the game. "Check, by the way."

"And then, once you had learned the truth, you threw the box away. No matter." Flameheart reached for his queen, reacting to Duke's check and pressing his miniature army forward before withdrawing his hand in satisfaction. "A bold move, but a foolish one. Try as you might, you have but one more move before checkmate." Flameheart rose, then, stepping around the desk and moving to the door of his cabin. "The game is over. Every battle needs a victor. Stand with me one last time at my coronation, and bear witness as your king takes his rightful place as ruler of the Sea of Thieves!"

Duke, however, did not follow, and when Flameheart turned to admonish him, to angrily accuse him of stalling for time, he saw that his former friend was standing by the Captain's Lockbox, one hand on the lid. "You were wrong," Duke said, softly. "I didn't throw anything away."

The fire in Flameheart's eyeless sockets blazed. "What are you talking about?" he demanded. "Answer me!"

Duke pulled back the lid of the lockbox. "Your biggest problem, *Captain*, has always been that you never can hold your tongue. Once we understood the means by which you'd been taunting me, Slate and I decided to gather some tribute of our own. To be placed in your Box of Wondrous Secrets so that, like any other offering, it would end up here. While the lid is open, of course, I can be heard quite clearly. *Now, Mister Singh!*"

Duke gave a mighty grunt of effort and tipped the lockbox onto its side. Immediately, a torrent of fine dark granules began to pour forth. They spilled across the floor of Flameheart's cabin in a great tide, trickling down between the floorboards, making their way into every nook and cranny of the *Burning Blade*. Flameheart stood aghast, unable to comprehend what he was seeing as the room continued to fill. "What is this foolishness?!"

"A message, of course," Duke replied. "A message to the

new king from all those pirates, shopkeepers, shipwrights and merchants across the Sea of Thieves who know that our freedom is more than just a dream, delivered to one spot by an alliance of ships from every outpost. Unless you were speaking literally, in which case – it's lots and lots of gunpowder. What's a coronation without fireworks?"

Flameheart gave an enraged bellow and shoved Duke aside, slamming the lid of the lockbox shut – but too late to prevent the torrent of deadly powder from coating every deck of his ship. "You won't do this! You can't!" he screamed, with an unfamiliar note of fear in his words. "Our kind... We won't... *YOU'LL DIE TOO!*"

Duke moved to the chessboard, peering down at the clustered pieces in the candlelight one last time before placing his king on its side and making his pronouncement. "I resign," he informed Captain Flameheart. "Stop the clock."

And then Duke knocked the candle over.

Jill felt, rather than saw, the explosion of the *Burning Blade*; first, a rush of arid air washed over the *Ophelia*, and then a great shockwave capsized the battered warship and sent them all tumbling helplessly into the sea. Striking the water so unexpectedly almost sent her into shock, but she forced her legs to start kicking out and away from the ship as it sank, so that the tug of the warship's descent did not consign her to the same watery grave.

She spotted a dark shape in the water nearby – Fontaine, unmoving and limp, a nasty bruise blossoming on his forehead. Jill redoubled her efforts, scooping the stricken pirate up in both arms as she kicked ever more furiously. The surface of the sea scarcely seemed more inviting, awash as it was with flaming wreckage and churning waves, but at least there was precious air to be found up there.

Jill's body, however, seemed to have different ideas. *This is the third time you've nearly died today*, it seemed to say, *and it's so nice and cool down here. Would a trip to the Ferry really be so bad?* She could feel the darkness at the edges of her vision now, the tug of sleep pulling at her from all directions. *It would be so much easier…*

Luckily, Jill knew herself to *still* be a very bad liar. She reached down into herself to find those final reserves of determination, summoning the last of her strength and breaking the surface of the sea to draw in air with a great, desperate series of gulps. She felt helping hands clutching at her, and briefly thought it must be the merfolk come to carry her home – but these were human hands, human voices, calling her name, asking if she was all right. Her answer was to roll over onto her stomach as soon as she felt the deck of the ship beneath her, regurgitating so much seawater she half expected to cough up a kraken as well. "F… Fontaine…" she managed.

"Out cold, but he's slept off worse." The voice was Slate's, and she looked up gratefully at her captain as he bent down to offer his hand. There were unfamiliar faces all around – but then, this was an unfamiliar ship, one that was practically packed to bursting with pirates who'd been rescued from the aftermath of the battle. The noise of the chatter and excited shouting from the mob was almost overwhelming, and it wasn't helped by the thunder of cannons as pirate galleons took pot-shots at what remained of Flameheart's fleet.

The *Burning Blade* had vanished in a cloud of smoke and shrapnel, and the remaining skeleton ships were left in utter disarray. A few continued to fight, but many others were trying to flee the scene or dive back below the waves to escape. Thinking about the skeletons reminded Jill of their absent comrade, and she tugged urgently at Slate's arm to get his attention in the chaos. "Duke?" she mouthed.

Slate shook his head sadly before moving to sit with Fontaine, who had been laid down on the captain's bed to recover, and Jill felt a hollow pit open in her stomach. Admittedly, it had been Duke's idea to leave the Box of Wondrous Secrets with DeMarco at the fort – a back-up plan, in the event that Flameheart somehow seized or destroyed the Ancient weapon – but, driven as he had been to make amends for his past, she had never imagined that he would willingly sacrifice himself if that was what it took to light the spark, and so extinguish the flame.

He could walk under the sea. If he has somehow survived, Jill thought sorrowfully, *he might be able to make it back to land, one day...* In her heart, though, she knew that there would have been no escaping that cataclysmic explosion.

The overpopulated galleon was in no position to chase down straggling skeletons, and so made its way slowly, if raucously, home. Dinger could be heard over the commotion well enough, and Jill caught a fleeting glimpse of Jewels and Karin below deck, but it was impossible to force her way through the crowd to talk with them. The two pirates sat quietly, trying to draw as little attention to themselves as possible. Anyone who had worked to abet Flameheart, however briefly, was going to find life very difficult in the coming days if their past allegiances were discovered.

Pirates poured down the gangplank and swarmed across Sanctuary Outpost as soon as the ship weighed anchor, chattering and exulting at the events of the day. The air of excitement was infectious, and before long even ships that had only witnessed the battle from afar were celebrating as the news of Flameheart's defeat made it from crew to crew. Grog barrels were rolled out on deck and their contents shared liberally around.

The *Ophelia*, of course, was the subject of much discussion and speculation among pirates far and wide, for almost everyone had seen her cutting a swathe across the sea and shrugging off cursed cannonballs, only for the fateful confrontation with an Ashen Lord to bring about her destruction. Few ships had been close enough to glimpse faces from the *Morningstar* aboard her, however, and before long, common consensus was that the ship had been crewed by phantoms and captained by the Pirate Lord himself. Jill was extremely grateful for the anonymity, and was content to recline in the sun and rest until everything stopped aching.

Little by little, the exuberant atmosphere gave way to a contented calm as pirates waded into the water, seeking merfolk – who had spent the day splashing and performing acrobatic leaps to mirror the excitement of their land-dwelling kin – to carry them home. Jill saw very little of this, for sleep had finally found her, and she was roused only when Dinger helpfully nudged her awake with the tip of his boot. She came to with a start, glaring, but broke into a wide grin at the sight of Fontaine, rumpled but recovered, standing alongside his shipmates. "I think," Slate said, as if conveying some great secret, "that the tavern might now be inhabitable enough for us to enjoy a well-deserved drink."

"So long as you do not rely on your quartermaster to provide the funds," Fontaine said, a little fuzzily. "I left all my money in my other ship."

"I'm sure Mister Dinger will be able to overcome his legendary shyness long enough to convince the tavern-keeper to open a tab," Slate said, smiling. "We have plenty to drink to, both in celebration and in commemoration."

Barely had the *Morningstar*'s crew taken their ease at a long bench in the George & Kraken when Karin's imposing silhouette briefly blocked out the daylight. She moved quietly inside and made towards a secluded corner table with Jewels in tow, but both stopped dead upon hearing their names called. Slate bade them sit down, sent Dinger to the bar to find another couple of drinks, and enquired as to what their next destination might be.

"Well…" Jewels began. "We've been talking it over, and the way we see it, Scraps is still out there somewhere. His soul, I mean, trapped in one of them cursed chests. Soon as we're done here, we'll be looking to find it."

Karin nodded. "If there's power out there to stuff a spirit into something, then there's got to be power to set it free. We won't stop searching until we learn a way. We owe him that much."

"And then I can give him a thick ear for feeding me dodgy stew," Jewels added. "But we'll save him, I know we will."

"You sound very confident," Fontaine informed her. "Do you have any idea where to start looking?"

Jewels gave him a bright smile. "Let's just say I feel lucky."

"And I'm incredibly stubborn," Karin added. "We'll find him all right. Until then…" She raised her tankard. "A toast. To Scraps, and to Duke. They should be here, and aren't."

They clinked their grogs as one, and those drinks became the first of many as the afternoon wore on. When the time came to light the lanterns, the two pirates got to their feet – after a few false starts – and bade the crew of the *Morningstar* farewell, staggering out into the evening air to begin their next adventure.

Once they had departed and Slate had stepped outside for a private moment in Tanner's Alley, Jill let out a long, deep breath. "I just find it so terrifying," she admitted to the others. "The idea of your spirit being ripped from your body like poor Scraps. When I thought Harkly had done the same thing to Slate, it was like knives inside of me." She cast her gaze down at her feet. "I don't think I could cope with something like that again."

"Should that day ever come," Fontaine said, sympathetically, "I am confident that you will rely on your wits and your skills to survive, just as you have done today. As you may need to do right now, in fact."

Jill wasn't immediately sure what he meant, and then she heard the voice.

"*AND JUST WHERE HAVE YOU BEEN ALL THIS TIME?*"

The colour drained from Jill's face as she turned, slowly, to face the furious woman behind her. If looks could kill, the one she was getting from Suki right now would have sent Jill to the Ferry quicker than any bite from Chomps. "First you do not come to work," the old woman began, berating her protégé with no concern for the stares and smirks of those in the tavern. "Then those I send to search the outpost for you tell me that you cannot be found. Now I find you here, wearing ruined clothes that reek of smoke, and you do not even think to apologise? To come to your poor old mentor and say sorry for the worry you have caused her? Well! I say to you that this is unacceptable behaviour for any shipwright, least of all my apprentice! You should be *ashamed*!"

"Madam." Eli Slate, returning to his seat, gave a graceful bow. "I believe this is a simple case of mistaken identity. You are not hectoring a delinquent shipwright, you are addressing a member of my ship's crew. A pirate."

Unused to anyone standing up to her, particularly a courteous older gentleman with a *very* fine moustache, Suki's mouth opened and closed a few times. "Well!" she began, and then a moment later, when words failed to materialise, she settled for "Well, indeed!" before stamping over to her usual table with the air of one who believes she has been thoroughly hoodwinked but isn't quite certain how, or by whom.

"Thank you, Captain," Jill said gratefully, "but I think my name is probably going to be mud around the outpost for quite a while, at least to the shipwrights."

"Fortunate, then, that our *Morningstar* can take us to *any* outpost, or indeed anywhere else we desire to go, and none may tell us differently," Slate replied, "Once we have reunited with her, that is."

"I thought you'd never ask." A figure detached itself from the shadows at the rear of the tavern and stepped forward, his slight smirk offset by two glowing, pupilless eyes. The same mysterious stranger, Jill realised, who had appeared in Slate's cabin... how long ago had that been? It felt like forever. "If you'd care to follow me..."

"I've still got half a pint here!" Dinger protested, but the others ushered him towards the stony staircase and down towards the den of the Pirate Lord, rather more woozily than the last time they'd been invited inside. The merriment had made it to Ramsey's tavern, too, and the ghostly band were surrounded by Pirate Legends – some living, some dead – leading them in a rousing chorus of a cheerful shanty.

This time, though, their guide did not lead them into the tavern, but continued to escort them along a jetty that led deeper into the cavern where the *Athena's Fortune* had taken its final rest. There was a shipwright here too, and Jill was interested but not startled to note that she, like her cohorts in the tavern, was a ghost. There was no time for introductions, though, for the Pirate Lord awaited them up ahead, standing next to a familiar grey and red hull with a broad smile on his bearded face.

"George was good enough to fill me in on your undertakings," he declared as they approached. "Ancient treasure vaults, a duel with Flameheart and a trip to the Sea of the Damned." He looked directly at Jill with a twinkle in his eye. "Not bad for your first voyage, eh?"

"I don't remember leaving my ship down here," Slate remarked, "but I must confess it's good to see her in one piece. I've already lost one remarkable vessel today."

"I think perhaps it's better that you did," the Pirate Lord said smoothly, tapping a finger on the head of his staff. "In my experience, no matter whose hands a weapon like that falls into, they become the wrong hands soon enough. As for the *Morningstar*, we've taken the liberty of repairing and restoring her. She'll be just the way you remember her." He gestured with his staff, indicating a large stack of boxes in which Duke's many journals and diagrams had been piled. "These secrets, however, are probably best kept tucked away down here. Who knows when they might be needed again?"

Slate nodded, placing one hand on the hull of the *Morningstar*. "The extra space will be appreciated, especially as I plan to make a study of that skeleton language. Flameheart may be gone, but his legacy lives on. There are plenty of dangers we've yet to face, and I wish to be prepared for them."

"Gone…" the Pirate Lord mused. "I wonder. Nothing really dies, not here on the Sea of Thieves." He laughed. "You're talking with the not-so-living proof of that. Even so, Flameheart's supporters have all but vanished. His forts are deserted, the bastion he had created in the Wilds is being picked apart by opportunistic pirates to the point of being completely dismantled, and crews can once again sail without fear of attack from skeleton ships. Instead, they can get back to what matters – a grand adventure, a glorious tale to tell and a gold coin or two to spend while they're about it."

Having said his piece, he gave Slate and his crew a final nod and began to amble up the jetty, back towards his tavern, whistling a cheerful tune to himself.

Jill shook her head. "The greatest pirate who ever lived… Is he always like this?"

Slate considered. "Actually, I'd say that that was one of his shorter speeches. I remember an occasion at Golden Sands…"

Once the anchor was raised, they eased their way back onto open waters and took up their positions around the map table, where Dinger glanced slyly across at his friend. "You're not fooling anyone, you know?"

Fontaine gave an audible groan. "Am I still concussed, or are you making even less sense than usual?"

"Well, I mean, a skelly who sacrificed himself to save the living? Magic boxes you can use to spy on people? A trip through a land of the dead? That's got to be enough to fry even your noggin trying to figure it all out." Dinger smirked. "You might say, there are more things in heaven and earth than can be dreamt of in all your philosophy."

Fontaine stared at him, astonished. "Do my ears deceive me, or is our dear Dinger actually misquoting the Bard? Perhaps we might make an aesthete of you after all."

"Not a chance!" Dinger exclaimed, horrified. "All that running and jumping sounds *exhausting*."

Even Captain Slate laughed at this, moving to stand with his crew. "It seems fitting that our newest addition should decide upon our next destination," he decreed. "What say you, Jill?"

This question stumped Jill, but only for a moment. She fished around in the pockets of her uniform jacket until she pulled out the treasure map that she'd purchased from the Gold Hoarders on her first day aboard the *Morningstar*. It was stained, smudged and singed around the edges, but the little red X of her first ever pirate quest was still just about visible. "We're already on a voyage, remember?" she pointed out, placing the tattered map for all to see. "That's someone else's buried treasure, which means it belongs to us."

"Hear, hear!" Dinger said happily. "I'm down to my last coin, and it's getting lonely. Let's find it some friends."

"I shall have to fetch you a shovel," sighed Fontaine. "Assuming I can find any of our belongings after such upheaval at the hands of clueless Pirate Legends. Doubtless nothing aboard will be in its proper place. Ah, *c'est la vie…*"

"Very well!" Slate barked, slapping the table as he stood. "You have your orders, all of you. To your stations, then, and don't dawdle. We've treasure to find!"

"Aye, Captain!" they chorused, and once more began the business of being pirates, setting their *Morningstar* on a path over the horizon to meet the new dawn. Another day of sailing free.

Epilogue

The Ashen Dragon

Their journey was almost at its end.

Captain Adara stood at the helm of her ship, the *Ashen Dragon*, and brooded. Despite their painstaking preparations, this fated day had not gone as planned.

Adara was fortunate to be here at all, she knew. She had been off the ship, ransacking the strange raft that had been commandeered by the traitorous Duke, when the *Burning Blade* was destroyed. That was why she had simply been tossed helplessly across the waves rather than slaughtered along with the rest of the crew. Pure luck, but her survival had allowed them to recover Flameheart's remains before any pirates could get their hands on them. The thought of her king's skull being used as some trophy for a bunch of squabbling swabbies disgusted her.

Adara had been pleased to see that the power and

protections upon Flameheart had prevented his lifeless husk from being obliterated entirely by the blast – no, not quite lifeless, she reminded herself. Even the *Burning Blade* had avoided total destruction, though what remained of her wreck had long since descended to the darkest depths of the ocean floor.

Whether she might one day be salvaged, Adara did not know – nor did she care, for she still had her king's last orders to obey. Flameheart had decreed that, if the impossible were to happen and he were somehow to be felled in battle, the *Ashen Dragon* would be chosen to ferry his body to a secret tomb, there to await his future resurrection.

Oh, he had been cunning, far more cunning than fools like the Pirate Lord would have believed possible, for Flameheart had turned the binding ritual upon himself. In doing so, he had secured his spirit not within a chest or other trinket, but inside his own body. This way he avoided an eternity in the Sea of the Damned, condemned for his crimes and denied passage back to the living world by the Ferryman.

The pirates Flameheart had fought so fiercely to destroy, however, lacked the respect to allow the *Ashen Dragon* to complete its final mission unimpeded. Two galleons had dared to stand against the skeletons as they went about their final duties, doubtless seeking to plunder whatever valuables they had aboard. If Adara had been acting alone, they might well have succeeded – perhaps even desecrated Flameheart's remains in the process. It was well, then, that she had surrendered command of her ship to another: Old Horatio, the last of the Ashen Lords.

When Horatio had bound the first pirate captain, trapping her soul like a miniature ship in a tightly corked bottle, the other galleon had broken off its pursuit and tried to flee – but the enraged Ashen Lord demanded they give chase. Adara and her crew scarcely needed the encouragement, such was their desire to exact vengeance upon flesh-kind for their master's downfall.

All too soon, however, the chase had been over, and Flameheart had been placed reverentially in his tomb – slumbering for now, but ready to reach out to those minds that might be receptive to his influence. Pawns, willing to orchestrate the release of his soul on one distant day when the Sea of Thieves had grown fat and lazy with the stupor of peace. There was one such puppet out there, she knew, who had foolishly peeked inside a Box of Wondrous Secrets and thus had the seeds of subjugation planted in his mind. In time, he would seek to gain the trust of others, paving the path for his new master's return.

Until then, Adara and those loyal few were to sail far into the east until they were needed once more. She watched, enthralled, as Old Horatio stirred up a great whirlwind, pouring the last of his energy into a sacrifice that would part the Devil's Shroud long enough to allow the *Ashen Dragon* safe passage. When the maelstrom finally dissipated, so too had the Ashen Lord, casting himself into the void to await his own inevitable rebirth.

With no Horatio to guide them and no more orders to follow, they made land on a rocky islet, where Adara bade them sleep, waiting patiently until the last of her crew dug themselves deep into the blackened soil before settling into the darkness herself. Their war was far from over, but for now, at least, the guns must fall silent. It was time to sleep.

Death felt a lot more uncomfortable than Duke had expected. It was cold, for one thing, and he was sure his back shouldn't be aching like this. *That would be singularly unfair*, he thought, *to retain the pains of life without having the body.* Then again... He began to suspect that he was missing one very obvious, and rather important, fact.

After a moment spent remembering how to do so, for it was something he hadn't had to think about in a very long time, Duke opened his eyes.

"Thought so," he said, blearily, staring at the back of his hand. After so many years adapting to a skeletal existence, it was at once extremely unusual and entirely familiar to see flesh-and-blood fingers wiggling this way and that as he flexed them. It stood to reason, then, that his back was aching because he was lying down on a hard wooden surface, something that human bodies tended to find disagreeable. He should stand.

He stood.

This, he decided, could only be the Ferry of the Damned. Even in his current confusion, the sputtering candles and great, hanging chains made that rather obvious. That wasn't the way things should be, though, was it? Had there been some sort of mix-up? Duke supposed it was possible, given the sheer number of souls the Ferryman must have dealt with in the wake of Flameheart's defeat, but...

Oh! Flameheart, yes, he remembered now. He'd tipped over the candle, hadn't he? They'd all have been blown to bits, he was certain of that. Well, if this really was the Ferry, there was only one way he was going to get any answers.

"Ahoy up there!" he called cheerfully, waving at the helm. "Nice day, isn't it? You'd be the Ferryman, yes?" There was no response from the wild figure at the ship's wheel, but Duke pressed on regardless. "The thing is, and I'm not trying to tell you how to do your job or anything, but I'm fairly certain I'm supposed to have been utterly destroyed. Reduced to dust, quite probably."

The Ferryman tilted his head the slightest fraction to glance down in Duke's direction. "Perhaps it should be so," he said flatly, "but there was...an intervention."

"Oh. Well, that's... good?" Duke was even more confused now. "I don't suppose they left me a note or anything? Something explaining what's going on?"

"These are... unusual circumstances," the Ferryman admitted. "It was decided that your actions aboard the *Burning Blade* were pure of spirit, and..." his tone grew stern, "...*despite* your many dark deeds in Flameheart's name, presented the possibility of redemption. I have been instructed to offer you... some would call it a second chance. To find the freedom you desire, and play your part in all that is yet to shape the Sea of Thieves."

Duke blinked, unsure what to make of all this. "Well that's a relief," he said at last. "I'm sure Slate and the others will be happy to know I've survived. And with all that I've learned, we'll be able to—"

"That is not to be," the Ferryman interrupted, icily. "All

recollection of your time upon the Sea of Thieves shall be stripped away the moment you step across my threshold – save for your name. It shall be as if you are a new arrival to these shores, with all the promise and peril that entails. As for the crew of the *Morningstar*..." The Ferryman hesitated, if only for a moment. "Quite some time has passed in the living world, and things are not as they were for Slate and his crew. A burden I shall attend to, in time."

There was a long, sonorous tone, as though a great church bell was ringing from far away, and the door to the Captain's Cabin creaked open. Duke started towards the portal, but the Ferryman held up a warning hand. "A chance is not a guarantee," he said forebodingly. "It is not my place to herald the future, but I would warn you... freedom always has its price."

Duke didn't quite know what to make of that, but reasoned that he wouldn't remember anyway, and that he'd had quite enough of the gloomy vessel and its curious captain. Somewhere on the other side of that door, a new world was waiting, and all he had to do was put one foot in front of the other. Smiling slightly in anticipation of the unknown, Duke stepped through the door, and came back to life.

"...Our numbers are small, but more of us are joining every day, yes? Before long, I should say that we will have a representative on every outpost across the Sea of Thieves – ah, but here now is our founder, who I am sure will be pleased to meet you." The booming voice of the squat, bearded pirate filled the tavern as he lowered his rotund frame into his customary seat, tray in hand. He passed one grog-filled tankard to the tall, wiry woman who sat opposite, flanked by piles of parchment, and claimed another for himself. "I see we have still not settled on an emblem."

"I'm not an artist, Faizel. Drawing's for people who like to sit still." Larinna accepted the tankard and took a deep draught before glancing up at Faizel's unfamiliar companion. "Who's this?"

"Ah! My new friend, who I met at the bar just now," Faizel said happily. "Duke is his name, and although he is a fresh face to our Sea of Thieves, I can tell immediately that he will make a fine addition to our growing group. Come, sit with us!" He patted a nearby stool encouragingly, sending the third and final tankard into Duke's waiting hand once he was seated.

Larinna looked at the newcomer appraisingly. "So, you'd like to test your mettle with the Bilge Rats?" she challenged. "We're not like the other Trading Companies, you know. We're all about embracing the days when things *don't* go to plan. Think you can handle that kind of excitement?"

Duke nodded and sat back contentedly, already feeling at ease with a drink in his hand and the soothing warmth of the tavern's fireplace, while Larinna began to talk of distant shores, incredible sights and all of the grand adventures that tomorrow would bring.

This, he thought with satisfaction, *is what being a pirate is all about.*

Acknowledgements

Special thanks to Adam Park, Peter Hentze, Shiying Li, Isher Dhillon, Mike Chapman and the entire Sea of Thieves team, Michael Beale and Davi Lancett at Titan Books, and Steve Gove and Kevin Eddy. Cover art by Thomas Mahon.

About the Author

Chris Allcock is a writer and game designer whose career began at Rare Ltd. in 2003. He has helped create a variety of acclaimed titles, including *Kameo*, *Rare Replay* and most recently *Sea of Thieves*. His published works include *The Art of Borderlands 3* and *Sea of Thieves: Athena's Fortune*. He currently lives in the English Midlands and is probably drinking tea.

For more fantastic fiction, author events,
exclusive excerpts, competitions, limited editions and more

VISIT OUR WEBSITE
titanbooks.com

LIKE US ON FACEBOOK
facebook.com/titanbooks

FOLLOW US ON TWITTER AND INSTAGRAM
@TitanBooks

EMAIL US
readerfeedback@titanemail.com